"What might at first seem like a cosy English mystery becomes a propulsive thriller with a healthy serving of gruesome murder. This book delivers a twisting tale driven by believable characters. Impossible to put down, the suspense is riveting and the twists and turns make the final reveal all the more satisfying.

A stunning debut."

Loraine Peck - author of The Second Son

"Surprising and fresh, dark but full of heart, 'The Cry of the Lake' is simply impossible to put down. From the first page you're fully captivated by the characters, and you won't want to put it down until you've found out the whole truth about what they've just done.

A truly remarkable story from an author with a bold new voice."

Cat Hickey, author of The Bellhop Only Stalks Once

The Cry of the Lake

Charlie Tyler

www.darkstroke.com

Discover us online:
www.darkstroke.com

Find us on instagram:
www.instagram.com/darkstrokebooks

Include **#darkstroke** in a photo of yourself
holding this book on Instagram and
something nice will happen.

For Mum and Dad

About the Author

Charlie signed with Darkstroke Books in May 2020 and The Cry of the Lake is her debut novel.

Charlie is very much a morning person - in fact, she likes nothing more than committing a fictional murder before her first coffee of the day. She studied Theology at Worcester College, Oxford and now lives in a Leicestershire village with her husband, three teenagers, golden retriever and tortoise.

Acknowledgements

Lisa O'Donnell – this book would never have been written without your encouragement and support. You are a fantastic writer, teacher, mentor and friend. Thank you for believing in me.

Thank you to Anne Glennie for your early comments and to Rufus Purdy for your excellent structural advice. Thank you to Laurence and Stephanie Patterson from Darkstroke for taking me on and guiding me through this process and again to Laurence for being my eagle-eyed editor.

Thank you to the family friends who never stopped asking about my literary endeavours even though I must have bored you all to tears: The Hunts, The Tylers, The Hopkinsons, The Reas, The Murrays, The Macks, The Lyles, The Prices, The Parrs, The Reddys and The Truslers.

Thank you Team Humpback for making the start of 2020 something to look back on and treasure.

There are a few of you who have gone above and beyond what is required: Diana Hallam with whom I started this creative journey, Debbie James, Rachael and Duncan Mack,

Natalie Hunt, Mary Price, Gillie Tyler, Matthew and Nicola Hopkinson, Chantal Cooper, Rhian Goodman, Viv Alston, Sarah Mettrick, Katy Ellis, Liz Ives, Hazel Neal, Sarah Koeberle, Becky Bennett, Marie Witting, Amanda Phillipson, Amanda Taylor, Emma Bargh and Christian 'Goonie' Totty. You are all superstars.

Thank you to my writing group the September Tribe for all your helpful comments during and after the CBC course. Sarah Beer, Robbie Glen, Kath Grimshaw and Loraine Peck; from across the globe you have kept me sane and been there to give advice on a daily basis – I'm so lucky to have met you. Thank you for your honesty, friendship and support. Sometimes, it's lonely being a writer...

Thank you to my brilliant siblings, James and V. It goes without saying that none of the family dynamics in the book resemble our childhood! A huge thank you to Mum and Dad for championing me in absolutely everything I do – you are the best and I love you to bits.

Finally, to Will, Ollie, Gina and Hattie – thanks a million for your patience, tolerance and optimism throughout this journey. Although I may not always show it, there is nothing as important to me as you four wonderful people and I'm very blessed to have you in my life.

The Cry of
the Lake

Chapter One

Lily

Death smells of macaroons.

Amelie was slumped over the kitchen table, face in a plate of meringues. Spearmint-green flakes stuck to her left cheek. Her glazed irises remained fixed upon a vase of spiky dahlias, cut and arranged by Grace that very morning. Every tangerine petal was bug and blemish free; my sister was well known locally for her green fingers.

My body sagged and my A level folders fell onto the floor.

"About time, considering this is all your fault," said Grace, appearing from the pantry in a veil of chlorinated steam. She threw a ball of latex at me.

Shit! This was really happening.

I peeled on the gloves, unable to stop gawping at Amelie's violet lips.

"Would you believe it?" continued Grace. "I ran out of black sacks. Had to nip out and get some more." She took a step closer towards me and lowered her voice to a whisper. "Where have you been?"

I reached into my tunic pocket for my phone. Grace cocked her head on one side so that her marmalade curls parted, revealing a tiny sliver of snowy hair against her scalp. She narrowed her eyes for a second then flapped her hands about her temples. "Never mind. You're here now." She leaned forward and pecked the top of my forehead. "We've got lots to be getting on with. You can start by bagging her up. The packing tape is in the top drawer of the dresser."

Grace wafted out of the room, her strappy sandals clicking

across the hallway.

For some reason Amelie wasn't wearing any shoes.

After I finished, I stared down at my handiwork; a black shiny parcel criss-crossed with brown tape. Grace stood there, leaning on the mop, her toe tapping to some hidden melody within her mind.

"We'll put her in the utility room for the mo." It was as though she was talking about an old hat-stand that was going to the charity shop. We lifted Amelie's shrink-wrapped body and set her down in front of the dirty clothes hamper.

Suddenly all the emotion of what I'd just done came flooding out of my body and I only just made it to the loo in time. I flushed then rinsed the vomit off my tongue with cold water from the washbasin. As I stared into the mirror Grace appeared behind me in the doorway, her reflected head perched upon my shoulder like a parrot.

Once again, she was Emily and I was Cassie and, in that moment, I could hear my heart thudding. I didn't want to go back there.

"Don't skimp on the soap. We're meeting Tom for supper at the pub. I don't know about you, but I'm starving."

I wasn't going to be able to eat a thing; my throat felt as though someone had scraped it several times with a butter knife, but I knew I'd have to pretend there was nothing wrong or Grace would fly off into one of her epic rages.

After I scrubbed my nails, I went into the kitchen and placed my phone on the worktop. Grace snatched up my hands in her own marble palms; eyes narrowed as she examined my fingers. Then she gave a small sigh and let them out of her grasp. She curled a stray lock of hair around her index finger and with her free hand she scrolled through my phone conversations. My speech board was full of silly chatter with Flo. We were trying to decide what to wear to Monarchy Day.

"Why did you tell Mr Briggs that you needed a homework extension?"

I reached for the pad and typed a message.

I left my book at Tom's.

There was a brief pause and she stared at me.

"Why are you crying?"

I put my fingers to my eyes, surprised by my wet lashes. I rubbed the tears away with the heels of my hands, but it was too late. There was a flash of movement, a thwack then warmth as the sting spread across my cheek.

"Do I have to remind you why we are doing this?" asked Grace, her voice soft and sweet.

I shook my head, trying to blink the moisture back into my eyes.

She re-tucked the stray curl behind her ear. "Do I need to tell you whose fault it is that a girl is dead?"

I placed a hand on my chest and hung my head, waiting for another slap, or worse. A few moments passed and, when I dared to look up, Grace was smiling at me from the hallway. The evening sun poured its golden light down through the lantern window, magnifying Grace's jagged shadow and imprisoning it behind the spindles of the bannister as though she were a caged beast.

"Come on. Tom will be waiting." Grace's almond-shaped eyes sparkled in the gloom.

She slammed the front door and linked arms with me, leaning her head on my shoulder. "You know Mrs Hutton? The woman with a backside the size of a mountain range." I forced a smile. I hated serving Mrs Hutton; she always spoke to me as though I was stupid and made a point of counting any change I gave her twice. "Well, she came into the café today and started telling me how the cheese scones she'd bought from me tasted a bit bland. *Apparently,* they weren't up to my usual standard. Of course, I feigned horror and said I'd add more mustard powder to the mix next time." Grace arched a pale eyebrow. "Anyway, when she turned to flounce off, I saw her skirt was tucked into her knickers." Grace's tinkling laugh rose into the sky. "Of course, I didn't tell her. Silly bitch. She must have walked the High Street with her puckered thighs and parachute pants on display."

My face ached from the effort of keeping my smile fixed.

"You want to know how I did it?" asked Grace. She flicked her crimson nails at the branch of an untidy sapling which dared to trail into our path.

I nodded and sang an Abba song in my head. The loud words in my thoughts drowned out her voice although I definitely heard her say *plastic bag*.

I had liked Amelie. She was one of the quiet ones in the upper sixth who hung around with the cool gang but never seemed to make it out from the side-lines. She always looked a bit lost when she was with them; as though she was trying to shrink into her blazer lining. But when she was on her own in the café, she was polite and chatty. She never displayed the awkwardness that most kids did around me. I guess Grace chose her because of her invisibility and, of course, there was the added bonus that she looked like Flo.

But I was the one who had got to know Amelie really well because, for the last six months, I was the one who had been stealing from her. I also knew that every Friday, during term time, she left the café, straight after the teatime rush, and took a short cut home along the dirt track which skirted Cupid's Wood and ran parallel to our garden fence.

We strolled along the mesh of narrow country lanes until we got to *The Bell and Bottle*. It was a hot summer's evening and the car park was busy.

As we walked across the dusty gravel, the hum of voices and laughter coming from behind the box hedge grew louder. The metal archway which joined the jade walls together was wrapped in clusters of sunny roses and, as I went under, the top of my bun caught on a stem. I paused to untangle myself and spotted Tom's bike propped up against the wall, its basket full of schoolbooks, just ripe for the taking. *When would he learn?* Free at last, I stepped into the beer garden.

Tom was sitting next to a pyramid of pastel sweet peas, nursing a pint of cider. As soon as he saw Grace, he grinned, his blue eyes disappearing into a bundle of laughter lines. He clambered from his seat and held his arms out to her.

"Hello, darling," he said. He kissed her on the lips then

wrapped his arm around her shoulders. Grace grinned and smoothed her floral skirt. Tom blew me a kiss. I tried so hard to smile that I thought the skin around my mouth would rip. "Right," he said. "What's everyone having?"

"Alright Loser?" came a familiar voice. I spun around to see Flo; her cheeks were patched with pink and her blonde fringe was glued to her forehead. She was wearing her usual uniform; faded *The Cure* tee-shirt, black skinny jeans and scuffed DMs. She had an empty tray under her arm which she slammed onto the table. I reached for the nearest glass, tipped a drowning wasp into the flowerbed, and stacked it on top of another empty one. "You not got your phone on?" said Flo. I shook my head. Grace had made me leave it behind. "Doesn't matter. Dad said you and your Mum were coming to meet him for a quick drink."

"Girls, can I get you anything?" asked Tom.

"Large coke behind the bar for me, Dad," said Flo. Tom nodded. "None of that diet shit either. I need sugar."

"I'll come and give you a hand, Tom-Tom," said Grace.

Peeling off my cardigan and draping it over the lichen-speckled bench, I moved to the next table with Flo.

"What are you doing later this evening?" she said, her voice swallowed by a group of sixth form rugby boys, not all of whom were eighteen and whose red, shiny faces indicated they had been there for some time. When they saw me they started giggling. One square-jawed boy stumbled out of his seat and started an exaggerated mime of walking into a large sheet of glass. His clumsy efforts received a round of applause.

"So, Lily,' he continued, 'if you answer this out loud, I'll give you a million pounds." Someone made a drum roll on the table. "How do you spell…dog?"

"How do you spell fuckwit?" said Flo, giving him the finger before adding to her wobbling tower of cups. The group fell about laughing and he blustered something about her being a gobby bitch, but by then Flo had moved over to another table, me trailing after her. The stacks of plastic glasses had multiplied and there was a yucky one in the middle, full of orange liquid and floating cigarette butts.

"So, what *are* you doing this evening?" she said. "Quiet one?" She winked. I meant to roll my eyes at her joke, but instead gave an involuntary shiver as the image of Amelie's body popped into my thoughts. She tilted her head in the direction of the boys. "Hey, you're not going to take any notice of those idiots, are you?"

Just then Grace emerged holding a bottle of juice and waving a bag of crisps at me. For the split second we made eye contact she glared, but in the next moment she was throwing her head back and fake laughing.

"Go on. Join them," said Flo. "I'm getting paid for this, you aren't. Shall I come and get you tomorrow morning? We can go for a run or something." I gave her a thumbs up. Flo and I were getting in shape for our beach holiday although I couldn't really get excited about it, as I knew full well it wasn't going to happen.

I moved to where Tom and Grace were snuggled together and sat down opposite them. Tom looked tired – his stripy shirt was crumpled, and he kept taking off his glasses to rub his eyes.

Grace pointed at the apple juice and I looked at Tom and put my hands together as if in prayer.

"My pleasure," he said.

"Do you want to come back to ours after this?" asked Grace, darting a glance at me.

He stifled a yawn. "I've got so much marking to do, but I'm happy to drop you home." Grace pouted and he tweaked the tip of her nose. "If I get it done tonight, then we can spend most of the weekend together. There's somewhere special I want to take you on Saturday." Grace tilted her head on one side and her left cheek dimpled as she fluttered her eyelashes. "No further questions," said Tom, then tapped the side of his nose.

"I'm intrigued."

Just then Annie walked through the doorway. Some of the boys saw her and nudged each other, pushing their alcoholic drinks towards those with legitimate IDs. Despite the late

8

hour she was still in her creased trouser suit; short, dark hair sticking up at awkward angles. When she saw Tom, her face fell, just for a fleeting moment, before giving him a huge smile which showed off the tiny gap between her front teeth. She gave Grace a slow nod and Grace returned her gesture with an icy smile, before planting a smacker on Tom's cheek. Annie's mouth twitched and she stalked off with her half pint of lager to the furthest table which was dimmed by the shadow of the wisteria.

"The one that got away," snapped Grace.

My mouth went dry.

Tom reached out and placed a hand on Grace's slender thigh. "The best thing that ever happened was her finishing with me because then I met you." You had to hand it to Tom; he was saying all the right words, but he couldn't stop himself glancing over to where Annie was sitting.

I liked how Tom never made a point of trying too hard to include me in the conversation. In fact, he'd always been very natural with me, from the very first time we met, although, he doesn't remember our first encounter because it was such a long time ago. Back then I was Cassie and I could talk.

I tried to take my mind off Amelie by focusing on the smells around me; cigarette smoke, the sharp scent of the salt and vinegar crisps spilling out of the packet and onto the table, but all I could think about was her stiffening corpse. Even though I knew it was impossible, I kept catching glimpses of Amelie's honeyed bob shining at me from various corners of the garden.

I shivered.

"Do you want to borrow my jacket?" said Tom. I shook my head and removed my cardigan from under my thighs and draped it around my shoulders.

Flo appeared again clutching a dozen wire-handled jars containing candles. She set them down and struck a match. The glow of the flame illuminated the underside of her chin and made her nose-ring glitter. As she set the lanterns on the tables, she caught sight of Annie and went over to say hi.

They laughed and I watched Annie capping Flo's shoulder with her palm. The lads were singing rude songs now; tapping their fingers on the edge of the table and suddenly from amongst the growls Flo's clear soprano floated into the inky blue sky.

I loved Flo's confidence – the way she carried herself; shoulders back, head held high. It gave the impression she was tall, and it always came as a surprise to me how petite she actually was. Her favourite band, *The Cure*, was a group no one else our age had ever heard of though she had made them the soundtrack to her life, not remotely embarrassed that the lead singer was older than her Dad. Nothing ever really bothered her or got under her skin. She had remained friends with her Dad's ex despite the heartbreak they had all been through when they broke up. The public reason for the split was the anti-social hours which went with Annie's job – Grace had started out as a shoulder to cry on. I didn't believe that for a minute; it had Grace's devious handiwork smeared all over it.

Flo was the best thing that had ever happened to me and luckily, in order for Grace's plan to work, there had been nothing my sister could do to stop us spending time together. Just then it struck me like a sucker-punch to the stomach – after they found Amelie there would be no more Flo. How would I cope? There was a sudden sharp pain to my shin, and I looked up to see Grace frowning at me. I blinked back my tears and busied myself trying to get the ice out of the bottom of my glass.

"Time to go," said Grace.

Tom and Grace kissed in the courtyard.

"So, we'll just walk my bike back and I'll nip you both home," Tom said, undoing the lock around the chain.

"Thank you darling. That would be lovely."

***

Grace killed the engine and rolled Tom's car into the clearing.

10

The sky was lit by the fattest of moons and the lake was awash with brilliant white light. We waited a few minutes then got out of the car. I was dressed in a dark tracksuit and had tucked my hair into a woollen hat. The air was cold, and my breath made little clouds which floated into the violet sky. Grace opened the boot of Tom's BMW and we lifted Amelie out. My heart thumped against my ribcage; this was the most dangerous part of the journey; we were no longer hidden by trees.

There were open fields to my left where the cows were lying in a corner, their hides illuminated so that they resembled a rocky outcrop. Cupid's Wood stood to the right and I could see the silhouettes of blackening bluebells and taste wild garlic on the tip of my tongue. Grace pointed to the lake. I screwed up my forehead. I had imagined we would be digging a shallow grave underneath the bracken and nettles.

Grace nodded her head towards the rickety pontoon which stretched out over one edge of the lake. The path leading towards it was lined with long, dewy grass which soaked into the fabric mesh on the tops of my trainers. My damp toes grated against each other and the ache in my arm muscles turned to burning.

We shuffled along the wooden boards and swung the body into the water. Amelie disappeared under the surface with a gurgle and cascade of bubbles.

I hung my head and tried to remember the words of the Lord's Prayer but before I got to *forgive us our trespasses* Grace had grabbed hold of my arm and dragged me back to the car.

Just as Grace pulled out of the woods and onto the main road a small dog, a terrier of some sort, ran out in front of us. Grace slammed on the brakes just in time and the creature stopped, turned its head and stared at us, its marble eyes glowing phantom-green in the headlights. Then it wagged its stumpy tail and trotted into the bracken; thankfully there was no owner in sight.

The moment we were through our backdoor Grace made me strip off. My grass-clumped trainers went into the sink.

She took all my clothes, even my underwear, so I was left naked and shivering. I made a dash past Tom, who was out cold on the sofa, and went upstairs into the shower. When I emerged my skin all pink and tingling, Grace was there with a small glass of milk and my pills. My heart fluttered. I had been worried she wasn't going to let me have them – that for some reason my behaviour this evening hadn't been up to scratch and that I needed to be punished some more. At least my refuge in sleep was assured. Grace had changed her clothes, but not yet showered. She watched me swallow the tablets and then ushered me into my bed.

"You did well," she said, tucking me into the sheets and smoothing back my hair. "Daddy would have been proud of us."

I wasn't convinced. I can't really remember Daddy at all, but I'm sure no father would be proud of their kids committing murder and chucking the body into a lake.

She stroked my forehead with the back of her hand.

Do you think he would have forgiven me by now?

She sighed. "Maybe. You were young, but…" Here it was again. The familiar ache of wrong-doing spread across my stomach, tying itself into knots as it coiled its way around my body. I closed my eyes. I wanted to recall what I'd said to Tom all those years ago but the broken fragments of what had happened lay hidden at the bottom of a lake, with only one tiny piece of the puzzle revealing itself over and over again in my nightmares. A lake which I was destined never to find.

"We still have lots to do," she said, turning off the bedside lamp. She picked Myrtle off my dusty shelf and stroked her hair. Myrtle was my worn mermaid doll with matted, woollen locks and buttons for eyes. A throwback from my childhood. The only throwback from my childhood. "We must sit tight and give nothing away." She laughed and pushed the toy back in its place. "Well, it's not as though you are going to blurt anything out, is it?" She was still laughing as she went out of the door.

12

Chapter Two

Flo

I sucked the froth off my cappuccino and gagged. Like a greedy bitch, I'd poured in far too much hazelnut syrup and the fake sugar made my tongue scratchy. I tipped it down the sink. The café was quiet after a crazy morning but two wrinklies remained, sitting by the window, slurping tea and fighting over a slice of carrot cake.

I couldn't be arsed. With only fifteen minutes to go before shutting up shop, I'd already stuck the closed sign on the door and sent Lily into the kitchen to start the final clean down which seemed to go on forever. Even though Grace wasn't there to nag us, Lily would still take her time. She'd tuned into some shitty classical music channel and the constant whinge of the violins, competing with the hum of the dishwasher, made me want to punch my ears, but I let it go.

There was something bugging Lily; she was moving about as though her limbs were made of wood and, every now and again, she stopped and gawped at whatever inanimate object was in her path. I was a bit pissed off that she'd cancelled our morning run last minute with the lame explanation that she was tired. I didn't buy it. Of course, I'd asked her lots of times if everything was okay and she had nodded and fake smiled, but the second she didn't think I was watching her, the weird spaced-out look returned.

My phone buzzed. It was Stella. *Apparently* I had missed a peng gathering last night. Dillon got with Helen and Dom had made an absolute tit of himself by vomiting over his trousers. But the best bit of goss was that Amelie Townsend, a girl in Dad's class who was a right beg, had gone AWOL. Stella's theory was that she was up to no good with some bloke from another village because *it was always the quiet ones who were the biggest slags.*

I couldn't picture what Amelie looked like. I left the wrinklies chatting shit and went into the kitchen. "Hey, Lil? You know who Amelie Townsend is?"

Lily had soap suds on her nose. The muscles in her jaw clenched but she carried on washing up the last of the cups and plates. She shrugged.

I couldn't stand it anymore. "For God's sake, Lils, what's bugging you? Is it something I've done? If you don't cheer up soon, I'm gonna sing." I opened my mouth and took a deep breath.

Lily dried her hands on her apron and pulled out her phone.

I'm fine, I promise. Sorry for being a fun sponge.

I gave Lily's shoulders a squeeze. "Hmmmm. Yes, now you come to mention it you are a wee bit spongy today."

For the first time this morning Lily broke into a proper smile.

"So, Dad told me, over brekky, that once we've closed, I have to get you straight round to ours for lunch. He's already got the food in – M&S finest range, don't you know." I gave a little bow and Lily rolled her eyes. "I've got to lay the table *nicely* whatever the fuck that means and chill a bottle of champagne."

He's asking her, then?

"What?" I said, drowning out my own voice as I shook open a new black sack.

"Yoo-hoo!" came a shrill squawk from the other side of the counter.

I dropped the bag and went through to hurry the women

14

out. Glad to see the back of them, I locked the door and grabbed their empty cups and plates. What was Lily going on about?

I put the dirty stuff next to the sink and leaned against it, waiting while Lily filled her bucket with floor cleaner which smelled like Dad's cheap aftershave. "What's Dad asking your Mum?"

Lily set the bucket down, water sloshing over the brim, and tapped her ring finger.

"Shit!"

Lily took the bucket into the furthest corner of the kitchen while I shoved the cups and saucers under the cold tap, processing the news. It was a good thing, wasn't it?

"No wonder Dad was a bit jumpy this morning. I should have known something was up – he was ironing his best shirt."

Lily swished the mop across the floor, making wet streaks on the tiles.

"Do you think your Mum will say yes?" I asked, grabbing the nearest, clean-ish tea towel.

Lily nodded and started attacking my feet with the mop.

"That will make us sisters, right?" I pulled Lily into a hug – her hair smelt of coconut.

Half an hour later we had closed the café and were on our way back through the village to my house. We stopped off at the newsagents to buy a bag of strawberry bonbons, my favourite, and a couple of bridal magazines.

I flicked through the pages, giggling at some of the awful big-fat-gypsy-wedding dresses. "They're a bit trashy, but at least it will give Grace something to look at."

***

There was a gentle pop and lazy, out-of-synch hooraying as champagne fizzed over the edge of the crystal flutes. Giggling, I licked the drops from my fingers and handed the first glass to Lily who hoovered the froth to prevent a secondary tsunami. Dad next, but none for Grace; she was tee-total. I poured her some sparkling water. We held our glasses up, chiming them against each other's and the evening sun caught hold of the emerald on Grace's wedding finger, throwing will-o'-the-wisps onto the table.

"Congratulations," I said. "To the happy couple."

Lily, my silent echo, nodded her head; her movements slow as though each expression was a real effort.

Grace blew me a kiss while Dad's crumpled stare hopped from person to person like the beam of a lighthouse. The sunshine was brutal in showing up the grooves across his broad brow, but at the same time the light made his eyes twinkle. I felt a burst of gratitude towards Grace. Okay, so I didn't have the same connection with her as I had had with Annie, Grace was a bit too prim and proper for my liking, but hey – she'd mended his broken heart. Dad was the happiest he'd been in ages.

I gulped my champagne, letting the bubbles burst on my tongue.

"You can, of course, start by calling me, Ma*ma*," giggled Grace, taking a dainty sip of water and wrinkling her small, pointed nose. She was wearing a short, pastel sundress which clung to her slender body. She didn't dress too badly considering her age.

"But of course," I said.

"In that case, I want to be *Pater*," said Tom, throwing his arms around Lily and making the champagne glass smack against her front teeth. She untangled herself and reached for the platter of strawberries; big, fat, bubble-gum-smelling berries picked from the row of netted plants at the bottom of the garden. She almost collapsed under the weight of the bowl and the veins on the back of her hands bulged. She was the total opposite of Grace; small and curvy, where Grace was tall and bony. She had big brown eyes and her hair, judging by the roots, was probably black although she had dyed it a shade of blue-blonde – what my Mum called *a blue rinse for the young*. Unlike me, she never had much skin on show. Even in this stuffy, June heat she was well-covered, wearing a gypsy blouse and striped culottes which came

16

down to just above her dainty ankles; a fine silver chain, dangling from one. She was barefoot and had painted her toenails with my favourite malted-chocolate varnish. I had always been desperate to know what her Dad looked like, but neither she nor Grace ever mentioned him and there weren't any photos of him up around the house. All I knew about him was that he had died when Lily was eight. Same time Mum walked out on me and Dad.

Lily gave me a small smile and plopped a berry into my glass. Something was definitely off with her; she could hardly meet my eye. Perhaps she didn't approve of Dad and Grace hooking up.

"Don't think that will make you the big Sis," I said, as black pepper from the strawberry swirled around the glass. I never did get why Grace insisted on sprinkling them with pepper and not sugar, but the sinking flakes reminded me I hadn't yet fed my carp.

"I am older than you by three months, so don't forget, Lily Bradshaw, if we are *forced* to share a bedroom, it means I get priority over absolutely everything."

Lily fluttered her long, dark eyelashes and tapped something into her phone then passed it to me. I had to hold it up to my face, squinting in the bright sunshine, so I could make out the words.

I have a lot of clothes…

Lily tugged at her blouse and widened her eyes, raising her palms to the sky.

Grace tutted. "Lily, darling, that's enough. We've talked about how rude it is to conduct private conversations when you're in a group. It's just the same as whispering."

Harsh! Lily hung her head. To be honest, Grace could be a bit of a bitch at times.

"Okay," I said, fishing out the strawberry by its spidery stalk. I took a bite and licked the sweet juice which oozed down my hands as though I'd pricked my fingers with a needle. "Let's just say we both have to agree before anything

17

goes up on the walls." We did our own private chinking of glasses to seal the deal.

I wiped my hands with a paper napkin and reached for the tissue wrapped parcel I'd hidden on one of the chairs. I handed it to Grace.

"What's this?" asked Grace, setting down her glass and tugging at the badly sellotaped joins. Dad came over and pulled her to his chest. Since he had started visiting the gym before school his body was less *Dad-bod*; certainly not ripped, but the saggy tummy was now only a gentle curve which peeped through a small gape in the buttons of his shirt.

Grace took out the bundle of bridal magazines and gave a little shriek. "Darlings. How terribly sweet of you."

"Lily and I thought you might like to get some ideas," I said. Dad clapped his hands with approval.

Grace turned the glossy pages slowly and looked up, narrowing her eyes. "Indeed. And do my bridesmaids have any particular ideas about colours?" Dad gave a cheer and Grace winked at him.

I launched in. "So, we were thinking jade and teal, but that silk which gives a two-tone feel. It's called Dupioni."

"Oh!" spluttered Grace. "I wasn't expecting such a precise answer."

Lily pointed at the little jug on the table which was bursting with sweet peas. "I'm on it, Lily," I said. "Dusty pink roses for the bouquet. And–"

"Sweethearts," interrupted Grace, flapping her hands about her face. "You know we can't afford a huge wedding. We need to keep it simple."

"No church?" I said, my voice wavering. "No marquee in the garden?" While we'd been waiting for the happy couple to return, I'd scribbled down a list of fit boys Lily and I wanted to invite. "No…no after party?" I continued, trying to keep the hiss of disbelief out of my voice.

"Well, I mean, Tom has been married before," said Grace sucking in the air through her teeth. Dad bowed his head. That was a classic from Grace. She always managed to squeeze, Nina, my super-neurotic Mum into the conversation when she wanted a certain topic shut down.

"But *you* haven't been married before," I chimed in. "Isn't it what every girl dreams of? To walk down the aisle in a puffy, meringue dress?"

Grace let out a burst of air; half laugh, half sigh. "No, Flo. Believe it or not, it isn't. I'd happily get married right here, right now with no fuss or frills. You guys are all we need." She linked arms with Dad and leaned into him, tilting her chin upwards. "Right, Tom-Tom?"

Dad kissed the tip of her freckled nose and nodded. "That's right, sweetheart." He stretched across the table and grabbed the neck of the sweating champagne bottle. "Neither of us has any other family." He topped up the glasses, ill-estimating how much remained, so that he was left with just a dribble. "And I really, really don't want to have to invite the rest of the science department along." He shook his head. "You know," he said in a loud whisper, hand over his mouth like a superhero villain, "they don't allow them all out in public at the same time. It's too dangerous." Grace was the only one who giggled at his crap joke.

"There had better be a cake," I said sounding more toddler than teen.

Grace threw back her head and laughed, keeping her eyes glued on Tom. "Yes, we can have a cake, but I'm sure as hell not making it."

My vision was growing fuzzy and wedding talk morphed into chat about heading into the village for fish and chips.

Just then, Dad's pre-historic phone rang. I sniggered. Hardly anyone ever called him on it, apart from me and now Grace, but when he answered his voice always carried an undercurrent of surprise, as though the novelty of speaking on such a modern thing would never cease. Emojis didn't exist in Dad's world and he had to make expressions out of punctuation marks.

Dad took the phone out of his shirt pocket and held it away from his face, squinting at the mysterious, incoming digits. He shook his head and put it back.

"We could get a taxi and go into town," he said.

The phone rang again.

"Answer it, darling," said Grace gathering up the glasses onto a tray and offering around the last of the squidgy berries which were sliding around in their black-speckled juice.

"What?" said Dad, his voice serious. "No. No. *Of course* I will." He put the phone on the table and rubbed his chin.

"What is it, Dad?" I asked.

"I'm sure it's nothing serious. But it seems one of the girls in my class has gone missing. Amelie. Amelie Townsend."

Chapter Three

Grace

I sat, legs curled up on the sofa, with Tom's arm draped around my shoulders. The heaviness of his body; the musky scent of his cologne and the graze of his cheek against mine made me feel nauseous. I suppose, if I were forced to be objective, I could see why Annie had been attracted to him and sometimes, when we kissed, the pit of my stomach whirred with a brief flutter of desire. Desire which was quickly followed by a flood of disgust.

Tom Marchant was a pathetic liar of a man and every ounce of his being repulsed me.

A thought struck me, and I had to swallow down my laughter. For the first time in ages, we actually had something in common; we were both murderers. *Hilarious*.

Today had been a good day for Grace.

I was still buzzing from the lashings of praise I received simply from saying yes to a man who went down to me on bended knee. When we entered the pub, Tom told the landlord our joyful news and he bought all those in the vicinity a drink to celebrate. A group of café regulars, sitting at a nearby table, clucked and examined the ring, all commenting on how it brought out the flecks in my eyes. There weren't nearly enough diamonds for my liking, but that was to be expected considering his paltry salary.

The only slight blemish on an otherwise productive evening was that DS Annie Harper hadn't been there. How I would have loved to shove my sparkling ring under Annie's snub nose, the silly whore. What was the saying? *Diamonds are a girl's best friend, but emeralds are for envy.*

I had never understood what Tom had seen in her. My only conclusion; that she was good in bed because she didn't have a lot else going in her favour with her androgynous haircut and sallow complexion. It had been really hard to break them up because, despite their incompatibility, they had been smitten with each other. I'd heard a rumour that Tom was desperate for more kids, but that Annie was torn between her biological clock and her career path. So, the first thing I created for this new version of Grace was an underlying broodiness.

The story of Grace so far was this: her partner had been killed in an accident at a tragically young age, leaving her alone with her special-needs daughter, Lily. Grace, however, carried on embracing life for the sake of her precious child and I liked to think that this element of the story gave her an air of vulnerability. Grace Bradshaw was young and beautiful and ready to find love once more. She was blossoming.

The wanting more kids aspect, however, wasn't enough to force Annie and Tom apart, so I manufactured a little 'incident'. There were lots of tears; Annie had said she was drunk and that she had no recollection of the man at all, but somehow the photo found its way into the school email account and the whole village had gossiped about it for weeks. Those crazy people and their alcohol dependence – pathetic but, at the same time, it made life so easy. There was a good reason why I had given up booze.

In the end Tom listened to the lovely, maternal woman with long, curly red hair who had recently taken over the running of his café. She had made him see with her soft, kind words that, without trust, a relationship was doomed to fail. Grace was sweet and naïve. Grace was whatever he wanted her to be and she made it so easy for him to fall in love with her.

Grace had Tom's trust.

But despite Annie's drab appearance I knew she was still a threat. I saw the way Tom continued to moon after her. They had a connection and it was something I couldn't manufacture or mimic because Grace was a piece of fiction and I wasn't built with those subtle, emotional intuitions – they had been forced out of me as a teenager. I also knew that, if I didn't take care, Annie would pluck Tom back off me before the job of destroying him was finished.

Thankfully, the fuss over the missing schoolgirl hadn't impacted on the good humour of the villagers – the general consensus was that there was nothing to worry about – Amelie was playing truant with a boy. Grace was allowed to bask in the attention she deserved. After all, it had taken a lot of hard work to become such an esteemed pillar of the community; someone who exuded warmth and love. I couldn't just throw it all away. Plus, it was fun playing Grace and I wasn't ready to return to being Emily – I had become quite fond of my creation.

Tom slid his hand up my blouse and fumbled with the lace edging of my bra, his breathing was shallow.

Typical. Trying to climb into my knickers now that he's gone and put a ring on my finger.

"More red wine, darling," I asked, leaning forward and dislodging his hand. Tom gave a grunt and nodded. I used my purity as an allure – promising him submission – total control over my body but only when we were married.

"I can't be too late," I said, giving a fake yawn. "Besides, darling, I'm not sure, as parents of two sixteen-year-olds, we should be promoting the idea that sex before marriage is a good thing. We should lead by example."

Tom slapped his own wrist. "You don't really believe that though, do you?"

"No. But we've got this far – what's another few weeks? Also, you know how Lily is – I need to be there to keep an eye on her."

"All the more reason for you to move in with me and Flo," he said as I filled his wine to the brim again and handed him back the glass. "The girls would love being together."

Give him a bit of encouragement.

I leant forward, showing him my cleavage. "As soon as we're married, we'll all live together…" I kissed him on the lips. He pulled back and gave a lazy grin. I chucked him under the chin. "So, let's get married as soon as possible. Then we can start a family of our own."

"What are you doing tomorrow?" asked Tom with a laugh.

I laughed too and tried to move away, but Tom grabbed hold of my arm.

"I mean it. Okay, so we can't actually get hitched tomorrow, but let's drive out and look at some venues." Tom held out his arms and I tiptoed forwards and wriggled onto his lap.

"I love you so much," he said, whispering into the hollow of my neck.

"I *love* you too."

Well done, Grace! Bravo!

We kissed again, then we talked about our future family. I told him what a wonderful father he was to Flo and how Lily adored him too. It wasn't a lie – he had a natural manner when dealing with kids. I remembered how he had talked to me when I was a teenager; made me believe I could trust him. How his honeyed words had led me to think that there was a way out of my miserable existence. How his lies helped shape who I had become.

His eyelids grew heavy and I turned off the lights and put some banal crime drama on the TV. Soon he was asleep.

Off I went into the kitchen to put on my latex gloves.

I had work to do and I pulled out of my pocket the pair of knickers Lily had stolen from Amelie's P.E. kit.

Chapter Four

Lily

Sleep was the time when my soul crossed to another world; an underwater universe where I was unable to free myself from the clutches of a beautiful mermaid who tried to entice me into the water. She sang, with a voice of unbearable sweetness, about needing my help. Her golden hair swirled about her pale face, offering glimpses of wild sapphire eyes and a neat, rosebud mouth. I wanted to go with her, to find out what secrets lay on the bottom of the lake, but I knew I mustn't and then she disappeared, and sadness deadened my limbs and left me hollow.

At other times, when I was working with Flo in the café, I wondered if I was dreaming with my eyes open. It was only in this sphere I could feel physical pain and it convinced me I was alive, though the joins of my double life were blurred and over the years I made peace with the fact I might never be certain of my reality.

Grace said it was my punishment for my part in what happened to Daddy.

I had always been a badly-behaved child; wild and out of control. I roamed around our mansion like a feral cat, slinking about the shadows and hiding in the shady woods which surrounded our father's estate. I had even created a whole bunch of imaginary friends to keep me company. Sometimes fragmented memories of this came back to me at the strangest times, popping into my head like fluffy clouds nudged along by a Spring breeze: dens woven out of fallen branches and bracken; thwacking the tops off puffball toadstools with a stick so that their chalky dust carpeted the damp moss; my sister telling me over the breakfast table that a mermaid lived in our lake.

School was as a torture chamber to me. My speech, although bursting to get out, was slow to reach my tongue so I took the focus away from my so-called stupidity by being disruptive. I spent more time being excluded from school than being in the classroom. All the time, my head was bursting with colours, smells and sounds.

Daddy was working for the government, destined for great things, and my behaviour, although quirky and endearing to start with, was becoming a source of much embarrassment. There was talk of special schools and even hospital. Nannies came and went until eventually I became unbearable and that's when I was sent to see Tom.

Even though it was a long time ago, I must have been about seven or eight-years-old, I could still picture Tom's crystal-blue eyes and recollect his velvety voice. He showed me how to make a safe place within my mind so that my bad thoughts weren't always there clawing at me, night and day. He promised he would help me take away the prickling under my skin.

I fidgeted on a spinning chair and he let me gobble up Haribos, three at a time, and he gave me a packet of crayons, really smart ones which twisted up and down, along with sheets of crisp, clean paper. He told me we were going to make a list of things which made me happy and he promised he wasn't going to go anywhere until we'd found a safe place for my scary thoughts; every single one of them.

And we got chatting and I remembered a day when I visited a huge oceanarium. Tom made me shut my eyes and describe it to him and thinking about walking through the glass tunnels with shoals of multi-coloured fish swimming over our heads made my knees jiggle with happiness. Tom told me I was a clever girl and that's what we would do: make an aquarium inside my head and fill it with fish of every colour – no sharks or stinging things, just happy, sparkling, rainbow fish. At the very bottom of the tank he

26

asked me if I could place a little treasure chest, right there, nestled among the smooth pebbles.

The next time I came to visit him, he sat opposite and stared at me with his cobalt eyes and, saying nothing, pushed a small wooden box across the table top. I lifted the hinged lid and peeped inside. It was full of keys; old-fashioned ones with ridged stems and knobbly collars. The sort of keys I was certain would open secret gardens or enchanted prisons. He watched as I examined them and then told me to pick one. I took my time and the sharp smell of the metal made the tip of my tongue tingle. Eventually I pulled out a small bronze key with a bow interlaced like a spider's web and the tips of my fingers bulged as I pressed them into the gaps between the woven metal.

Tom took it out of my hands and said I had found the key to my treasure chest and now it was time to put my bad thoughts inside and lock them away. Was I ready? I said yes and he made me close my eyes and think about the aquarium and describe what my fish were doing.

Then he told me to recall the thoughts which frightened me, but I wasn't to tell him, I was to put them into the casket, one at a time. Thought by thought. There was no need for me to say them out loud which was good because they were a bit of a tangle and some didn't make any sense. I put them away, piece by piece, like they were parts of a jigsaw puzzle. When I was done, he asked if I had shut the lid.

Yes!

He gave me the key.

Had I locked it?

I nodded.

And there sat the casket, hidden by lots of emerald weed with my beautiful fish swimming all about it, not bothered by its presence one little bit.

Tom asked me what I wanted to do with the key, and we decided I would give it to him for safe keeping. He tied a silver ribbon around the top so he would remember it was mine. He said we couldn't leave the treasure chest on the bottom of the aquarium for ever; we would need to move it to

27

make way for another ornament and did I have anything in mind. I said I fancied the idea of an open chest with glittering treasure spilling out: gold, pearls and rubies to sparkle alongside all the silvery fish scales.

Some happy weeks passed and then it was time to unlock the casket and take out one of the thoughts. Tom took me outside, and we sat on the lawn with the sun peeping through a canopy of lime-green leaves and the blanket which we sat upon, though soft, also made me want to scratch the underside of my thighs. Tom asked me if I was ready and I nodded. He handed me my key which I clasped in both hands and then I shut my eyes and he took me over to my beautiful aquarium.

He told me, when I was ready, to take a piece out of the chest and I did.

He asked if I could describe it to him and I did.

With a shaky voice he told me to lock the casket, but rather than making me swim back through the warm aquarium water, racing alongside my rainbow fish, he fell quiet. Startled by the silence, I opened my eyes. His face had gone very pale and his brow was all wrinkled. I gave him back the key for safekeeping.

Then my world stopped spinning and, from that moment onwards, I didn't utter another word.

It was only much later, when my sister was restraining me, that I realised Tom never told me what to do with the extracted jigsaw piece and it stayed with me all the time and became another thing Grace told me I must hate him for.

So much time passed, and I became scared of finding my aquarium. I was frightened it would be in a terrible condition with all my fish suffocated by overgrown algae; their skeletons stuck fast in an emerald soup of stinking, rotting flesh.

At the very beginning of our new life together my sister said we had to 'wait for the right time' and when we first moved to our cottage by the sea, I wondered every day, at breakfast, if it was 'the right time.' It was in Norfolk that we changed everything about ourselves. She allowed me to choose my new name and I chose Waterlily, but she, being a typical grown-up, said I had to be just plain old Lily. If you ask me, Grace was a spectacularly unadventurous choice.

Between visits to the speech therapist, hospital, primary school and collecting shells on the beach, we carved a life for ourselves and I forgot all about finding the elusive *right time*. Then one day, Grace said *it* had arrived and we were to leave.

We moved to a place called Rutland Water and Grace took over the running of Tom's café and that's how she trapped him. I didn't actually remember him until Grace told me I simply must do, but he didn't recognise me either. Not even a flicker from those big, blue eyes.

Chapter Five

Flo

Annie, or DS Harper to the rest of the planet, came into assembly on Monday morning. Her dark hair was wet and slicked back as though she'd dipped it in the washroom sink just before entering the hall. Sun streamed through the dirty rectangular windows, throwing half of the hall into darkness though the pupils on the other side of the room had to hide their eyes from the nuclear glare. Annie stood behind the lectern, her thin mouth painted a slutty shade of red, ridiculous Easter-egg bow dangling around her neck. She scowled into the huddle of blazers and spotty faces, her eyes flicking from right to left – she'd gone way too emo with the kohl. I managed to catch her attention and gave her my best reassuring smile, but she completely ignored me.

She must have been wetting herself. Annie was the coolest, most unflappable person I'd ever met but standing in front of a room rammed with teenagers would scare the shit out of even the toughest of coppers. Dad, dressed like a tramp in a manky velvet jacket, was standing next to his class and avoided catching Annie's eye by staring at the tips of his old-man loafers.

I closed my eyes, trying to remember the last time I'd seen Amelie. I raced through my memories one by one, like I was clicking through my kiddie's view-master. I was a complete fraud, already finding it impossible to recall her image. Here was the whole school fizzing with excitement and all that was running through my head was this: if I went missing would anyone else, apart from my besties, be able to describe

30

me to the police.

Stella nudged me. "I reckon if they have to do one of those TV re-construction thingies they'll ask you to do it."

"Oh?"

"Yes – you look really similar. It's the hair."

That was it – I knew exactly who they were talking about. I grinned. "Fame at last."

Lily was on the other side of the hall, daydreaming as usual and staring up at the ceiling. Sometimes she really didn't help herself with the whole weird vibe she gave off.

The headmistress, Ms Phibbs, clapped her fat hands together and we all shut up. She nodded to Annie.

"Some of you will already know me," said Annie. A few sniggers swept around the room and the tips of Dad's ears burned as everyone turned to stare at him. Poor Dad and those fucking awful photos. I glared at any of the rubberneckers who dared to meet my eye. Annie gave a sigh, folded her arms and scowled until the room fell silent again.

"I'm DS Annie Harper and I've come here this morning to talk to you about Amelie Townsend." She strode out from behind the lectern, square heels clipping the wooden floor of the stage. She was wearing a knee-length kilt – things were serious. The last time I'd seen Annie wearing a skirt and heels and, for that matter, face powder was when she'd been on the telly to give her opinion about a team of robbers who kept thieving the cash machines from our neighbouring villages. She was often accused of being too intimidating and the *female* get-up was meant to soften the edges, but I thought she looked even more scary when she was made-up; like a freaky doll from a slasher movie. "We're beginning to get quite concerned about Amelie's whereabouts."

Whispering.

Annie pressed her lips together. "Now there are a lot of rumours already flying about so, do me a favour will you, and block them out of your mind. What I want you to think about is what *you personally* know about Amelie. Fact not fiction." Annie started pacing across the stage, lost in her own thoughts. "The last sighting we have of Amelie was when she left school on Friday afternoon. We need to know where she went. Was she meeting anyone and if so who? Did she have a boyfriend or was there someone she had a crush on?" I sucked in my breath and Stella dug me in the thigh, rolled her eyes and mouthed *crush!*

"I want you to know that we are searching through her belongings so if there is anything to find we will find it…" She stopped pacing to let the words hang in the air. The atmosphere in the room was spiky and my shoulders ached from trying to stand up straight. "So, if there is anything, anything you can think of that might help us…"

Annie nodded at Phibbs.

"Right, off to class now please," said Phibbs, playing with the string of fake pearls around her neck. Everyone started talking at each other as we bundled out of the hall. "All apart from Upper Six M, that is," she shouted. Dad looked up at the stage. "DS Harper wants to have a further chat with you and her classmates. So, Mr Marchant, if you wouldn't mind taking yourselves into the common room. I've organised some teas and coffees to be sent your way." Dad rubbed his forehead and nodded.

For the rest of the day, school was full of gossip about Amelie, the rumours growing worse with each passing minute. Nearly all of the chat was based around her running off with a boy because *the copper wouldn't have mentioned a boy unless there was something in it*. I had been in the loos at first break and overheard one of her gang saying Amelie had *almost certainly* hinted that she was seeing someone but wouldn't say who it was. None of the boys had owned up to it being one of them. Amelie wasn't a stunner, but nor was she a minger, so there was no reason for them not to come forward.

By second break it was Salem all over again. Carl Flack, a bit of a loner who liked to spend his free periods doing fuck knows what in the science block, was the favourite suspect amongst us sixth formers. Stella said she knew for a fact he had a bit of a thing for Amelie, but, as I pointed out, he had a bit of a thing for any girl who didn't cross to the other side of the corridor when he approached.

At lunchtime someone dared to switch channels from *Doctors* to the local news bulletin and there was Annie, looking awkward, standing on the steps of Oakford police station. She was making an appeal and afterwards a picture of Amelie flashed across the screen. It was one of those official school photographs with a swirly blue background. I definitely remembered who she was – I'd seen her with Dad. I'd walked in on them one break time. Dad had been helping her with her oh-so-very-important Oxbridge homework.

By the end of the day, Carl, oblivious to the lies, was lucky to escape without being lynched.

I was relieved by the change of scene when I entered the café, but unfortunately the Chinese whispers didn't stop there; *Lake View Café* was bursting with gossip too.

I slung my blazer on the peg behind the kitchen door and tied on my apron tight before launching myself into the task of mixing milkshakes for snotty, ungrateful kids. I hated the afternoon shift on a hot day as all it seemed to involve was standing by a blender, whizzing up ice cubes while my nostrils filled with the sickly scent of burnt caramel and butterscotch. Still, the grinding sound was the perfect way to drown out the ever-increasing flow of shit.

"Hey, Flo," shouted a familiar voice.

I spun around. "Hey, Annie," I said, loosening my apron strings which were almost cutting my waist in half. I squirted cream onto a milkshake then popped a lid onto the plastic cup before stabbing it with a straw. I handed the sickly mixture to a Year Seven boy who was leaning his greasy forehead against the glass counter, gazing at Grace's rainbow cake.

"Thank you," I said in my most patronising voice.

The rude shit said nothing and walked out, leaving a smudge on the counter.

I turned to Annie. "You did good this morning."

Annie grinned. Her lipstick now resembled a stain of raspberry jam and her dark hair had dried into its usual guinea-pig rosettes.

"School kids," she said, and mimed being hung on a noose.

"I know, right?" I pointed to the nearest table where a group of younger kids were throwing sachets of sugar at each other. "Hey! Cut it out," I shouted, "or piss off." I turned back to Annie and they fell about laughing. "Can I get you anything? On the house, obviously." I whispered the last bit because although Dad technically owned the café, I wasn't sure Grace would approve. Not to me giving out free drinks, but because it was Annie.

It wasn't obvious to most people that Grace had beef with Annie because she always went out of her way to be super nice about her, but face-to-face Grace couldn't hide her dislike. I suppose I couldn't really blame Grace; Annie had broken Dad's heart and chipped a bit off mine while she was at it.

"No thanks, Chick. I've actually come here to speak to Grace." She paused. "Well actually you and Lily too."

"Grace isn't here. She's taken Lily somewhere. Dentist, doctor, hairdresser. Take your pick. I'm afraid I wasn't listening."

"You'll have to do then." Annie eyed the empty kitchen, but just then the café door opened, and a stream of brats came piling in. I groaned and reached for the chocolate powder.

"I can multi-task," I said with a small smile.

Annie slipped through the hatch and rolled up her sleeves. "Me too. And I haven't forgotten how to make a Frappuccino either," she added, going through to the kitchen to wash her hands. I grinned and chucked Lily's apron at her.

"It reminds me of the good old days," I said. Annie was about to say something in return but instead clamped her mouth shut and busied herself at the other end of the counter. We worked side by side until the rabble had spilled back onto the hot pavement and I watched, jealous, as the kids crossed the road and sat by the edge of the lake, soaking up the cool breeze.

"I'd forgotten what hard work being a barista is." Annie

34

leaned her elbows onto the patch of work surface nearest the till. She arched her back and her spine clicked. "I gather Amelie was a regular here. Did you know her?"

I shrugged. "Not really. She came into the café a fair bit. She seemed sweet but quiet. Always with the popular girls – a bit of a beg."

Annie nodded and untied her apron, leaning into the kitchen and hanging it back behind the door.

I shoved a biscuit under her nose; a misshapen cookie with cracked smarties bursting from the surface. "They need eating up."

"And who might the popular crowd be?" Annie took a large bite of the cookie and held an upturned palm under her chin.

"Bea Harding and Tessa Pike. Silly bitches, the pair of them."

Annie reached into her jacket pocket and pulled out a notebook. She asked me to repeat the names before scribbling them down. "Did she come into the café last Friday, either before or after school?"

"I don't think I saw her after school, but I honestly wouldn't be able to say for sure because she was never really on my radar. Lils and I don't work before school. Grace and another couple of women do that shift but, even then, Grace is normally out the back baking and making up sandwiches, so I doubt if she'd remember either. In fact, Grace hardly ever serves front of house."

Annie dusted crumbs from her blouse and made a note of the names of Grace's other employees.

"I know you can't really say but…" I said, my voice doing that silly up-speak at the end.

Annie raised an eyebrow.

"Well, it's just that everyone is saying there was a boy involved."

"Did you ever see her on her own with a boy?" asked Annie.

I shook my head.

The sugar-throwing group of kids got up to leave, scraping

their chairs across the floor before they trundled out, giggling and whipping each other behind the knees with their jumpers. I armed myself with a j-cloth and spray before ducking under the counter. I started to stack the plates and then launched myself out of the café, sending the bell above the door into a frenzy. I peered along the High Street, but the group had already vanished down the side road which led away from the lake and towards the park.

"So typical," I said, coming back inside, waving a slim, pink fluffy pencil case in the air. "I could literally start my own shop with all the shit that gets left behind."

I opened the cupboard next to the milk fridge and pulled out the large plastic box with *Lost Property* written on the side. I dropped the pencil case into it.

"Can I have a look at that?" asked Annie.

I handed her the crate. "Go for it. There's even a tiny china doll in there. I found it slap bang in the middle of a table, sitting up against the saltshaker."

Annie peered inside the box.

I picked out the doll and dangled it by its woollen hair. "I know it's missing a leg, but it looks vintage, doesn't it? If no one claims it by the end of the month, I'm going to take it into town and see if *Kamble's Antiques* will give me some cash for it. What do you reckon?"

Annie grunted and, reaching inside her jacket for a silver topped pen, leaned in, poking around, like she was playing a game of *Operation*. After half a minute, she put her pen back in her pocket and folded her arms.

She moved towards the door. "I'll pop in another time to speak to Lily and Grace." She paused. "Oh, and do say hi to Tom," she added, the words tumbling out of her mouth. She left, and my stomach lurched. *Damn!* I hadn't told Annie about the engagement and that had been the perfect opportunity. I didn't want her to hear it from someone else. Somehow, I'd let things fall back into how they use to be; the same easy friendship which allowed Grace and the wedding to vanish from my thoughts – or was it just wishful thinking?

Chapter Six

Grace

I was re-arranging all the items in my glossy, wicker hamper bought specifically for Monarchy Day. I had picked a polka dot tea-dress to wear for the special occasion. In my youth I hadn't always been great at knowing how to dress myself, but as Grace, I always made sure I had the latest Joules catalogue to hand – that way I knew I would always look perfect.

I was truly delighted with my choice of linen napkins, and tied up each one with black ribbon. In the super-expensive homeware boutique in Oakford I stumbled across a set of champagne flutes made of thickened glass, ideal for al fresco dining. Plastic simply wouldn't have done, but cut-glass would have been too fragile. These were perfect for magnifying the contents of the bottle of vintage champagne which took me five minutes to zip inside its shiny, refrigerated jacket. I was delighted to note that there wasn't a Tupperware box in sight. I wrapped the smoked salmon sandwiches with the cutest beeswax paper and string, and tucked them next to the kitsch, china plates I found in one of the charity shops – shabby chic.

Okay, so it wasn't Henley Regatta we were attending, but a dance around a slimy pond crawling with horse flies, but one still had one's standards. After all, this was our first official outing as an affianced couple and, already I could see the sand in the egg-timer slipping through the funnel. There wouldn't be much more time for me to enjoy my engagement celebrations.

Emily would never marry. She was tainted goods.

There was a knock at the door.

I went to answer it, leaning into the cloakroom on my way past to check myself in the mirror. I pinched my cheeks, pleased with my elegant silhouette although, ideally, I would have liked to lengthen my frame with a pair of sky-scraper heels, but they would have been far too impractical for the walk through Cupid's Wood to the well.

I opened the door and there was DS Harper. Off-duty by the looks of her dreadful outfit.

"Oh!" I said, stretching my lips into a dazzling smile. Little did she know it was one of pity. Annie looked awful; her skin was damp and shiny, and her denim dress hung off her frame as though she hadn't zipped it up at the back.

I stepped onto the gravel drive and breathed in the humid air which was buzzing with excited chatter. Each household, like me, was packing up their picnics and searching for the right equipment; flasks, folding chairs for Granny to sit on and rugs still patched with crusted debris from their last outing. The sky was a hazy grey blanket and as soon as I stooped to pick up a stray sprig of geraniums, pressure needled against my temples, warning me the sun was moments away from scorching through the clouds. A timely reminder to bring the sunscreen. The flowers in my hand smelt earthy and drips of dew slid onto my fingers.

I bit my tongue to stop myself telling Annie that the dolly bow at the back of her dress made her look like the prize draw for a WI raffle.

Annie squinted at me. "Good morning, Grace, can I talk to you for a minute?"

"Of course, of course. Let me make you some tea. You look tired. Some raspberry leaf and ginger perhaps to get rid of those dark bags under your eyes." My lips glistened with my honeyed words.

"No, really, no thanks." Annie shifted her weight from one foot to the other. She was wearing scuffed Mary-Janes. *Simply ghastly.* "I've a few things to do before heading off with everyone else to the well."

I pretended not to listen and retreated into the house. I

heard Annie sigh and wipe her feet on the door mat before following me into the cool hall. Annie's breath smelt of coffee. The poor creature had really let herself go; she was pencil thin, her limbs all sharp angles – presumably the result of a diet of loneliness.

The engagement ring.

I spun around. "Well this is a lovely surprise." I reached out and clasped Annie's hands. I squeezed them hard, pressing the jagged emerald into Annie's palm. Annie glanced down, a look of bewilderment sweeping over her face before she jerked her hands away as though she had been stung.

I had to grind my feet into the floor to stop my body from quivering with delight.

I turned on my wedges and stalked into the kitchen. I really couldn't have planned this any better. All those years ago, when Grace was just a spark in my imagination, that very moment which had just elapsed was the perfect opportunity to sit back and admire my masterpiece. Grace, the lavender-scented, perfectly attired, ideal girlfriend.

There, sitting in the middle of the kitchen table, sat the picnic hamper, my straw sunhat lying against it; ribbon around the brim. When I went out to water the passionflower first thing, I had picked a couple of roses which now stood in a glass milk bottle next to the basket. I took a photo of it for the café's Instagram page and the likes were already pouring in. I fluttered my eyelashes at her and organised myself into a balletic first position.

"Wow," said Annie, her eyes wide with admiration, although for some reason the corners of her mouth were twitching at the same time. "There's me with my corned beef sarnies and bag of Monster Munch, pickled onion flavour of course."

Of course?

"Dave's bringing the sausage rolls and a scotch egg to share."

"Is Dave your...your other half?"

"Oh no." She gave an unattractive snort, but didn't say

anything to provide an explanation as to who Dave was or why the crisps had to be pickled onion flavour. She jerked her head towards the table. "You must have been up at the crack of sparrows to get that all ready."

I wafted a hand across my face. "Oh! It's nothing. Just a few smoked salmon sandwiches, freshly baked scones with homemade jam, strawberries and pink fizz to round off the celebrations. After all, it's not every day a girl gets engaged." I threw back my swan-like neck and a delicate volley of laughter escaped my lips.

"Is Flo not coming with you?" Annie wrinkled her brow. There was a pause and a flash of confusion passed through my mind. I'm ashamed to say, for a few seconds, I may have gawped.

Annie cleared her throat. "It's just that Flo hates fish, doesn't she?"

Stupid woman, how could you have forgotten?

"Oh, well, of course, there's ham in there as well." I smoothed my skirts in a calm, sweeping motion whilst a swirl of anger burrowed itself into my stomach lining.

"Is Lily here?" Annie peered into the basket.

I wanted to say no but there was a thud from upstairs which jingled the light fitting. I shook out a clean tea towel and draped it over the basket, forcing Annie's fingers to retreat. "May I ask what this is about? You look as though you're…off-duty." I clamped my teeth together and gave Annie another brilliant smile.

She winked. "Ah, but I'm never off-duty."

Cheeky bitch.

I walked into the hall and called up the stairs. "Darling, please can you come down. Now."

Annie had moved to the kitchen window, her gaze settled on the dahlia bed which, from this side of the kitchen, was a blur of angry reds.

"Your garden looks amazing," she said, turning around and leaning against the work surface. "I'm guessing Tom's not involved." She gave a dry laugh. "Despite all his best efforts, he never was much of a gardener."

I laughed, perhaps a little too loud. "Yes. I think I've got my work cut out there."

"Have you set a date?"

"Absolutely! Tom and I don't see the point in waiting. We're getting married in a couple of months. Naturally, it makes sense to move into Tom's house – it's so much bigger than this place plus there's room for a…" I paused and lowered my gaze; demure, "…a nursery. You know Tom – he's just crazy about kids."

Annie swallowed and ran her finger around the neck of her disgusting blouse. "Well! Congratulations, indeed."

"Oh, thank you," I said, trying to hide the fact I was relishing Annie's discomfort. "At first I thought I would miss living around the corner from the café, but if Tom has his way, I doubt I'll be working there much longer." I patted my stomach. "He wants to put the café and this little house on the market this autumn."

Lily sauntered into the room and Annie's body sagged with relief.

I gave Lily an optical sweep; the gypsy skirt was too long, the linen shirt too baggy.

Lily nodded at Annie.

Annie rubbed her hands together. "Hi Lily. Right! I just wondered if either of you recall seeing Amelie in the café on Friday."

Lily shrugged.

Maybe, but I couldn't say for sure.

I shook my head.

Annie paused then gave a thin smile. "Ah well. Don't worry, I'll show myself out. By the way, you look lovely, Lily."

When I heard the front door close, I turned to Lily. "Well done." Lily's face remained devoid of expression and she turned away. Lily went back upstairs. There was a slam then the dull, thud, thud, thud as her music reverberated through the ceiling.

41

She was cross with me because I had halved her dose last night and she had suffered for it. I had sat there in the corner of her bedroom and watched my sister writhe around, kicking off the sheets, murmuring and fretful as she played out her nightmare. What the selfish bitch didn't understand was that, although I had to punish Lily for her disobedience, I was the one who really suffered not her. She would never be able to comprehend what I'd lost or how my heart split in two each time I heard her voice; a most cruel reminder of my beloved.

Chapter Seven

Lily

It was Monarchy Day and there we were in the middle of a field which was supposed to be the place where King Charles I watered his horses after he was defeated at the battle of Naseby. The well was so far from picturesque that ramblers often missed it completely. Imagine a fairy tale well; circular brick walls with dainty wooden bucket swinging from a slate roof – now scrap that: King Charles' Well was a sunken rectangle of green slime, surrounded by a mesh of wire and avoided by all living creatures. Once a year, in June, the villagers came together to dance around it and give thanks for *our blessed monarchy* before peeling back to the other pub in the village – aptly named, *The King's Head*.

Grace was dressed as though she was attending Royal Ascot. She wasn't a natural at marrying the right appearance to the right occasion – I sometimes wondered if she could see colours at all. She had picked her outfit straight out of her latest catalogue. The original model was wearing a fascinator with magenta plumes but even Grace, despite her missing link to reality, was aware that this was a bridge too far and instead had tied a black ribbon around her straw gardening hat.

Grace was acting her part to the fullest and this particular episode was worthy of an Oscar nomination. Every movement and utterance was designed to be seen and approved of; if she could have given this sketch a title it would be *a match made in heaven*. She liked to think that all eyes were upon her as she fluttered around the field, shaking out the picnic blanket which smelt of chemicals. Tut! Tut! She hadn't thought to iron out the tell-tale creases which showed the rug was a recent purchase and that we didn't usually picnic with such panache. Grace was laughing, her speech too loud and high-pitched; *pass the napkins, darling* and other such nonsense.

Meanwhile, every other thought of mine was perforated with worry. Even with my back turned, I could envisage the rickety pier stretching out towards the glittering water; Amelie's body snagged up in the weed beneath.

Tom came rambling across the field and Grace, catching a glimpse of his gangling frame, went running towards him like something out of the Sound of Music; freshly dyed, copper mane streaming behind her, floaty dress billowing in the breeze. She kissed her fiancé full on the lips causing Mrs Nayler, who was laying out her tatty old plastic ground sheet next to us, to coo something about young love.

Then I saw Flo and despite half my brain being in shadow, I couldn't help breaking into a smile. For some inexplicable reason, Flo was dressed in full morris dancer attire.

"Don't you dare," said Flo. She threw herself down next to me, jingling as she did.

I bit my lip and allowed my gaze to wander up and down her entire outfit before giving one of the bells on the hem of her knickerbockers a rattle, producing a good solid top C.

Flo raised her knees into a bridge and buried her head in between so all I could see was her fair hair which she had scraped back into a short ponytail and tied up with ruby ribbon. I patted her between her shoulder blades.

"Bloody Dad volunteered me," she said, talking to the blanket.

I held my phone under the bend of her legs.

I think you look lovely.

"Piss off. I'm meant to be meeting up later with Steve and the band. I can't do that looking like this."

You can go back and get changed as soon as it has finished.

Flo sighed. "Apparently Amelie was due to do the stupid fucking dance around the well and because of her being missing and all that, they were going to call the whole thing off. But Amelie's Dad didn't want them to because he thought Amelie wouldn't want them to, so Dad said I'd step in." She sucked in her breath.

I carried on stroking and patting her back as though she was a toddler I was trying to calm down after a major tantrum.

"I even had to go to a rehearsal first thing this morning. You wouldn't think it was hard to join hands and move around in a circle, but I managed to fuck that up. I actually tripped and pulled a couple of old dears down with me."

It was too much and my body started shaking with bottled laughter. Flo felt the tremors and tipped her head on one side, left ear glued to her kneecap. Her cornflower eyes darkened, but after a few seconds of holding my gaze, the edges of her mouth twitched. "It's sooo not funny."

I nodded, my vision cloudy with tears.

I especially like the ribbons around your ankles. It's a good look.

"Hi Lily," said Tom sitting down next to me and taking up the rest of the blanket with his long limbs. He stared at the overflowing hamper. "My goodness, Grace, you've done us proud."

"Oh, it's nothing." Grace beamed, tapping Tom's thighs until he tidied them away into a cross-legged position. She clapped her hands together. "You do the champers, darling and Lily you hand out the plates please."

All around there was the rustle of people unwrapping parcels of food or prising the lids off plastic tubs.

Annie walked past swinging a jute bag, bottle of Dr Pepper peeping over the brim. She was deep in conversation

45

with a tall, unshaven man who was carrying a beach towel under his arm.

"Hey!" called out Flo. Tom waved.

Annie gestured for her companion to continue on without her. She came over and stood in front of us, blocking out the sun. "I hear congratulations are in order." Tom opened his mouth to say something then snapped it shut.

"Sandwich anyone?" said Grace, placing the perfect triangles in a central position.

"What are they?" asked Flo, wrinkling her nose at the smell.

"Smoked salmon."

Flo sighed.

Annie put her hands on her hips. "Don't worry. I know for a fact that Grace has made you your own special ham ones."

Grace's eyes narrowed as Flo rummaged around in the hamper.

"I can't find them," said Flo.

Grace cleared her throat. "They...they must have fallen out."

"How odd," said Annie, raising an eyebrow. "Flo, you're welcome to come and have one of my corned beef ones."

Flo shrugged. "Ah, thanks Annie, but you're alright. I'll beg a sarnie off Stella – she's bound to have marmite or something else normal." She rose to her feet and sauntered off with Annie in tow. Stella, clapping eyes on Flo's outfit, laughed as though she were a crow caught fast in a trap.

Grace cast her gaze to the ground. "Sorry, Tom. I can't think where those pesky ham sandwiches have got to."

He waved his hand across the open basket. "Don't be sorry. This is amazing. Thank you so much." He opened the champagne and the cork, as it left the bottle, gave out a loud pop and flew into the air. He winked. "I'm getting a taste for this, aren't you?" Grace held up her bottle of Perrier. "Oh! That was a silly thing to say," he added, slightly shame-faced. He poured the frothing, pink liquid into the glass goblets and, dressed in his cream linen suit, it would have been easy to mistake him for a character out of The Great Gatsby.

"Any more news about…?" Grace widened her eyes and licked her lips.

Tom shook his head but leaned in. "What the head, Ms Phibbs, has told me," he whispered, "on the *q t*, is that the police are almost certain there was a boy involved. Sounds like she's gone off with him, whoever he might be. Apparently, they found a burner phone in her locker at school. It appears that was how they communicated. They are trying to trace the other number as we speak, but they think the device is most likely switched off."

Grace swallowed and gave an involuntary shudder. Tom patted her arm and gave a sympathetic sigh, but, if he had looked closer, he would have noticed her pupils had dilated, reducing her irises to slivers of lime.

Grace sighed. "What a silly girl! But," she tilted her head on one side, "I do know how it feels to be hopelessly in love."

Tom gave her a peck on her nose before taking a huge bite of sandwich.

The field was filling with a rainbow assortment of chairs and blankets whilst loud chatter, buzzing and laughter drifted up into the hazy blue sky. The pale, white sun burned fierce behind a sheen of fluffy clouds but thankfully there was a gentle breeze. Every so often the stench of stagnant well water wafted across the clumpy grass, mingling with Grace's coconut sun lotion. Someone had put red, white and blue bunting around the wire which surrounded the well and the triangular flags slapped against the corner posts like waves lapping against the shore. Lining the edge of the field nearest to the village stood a row of horse chestnuts, their blossom like hundreds of upside-down wedding cakes.

Flo returned to base camp, dusting flakes of pastry from her top. Grace and Tom had finished eating and she was sitting, her back leant against his chest with his knees either side, like she was reclining in a comfy armchair. Tom kissed the top of her head then rested his chin on her shoulder.

The sound of a gong cut through the noise and people sat up and re-positioned themselves so they were facing the well.

The mayor buttoned up his scarlet jacket and picked up his tri-cornered hat which he'd been using to stand his wine bottle upright. Mrs Mayor helped winch him to his feet.

From varying positions throughout the field, all those in white knickerbockers, Flo included, rose to their feet and picked their way through the sheep droppings towards the well. Flo's jaw was set.

"Break a leg," said Tom and Flo mumbled something unrepeatable.

A tall man with a snowy handlebar moustache picked up a drum and held it above his head. He nodded at a plump, pink-faced woman who raised a flute to her lips. Then three women started singing a jolly tune about a frog and someone called Roly which made no sense, but which Tom hissed was all about King Charles. Meanwhile, the jingling white-walkers linked hands and circled the rectangle, stopping every ten steps to clap their hands and bang their knees before re-grouping to move in the opposite direction.

Flo's face flushed maroon with embarrassment. I filmed the whole thing with my phone. The local newspaper was there too so no doubt tomorrow she would find herself on the front page of The Rutland Chronicle. It should have been hilarious, but I kept thinking about how it should have been Amelie there dancing around the well, not Flo, and the champagne burned an acidic trail down the back of my throat.

Next, the Mayor and some grey-haired woman with a large, wooden cross around her neck kissed the long stick she was carrying.

"Today we give thanks for our blessed monarchy," she called out in a reedy, high-pitched voice. "As this well gave King Charles' horse sustenance in its time of need, so we give thanks for our life-giving water and pray that it will ever flow eternal and quench the thirst of all those who should desire it. Please join me all for a few minutes' silence to offer up our own prayers for the Queen."

Just the thought of drinking from that well made me gag. In years gone past, the vicar had to draw a cup of gloop from the stagnant pond and actually swallow it. I bet the last one to do it died of typhoid.

The woman bowed her head, kissed the stick again then poked it into the well. There was silence, then from the shore of the lake came a piercing scream.

Chapter Eight

Flo

I stumbled through Lily's front door and we spent a couple of minutes scrabbling around turning on every single light switch. The house smelt of lavender pot-pourri and public swimming pools. I had never seen such a clean and tidy home – unrealistic standards for me and Dad to keep up with when we all moved in together. I mean – there was literally no clutter anywhere. No photos either; just a few black-and-white nature prints – the sort you'd find in a show home.

I couldn't get the dreadful image of a dead body out of my mind and I'd been grateful for Lily's silence on the way over. I didn't want or need to add anything to Stella's endless stream of possibilities about what we'd just seen.

A body. A dead body washed up onto the shore of the lake.

After the police had taken down names and addresses, the crowds, stunned into a spooky silence, trailed back towards the village. The smell of the charring hog roast and crispy crackling, waiting for us at the King's Head, made my stomach turn. The sad twangs of a bass guitar drifted into the sky as the band, unaware of what had just happened, continued with their sound check. But, regardless of my stupid morris dancer outfit, I was no longer in the mood for trying to catch Steve's attention. The whole thing would be cancelled out of respect anyway, although the pub said it would remain open for those locals in need of something to calm their nerves.

That's when Dad begged Grace and Lily to stay the night: Grace in the spare room and Lily on an inflatable mattress in with me. It was weird that they didn't stay over more, but I reckoned one of the reasons was because Grace was hung up about what the older women in the village thought of her – she didn't want them to think she was a slag. I also knew about Lily's night terrors and all the pills she had to take to keep her dreams in check and Grace never ever let her go on sleepovers, not that she got many invites.

While Lily creaked around upstairs, packing an overnight bag for her and her Mum, I raided the cupboards. Five or so minutes later Lily came back into the kitchen. She was pale – her eyes red rimmed.

"Where does your Mum keep the booze?" I asked.

Lily pointed to a corner shelf underneath a neat row of cookery books.

"Oh!" The so-called spirits consisted of a startling violet liqueur, an almost empty bottle of sweet sherry and an evil-smelling cooking brandy. I did eeny-meeny-miney-moe then picked up the brandy along with a couple of tumblers. I sat down at the kitchen table and poured a generous measure for each of us, pushing a glass towards Lily. Lily sniffed at it and wrinkled her nose.

I gave her arm a gentle punch. "It is good for shock." Just then my phone rang, and I jumped, sloshing brandy over the rim. Lily grabbed a cloth from the sink and mopped up the spillage. "For God's sake, Dad. Yes, we're on our way." I dropped my phone onto the table and knocked back what was left in my tumbler before pouring myself another double helping. It tasted disgusting.

"How in the hell do you think she got there?"

We don't know for sure it's Amelie.

Lily pinched her nose and took a sip of brandy.

"Stella saw her, you know." I was still wearing my morris dancing outfit and the bells jingled as I ran my fingers through my greasy hair. "Well, she didn't exactly see her, no one did, but she said there was definitely a foot, bursting out of the corner of the bag."

51

Lily's skin was almost green, and she took a bigger gulp, dark eyes staring at the bottom of her glass.

I stood up and paced around, the soles of my dumb-looking leather slippers slapping against the lino. "It's got to be murder hasn't it? I mean she was all wrapped up. And what do you reckon – someone local? I mean, to put her there a few days before Monarchy Day was either really stupid or really nasty."

Or they didn't know the importance of the well.

I patted my stomach. "No. My gut tells me it was planned. Someone wanted to shock the whole community. I mean, half the county was there."

Lily drained her drink and I poured her another which she downed. A pulse flickered at the corner of her left eye.

"It's really shaken Dad. In fact, I don't think I've ever seen him so upset. He never talks about his students, but I guess he must be close to them – I mean he sees them every school day. You can't help getting attached, can you?" I thought of the time I'd gone into the classroom without knocking and found him with his arm around her. They hadn't seen me, and I'd made a quick exit. There was nothing in it, I knew that. I did.

The phone rang again. "Alright," I shouted. "Yes. Yes. We're leaving now."

When we got back to Spinney Cottage we went in through the back door and straight into the kitchen – Dad only ever turned the Aga off if there was a worldwide drought, so it was currently leaching heat. The kitchen table, tucked into the alcove under the bay window, had a half-empty bottle of whisky plonked in the centre. Dad's upper body was stretched across the painted pine surface, head cradled in his hands. Grace was leaning against the oven; pink cheeks to match her dress.

Dad looked up when we came through the door and asked if we wanted a nightcap. Grace was drinking Baileys, ice cubes clinking against the sides of her glass. I'd never seen her drink alcohol before. I pointed at it and Grace reached into the wooden cupboard behind her head to grab me a tumbler.

Lily pointed too, but Grace lifted the kettle onto the hotplate and waved a peppermint teabag at her. "Not before you go to sleep, darling." There was a fraction of a pause. "Have you–"

Lily nodded and pointed at me.

"Yep. I saw her swallow them." Grace's nostrils flared as she went to dispense a couple of rocks of ice from the freezer.

"Actually, I think I'd rather have tea," I said, and Grace squeezed my shoulder with approval as she walked past.

"They've identified the body," said Tom. "It's Amelie."

The silence was as smothering as the heat from the oven and after a few minutes I caught Lily's eye and jerked my thumb to the ceiling. Lily nodded and we kissed Tom and Grace goodnight and took our teas to my bedroom. I closed the door behind us.

"It's quite sweet our parents have got each other." I stripped down to my underwear and put on a pair of crumpled cotton shorts and my favourite of Dad's old *Cure* tee-shirts.

Lily pulled at the string of her teabag, tears spilling down her face, but before I could say anything, she leapt to her feet and pointed to my en-suite bathroom, bundling her lavender pjs under her arm. When she returned, she jumped onto her mattress and pulled up the duvet, covering her entire body. "Okay, okay. I get the message. You really need your beauty sleep." Lily stuck out a hand from under the covers and gave me the V-sign.

***

I woke with a start and rolled over; I could hear gushing water. I looked across to Lily's makeshift bed and did a double-take – it was empty. The taps in my bathroom were running – surely Lily wasn't taking a bath at this time of night? My dry mouth tasted disgusting and the room smelt of sour milk. I hadn't bothered to brush my teeth after the peppermint tea – telling myself that drinking it gave just the same protection as Colgate. Not true.

I reached out to the bedside table for my phone and saw that it was 3am. I was wide awake. It was as though someone had flipped the 'on' switch in my head. What the fuck was Lily doing? I crept out of bed and knocked on the door.

With a start, I realised that the soles of my feet were wet. I lunged for the handle of the bathroom door and pushed it open. The room was in complete darkness, so I pulled on the cord and there was Lily sitting in the bath, still wearing her lilac pyjamas, cold tap chucking out water.

My initial reaction was to laugh and ask her what in the hell she was doing, but then it was clear that although Lily's eyes were open, she wasn't fully conscious. Her lips were bluish-purple, and her jaw was moving. It was very cold in there and my teeth started chattering. As I moved closer, I realised Lily was singing *Down To The River To Pray* on loop. This was weird in itself, because it was the first time I had ever heard Lily's voice, but though she was singing the words of the folksong softly, the notes had a strange metallic ring to them. I shivered. Lily's dark irises stared into mine and filled my body with an overwhelming sense of dread, making my eyes fill with tears.

Suddenly Grace, appearing from nowhere, barged past me and turned the tap off, pulling at the plug. She whipped around to me and pressed an index finger to her lips then pointed to the towel on the radiator. The draining water gurgled and slurped.

Grace lifted Lily to her feet and wrapped the towel around her. "Go and get some pyjamas from the airing cupboard," she said to me, her voice calm and at the same time bossy. I swallowed down my terror but as I ran out of the room, something slimy caught between my toes. I looked down and pulled a string of pondweed from around my big toe, wondering how it had got into my bathroom.

Then I heard Grace say in a very firm voice: "Myrtle, it's

not your time. You need to leave. Now."

My mind was spinning with what I had just seen, and I was desperate to know who the fuck Myrtle was. I rushed back with a pair of my own pjs. Grace had Lily enveloped in her arms and was kissing her matted hair.

"Thank you," said Grace. "You go and sleep in the spare room. I'll stay here with Lily." I climbed into the cold guest bed, eventually drifting into a fitful sleep and dreaming about a silvery ghost who called herself Myrtle.

The next morning when I went downstairs, I found Grace in our kitchen, drinking coffee and staring out of the window.

"Is Lily okay?"

"She shouldn't have drunk spirits with her medication," said Grace, her voice sharp.

I shifted from one foot to the other.

Grace sighed, but still didn't look at me. "No harm done. She's fast asleep now and probably will be for most of the morning."

"Where's Dad?"

Grace shrugged.

I was about to open my mouth to ask who Myrtle was and why Lily could sing in her dreams, but something in Grace's manner made the words evaporate on my tongue. She didn't offer me a cup of coffee although the cafetière was three-quarters full and carried on gazing out of the window.

That's when I remembered the fish. My poor little, hungry carp.

Pretending that I didn't mind getting the cold shoulder from Grace, I wandered over to the back door and pulled the nearest jacket off its peg, draping it about my shoulders. I slipped on my trainers and stepped outside. The grass was sopping, and my rubber soles squeaked as I walked across the lawn. I headed towards Dad's shed at the side of the garden and, as I opened the door, the smell of grass clippings, petrol and creosote caught the back of my throat and made me cough. I picked up the plastic bucket of fish food and followed the crazy paving path towards the pond, knocking my shins against the handlebars of Dad's abandoned wheelbarrow which, thanks to a face full of early morning midges, I didn't see in time.

The pond was screened by a wall of wildflowers and feathery grass, but you knew it was there before you saw it; the surrounding air was heavy with the stink of stagnant water and there was a sound like someone taking a pee as the pump struggled to make the current flow.

I turned the corner and was blinded by a brilliant light which bounced off the surface of the pond. Then I took a step backwards, blinking fast as my eyes tried to make sense of what I was seeing.

I stood there squinting, the pail of fish food rattling by my side. Then I forced myself forwards, my heart hammering against my ribcage as the vision in the pond grew clearer: seven white and speckled orange bodies floating on the surface, eyes glazed open, mouths tiny dark circles.

Chapter Nine

Grace

My body trembled with pure rage as I clawed at the blooming patch of sore skin which coated the back of my right hand. Tom didn't have any calamine lotion. Indeed, the last time I looked in his medicine cabinet all I found was a battered box of Alka Seltzer, some ancient cologne which smelt of church incense and, of course, the little clue for the police I had hidden there. Thankfully, I knew that the manifestation of this skin irritation could be passed off as anxiety; solidarity with Flo.

I was furious with myself. Of all the crazy, stupid things to go and do and all because I'd had a couple of glasses of Baileys – and a few whisky chasers.

Tom, Flo and I stood by the edge of the pond, staring at the motionless bodies of the carp; a few fat bluebottles hovered over the surface. A pigeon tucked away in the boughs of a lacy-leafed birch gave out a mournful coo which drowned out the buzzing. Tom could barely make eye contact with me. I held out my hand to him, but he brushed my fingertips away. How dare he, of all people, ignore me.

Flo, the spoilt little drama queen, was lapping up the attention. Her eyes were puffy from her incessant snivelling. It was laughable. I tried and tried but couldn't fathom how Flo was able to muster any sadness over the death of those seven, soulless creatures. Nevertheless, I needed to rectify the situation with Tom. I took a step forward and positioned myself directly in front of him, forcing him to meet my gaze. I leant up and kissed the underside of his neck.

He recoiled.

I gulped down my disappointment. He had reduced me to nothing before, but I was strong – this time I wouldn't crumble to pieces. I turned and gave Flo my best sympathetic smile whilst in my head I acknowledged that this was a good thing; a timely reminder of Tom's capacity for cruelty. The tickling trace of ammonia, hanging on the early morning breeze, made my nose twitch.

"Who would do such a thing?" asked Flo.

Tom placed an arm around his daughter. "I have no idea," he said, his voice soft like balm.

I tried not to roll my eyes at his ludicrous over-indulgence. "Oh, but darling girl, it was such an extraordinary day, full of extreme emotions. Maybe *you* did it by mistake."

"Don't be so ridiculous," snapped Flo, and Tom enveloped her shoulders in a bear hug.

I clenched my fists, letting my fingernails dig into my palms. Tom may have been horrified at my behaviour last night, but I wanted to shake him: *who made me like that?*

The back door of the cottage creaked open and Lily appeared, holding a tray, her useless tongue poking out with concentration as she made careful steps across the lawn.

Lily set the tray down on the low, brick wall which skirted the border of the pond area and the orchard. The blossom from the apple trees had long since disappeared though the petals lined the grass underneath like used confetti. Tom's school briefcase, his one-time doctor's bag, sat there, wide open and the initials P.T.M glowed in the sunshine. I had to gulp down a snigger – did the marvellous Dr Marchant think he could resuscitate the fish with his rusty medical skills? Or maybe a bit of cognitive therapy would make them rise from the dead.

"Do you want sugar in yours?" I said to Flo before Lily handed her a cup. That's what you did when someone was in shock, wasn't it? That's what Frank always used to do – add a few spoonfuls of sugar and, God knows what else, to my tea. Flo pulled a face like she had sucked on a piece of lemon. Lily gave me the mug with a chip on its edge but avoided looking me in the eye as well she should. I was furious with Lily. Yet again, it was her selfish actions which had caused this premature avalanche of events.

My throat tightened as I recalled what happened last night; how one careless moment of alcohol-fuelled desire, followed by rejection, might have destroyed my whole five-year plan. I had to stay calm.

"Flo, dear. What do you think we should do?" asked Tom. I seethed. Was I now invisible?

There was a creak and slam as someone entered through the side gate. Startled, I looked towards the corner of the house, wondering who would be so ill-mannered to think they could use the back entrance.

"I called Annie," said Flo. She swept her hand over the surface of the water. "As soon as I saw this I knew it wasn't an accident." Sure enough, there she was the stupid cow, walking across the lawn with a large, cube-headed PC trotting after her. He had a bulky camera dangling around his chimneystack of a neck.

You called the police for a couple of dead fish was what popped into my head, but instead I swallowed my words. "Quite right. Good call." A sudden thought buckled my knees and I stumbled forward spilling my tea; I hadn't put my nightshirt in the wash – it was still hanging over the chair in Flo's bedroom. There would be traces of chemicals on it.

"Tea?" I asked, glossing over my own clumsiness with a dainty laugh, and offering Annie my chipped cup. She shook her hand. "Suit yourself." I put the cup back onto the tray. "So awfully good of you to come – I mean, what with all that's going on, I wouldn't have thought a shoal of dead fish was a priority for the police." I laughed again.

"Why not?" said Annie, her silver eyes unblinking. I hated the way she questioned every throw-away comment I made, as though trying to catch me out. "This morning all of Flo's fish are dead. That seems like a pretty big priority to me."

"You can't possibly imagine the fish murders are in any way linked to Amelie's death."

"Why not?" There it was again. I could feel my body

tensing with anger. I knew what I needed, but the whisky bottle was out of reach for the time being.

I moved away, but Annie held up her hand. "Could you just wait here a minute? I've got a few questions."

I sat down on the low wall and brooded about the nightshirt. And the whisky.

Next to Tom's bag were a couple of small vials containing cloudy brown water and Annie pointed at them.

Tom rubbed his hands down his thighs. He picked up one of the test tubes and held it out to Annie. "I've run some experiments. It's $CH_{16}O_4$. Otherwise known as metaldehyde a.*k.a.* Slugit."

Annie's eyes opened wide. "Wow, Tom. That's impressive," she fawned. "And you worked that out from just taking a couple of pondwater samples."

Tom gave a small crooked smile. "I'm not that smart." *You're not wrong there.* He took hold of her arm and pointed it towards the water. Annie stood still for a moment, and I caught the look which passed between them; a flash of mutual understanding.

"Remind me. What am I looking at?"

"See. On the bottom of the pond. There is a load of blue pellets."

"So definitely done on purpose?"

Tom nodded. "Yes, and with pellets taken from my shed."

"Don't you keep the shed locked?" asked Annie.

Tom shook his head and Annie wrote something down and then turned to *the bereaved*. The flabby policeman was walking around the pond, stopping every few seconds to take a volley of photographs.

"Right. Well the fish look as though they've been dead for a while. Did any of you hear anything strange last night or did something unusual happen? Talk me through your evening and let me be the judge of what is relevant."

Flo sat down next to me. "I woke up in the middle of the night because," she paused, "because I heard Lily in the bathroom."

Annie raised a badly plucked eyebrow. "She stayed the

night?"

I put my arm around Flo. "We both did. After yesterday we just felt the need for company. You know how it is?" I caught Tom's eye and gave a coy smile, though he responded as if I were Medusa.

Annie looked up at Flo who, in turn, stared at Lily. "It turns out Lily wasn't feeling well, and she was making these funny noises, so I went into the bathroom." She closed her eyes. "Then Grace came in and helped Lily. She'd sort of fainted."

Lily was staring into her teacup.

"After you went into the bathroom, how long was it before Grace came in?"

Flo shrugged. "About five minutes."

Shit. The nightshirt.

Annie gave me a sideways glance. "And where did you appear from?"

"I was in the guest room," I said. The corners of Annie's mouth twitched. "I heard a noise and came running. Anyone who is a mother will tell you – childbirth makes you a light sleeper." I smiled at Lily who avoided eye contact whilst Tom made an irritating clicking noise with his tongue.

"It's not a deep pond," said Annie. She folded her arms so her blouse rode up her waist, revealing her concave stomach. She was far too thin – skeletal.

The nightshirt was now an overwhelming source of concern and I leapt to my feet. "Coffee time," I announced, seizing the tray and storming off before Annie could stop me.

I was shaking as I went into the kitchen. I took a gulp of whisky. There wasn't much left from last night, so I finished it off and threw the bottle in the recycling. Then I set the kettle on the hot plate and made a dash for Flo's room. There, on the back of the dressing-table chair, was my nightdress, the hem speckled with tiny dots of cobalt blue – unnoticeable at first glance, but not under close scrutiny. I ran downstairs and threw it into the washing machine. Of course, Tom didn't have any stain remover products, so I'd settled for the hottest wash possible.

I needed more time. Time when I wasn't being observed.

The kettle whistled and brought me to my senses. I had to calm down and get a grip. I'd been terrified this morning when Flo came creeping into the kitchen, expecting her to ask me what I'd been doing by the pond. But when Flo didn't mention it, I realised she hadn't seen me, and I could still get away with no one finding out I'd slaughtered the fish.

I'd been in such a rage and it all stemmed from Tom's rejection. Drunk and aware my time with Tom was nearing an end, I'd decided to override Grace's prudishness. He'd seemed very pleased to start with and then, when it was over, hurt and confusion pasted across his face, he banished me to the guest room.

Furious at being cast aside by *him*, the hurt and humiliation mithered on all night preventing me from sleeping until, in the early hours of the morning, I got out of bed and went off into the dark to kill the fish. It was only when I glanced up at the window and saw the light on in Flo's room that I came to my senses and ran back inside just in time to rescue Lily. Tom, all the while, sleeping through the commotion like a well-fed baby.

She didn't know it was me!

I filled the cafetière with hot water and the tempting hazelnut smell put a stop to my alcohol cravings. I knew I could do this. Full of resolve I strode back across the lawn.

"Anyone for coffee?"

Tom tipped out the dregs of his tea and held his mug out for me to fill.

He caught hold of my hand. At last, I thought; he's deigned to forgive me. "Hey," he cried, pushing off his glasses to examine my hand further. "What did you do to your wrist?"

"Nothing," I said, snatching it back off him. Whilst caught up in the black mist of rage last night I'd forgotten to put on gloves and the chemicals had irritated my skin. "I had a fight with a patch of stinging nettles."

The waterlily pads were curling up around the edges. Flo fished out the carp with a long-handled net and plopped them into the wheelbarrow which, only last night, I had used to transport the slug pellets from the shed and down to the water. Thankfully, when the bedroom light went on, I'd had enough presence of mind to wheel it away from the pond, abandoning it on the other side of the grassy divide. No one had noticed – the garden, like the house, was always such a mess.

Tom smoothed his fringe out of his eyes. "Why would anyone come into the garden in the middle of the night to poison some fish? Unless they were a crazy person."

Tom stretched out his legs and put on a pair of rubber gloves and waders which came up to the top of his thighs. "If it's okay with you Annie, I think it's best if I drain it before any other creature comes into contact with the poison." I wanted to shout *no*, but Annie nodded, and he clambered in, wading through the dark water, momentarily stopping his journey to pick up the remaining carcasses for Flo's net.

Flo looked up from her funeral pyre. "Grace are you okay? You're bleeding."

I stared at my hands. I'd been pulling at the skin around my fingernails.

I nodded, dragging my eyes back to the pond, willing Tom to stop.

At the far left-hand corner of the pond, he stooped and fiddled around with something under the surface. There was a glugging sound and the water level lowered until the dark weed, which coated the bottom, was visible. A frog hopped out from underneath the base of a jaundiced lily pad.

"What's that?" asked Annie, pointing to a mound of rocks stacked against the opposite side of the pond's rectangular shell. Tom, slipping and sliding, went over to take a look. I hoped he would fall over and bang his head, but instead he shrugged and looked at Flo who mimicked his body language. There was black plastic poking out from underneath the stones and he began to disassemble the heap to reveal a bag which he picked up and placed at Annie's feet.

I stifled a groan. They weren't meant to find this yet – it

was too soon.

Annie put on her gloves, opened the sack and pulled out a pair of black shoes. Small, black lace-ups. School shoes tied together with a pair of white, lacy knickers.

Chapter Ten

Lily

Grace and I left Spinney Cottage. The white and blue police tape which boxed in the empty pond rippled in the breeze whilst Tom and Flo continued to stare at each other with bewildered expressions.

Annie's reaction to discovering the shoes and pants was strange; quiet, contained. She refused to communicate further without the use of stock police phrases; *no comment, process the evidence.* Flo took it very badly saying for God's sake why was Annie being such a prize bitch and how could she possibly think they had anything to do with either item. Annie rebuffed her with silence. She moved everyone away from the scene and made a few phone calls. Within ten minutes an army of police people arrived, and a cloud of suspicion fell over the house.

Grace couldn't keep still, her eyes darting all over the place. This wasn't part of her plan and she was fidgety and awkward – my sister at her most dangerous.

Annie sent the ginger-haired constable off to the police station with the bagged-up shoes.

Eventually Annie came over to us, female police officer at her side. She told Tom and Flo they needed to pack a bag and go and stay with Grace for a couple of days. The police officer would accompany them into the house.

"Fucking hell, Annie," said Flo. "Do you really think that's necessary. Besides, don't you need a search warrant or something?"

Annie nodded. "It's being sorted."

"Well until then, I'll bloody well go where I like in my house." Tom reached out and put a hand on her arm. He shook his head and gestured for the policewoman to lead the way.

Grace gave me a sly grin which knocked me off balance.

Having Tom staying at ours obviously wasn't part of her great plan, but as he crossed the lawn, she called out to him that she would hurry back first and get the rooms ready. The lies were coming so fast, I couldn't keep up.

Either Tom didn't hear her, or he was ignoring her. She clenched her jaw.

We took a right turn out of Tom's house and wandered along the broken tarmac path which led into town, Grace muttering all the time under her breath. It was as though she was having some kind of conversation with herself; her expression swinging from fierce to sad and back again; her emotions suspended from the rocking pendulum of a grandfather clock.

Fat white clouds were building themselves into enormous haystacks in the sky and, as they assembled, brought with them a chill to the air that nipped at my bare toes.

Through the tall row of wispy ash trees, I saw that the lakeside car park was already full. We slipped through the red and white barrier and took the narrow gravel path which led down to the lake. There were people everywhere, only they weren't smothered in their usual Lycra outfits – they were dressed in smart clothing; all designer jeans and jackets.

It hadn't taken long for word to reach the wider world that Amelie's body had been found.

We emerged from the brick archway which led onto the cobbled road lining the south side of the lake. I blinked. The lake had disappeared, replaced by huge white vans parked on the green verges, wires trailing all around, strangling the *keep off the grass* signs. One of the journalists was perched on the war memorial, eating a sausage roll, her bare calves pressed against the engraved names of the fallen.

We stopped outside the café. "Wait here," hissed Grace, fishing the keys out of her pocket and unlocking the door.

The clouds had turned battleship grey, casting monstrous shadows everywhere.

I stood in front of the windows, a pinching sensation at the back of my neck – this was serious. This was real. Someone a couple of metres away was making a broadcast; the light of the camera shone onto the presenter, making their skin glow an eerie pale blue. The logo on the nearest van belonged to a regional news team and I recognised the tiny female reporter who was busy typing onto an iPad. Sandy something-or-other.

Loud hysterical chattering, interspersed with pinging, punctured my train of thought. The self-appointed cool clique had arrived – faces lit by the activity of their phones as they created hashtags and facebook pages to advertise their own personal traumas. I wondered how many sad face emojis Amelie's disappearance had generated. Their leader, Bea, was wearing very expensive pistachio-green shorts with tight black tee and white trainers. Her caramel hair was piled on top of her head in a dishevelled bun, escaping tendrils coiled around her neck. A hairstyle which had been constructed with care. Bea's face was thick with a biscuit foundation, as though mindful of the possibility of a TV appearance for which pancake was essential to blot out the shine.

There was a gentle tap on my wrist, and I turned to find myself looking down the bridge of a nose which belonged to Sandy, the TV reporter.

"Hi. I'm Sandy Baker," she said with a faint Birmingham inflection. I nodded. She was incredibly small – her feet wedged into patent, aqua heels were, at the most, a size three.

"I'm a reporter with *East Midlands Today*. Can I ask you a few questions?" Before I had time to shake my head, the camera was angled at me, drenching my body in white light. My gaze was drawn to a hypnotising crimson dot which encouraged my useless tongue to stick to the roof of my mouth.

"Did you know Amelie?" asked Sandy.

Someone barged into my shoulder, knocking me to one side.

It was Grace.

She placed a flattened palm in front of the camera lens. "Have you no shame? Someone has died and all you want is salacious gossip." Sandy raised an eyebrow, but the cameraman continued filming.

Grace grabbed me by my elbow and frog-marched me away. Her breathing was fast and shallow. Beads of perspiration coated her upper lip. She hadn't wanted to be there when they found Amelie's shoes and she hadn't wanted to draw any attention to us. She had failed spectacularly on both counts.

"Did you know her?" called out Sandy to the back of our heads.

Two minutes later we arrived home and I was banished to my room. With a sinking heart, I heard the clunk of a key turning in the lock.

***

I looked down into the dark water, my own reflection swallowed by her heart-shaped face which smiled up at me, just below the surface. Her hair had spread into a blonde fan around her head and it gyrated in slow-motion, fighting against an underwater eddy. Emerald weed rose from the depths and twined around her wrists as though she was off to the opera, wearing her best feather boa. Her ruby lips were parted and, though she was singing, I could only catch hold of a faint melody, but it was enough to set my heart on fire and my body trembled with the need to hear more. She carried on, the notes leaving her rosebud mouth as a funnel of bubbles and I heard her voice reverberating within my chest, tickling against my ribs.

O sisters, let's go down,
Let's go down, come on down
O sisters, let's go down
Down in the river to pray

She raised a slender finger and beckoned me closer. There was something about the scent of the water; the bitter aroma of the algae which warned me against reaching out to her. My mind, however, was slower than my body. As I leant over, an arm shot out from beneath the surface and clutched at my wrist. I was paralysed with fear. This arm was fleshless – it was bone, the fingers were knives pressing into my wrists, but she had no strength to pull me under. Only one arm emerged from the lake and the rest of her body was surrounded by water. I remained rooted, staring at her face as her white skin peeled away, leaving a skull; eyeballs bulging from the sockets while her teeth crumbled into the water and settled as ivory flakes on top of the sediment.

"Help me," she screamed and now my face was an inch away from the surface of the lake. I felt tiny water droplets splashing against my cheeks. "You have to look. You have to find me. You. Have. To."

Her voice morphed into a wailing – a song of unbearable lament which thudded around my eardrums, sending waves of sadness into my heart.

"It was you who let me out and now I can't return. Only you can see what has become of me. You must unlock the casket, my darling girl, I loved you so much. Do this for me."

Then I saw it. To the left of her was a chest, hidden amongst the pebbles and silt at the bottom of the lake. It was barely visible but for a greenish-gold lock at the base of the lid which, at that very moment, caught a moonbeam and caused a splinter of light to pierce my eye.

Tears streamed down my face and dropped onto the water. For a few seconds my vision clouded and, when the fog lifted and I looked again, I saw she had disappeared. My insides ached and I sobbed. I wrung my hands together, my heart churning. The casket had vanished too. I was staring into an empty cavern of blackness. Guilt flooded my body and I began to howl.

***

I sat up. It was dark. Something bit into my ankles. I rubbed my eyes with my hands as familiar silhouettes registered within my mind. I was at home, lying on my bed. As I shifted on the damp mattress the pinching in my legs deepened. My pyjamas were soaked with sweat and as I shifted into this other sphere of existence, my skin chilled to gooseflesh. I cast my gaze towards the end of the bed; both of my ankles were tied by a washing line to the iron railings of the bedframe.

"Lily," said a familiar female voice. It was Grace.

As the sweat evaporated from my body, my teeth started chattering. I thrashed around, trying to locate her. She was sitting on the armchair in the far corner of the room beneath the windowsill. Her body cast a chequered shadow on the wall as the grey dawn filtered through the gingham curtains.

"I'm sorry this had to happen," she said, her voice harsh.

I hunched myself over trying to pull at the plastic-coated cable, but my fingers were trembling and could make no inroads into the knots.

"You left me no choice." My mind stumbled around trying to pull ideas out of the creases of my memory. What did I do?

I mimed putting pills on my tongue and I heard the creak of her smile, her pearly teeth glinting in the gloom.

She narrowed her amber eyes. "Why didn't I give you your medicine?" She drummed her long fingers on the arm of the chair. Experience had taught me how to play this game. The rules were always changing, but the skill required to partake remained the same: buckets of patience. I thought back to yesterday, racking my brains to pinpoint what had caused this outburst. Sometimes I had to use fairy steps to retrace my journey towards the tipping point; the trigger; the switch.

Grace folded her hands across her chest. The hairs on the back of my arms stood to attention; a premonition of what I was about to see. In the next second the blade appeared – it shone as the first rays of sun peeped under the curtain hems. Grace held it underneath her chin, running the fingertips of her left hand across the point of the blade.

"You," she said, her voice deepening.

I knew this bit. It was as though she was telling me a favourite bedtime story – her favourite not mine. "I gave up everything for you." I steadied my breathing and began counting to ten.

"Tom Marchant may have been the one who forced Daddy to kill himself, but you…you were the one who told the lies in the first place. Didn't you?" She was staring at me.

I nodded, but I really couldn't remember.

Grace always listened to my nightmares. I think she enjoyed watching me suffer; saw it as my eternal punishment for bringing Tom into her life.

"When Daddy killed himself, who was left to pick up the pieces?" Her voice had taken on a sing-song tone.

I pointed to her.

"Who had to abandon everything just to bring you up?"

I bowed my head and pressed my palms together as though in prayer. I had learnt over the years that sometimes this obsequiousness softened Grace's thirst for blood.

Not this time.

She widened her eyes in mock surprise. "Then why are you being like this?"

I hung my head.

"You are being like this because you are bad. You were born bad." Grace sniffed and this intake of breath was my cue to act. I knew if I didn't get to the thing that displeased her soon my punishment would be more severe. A broken arm once.

"All I've ever done is love you."

I placed my hands on my heart. A gesture of love. I suppose deep down I did love her, but, if we were to get the scales out at that moment, my hate for her would have tipped the balance.

"You don't," she said, and a bubble of spit flew into the air. "Otherwise you wouldn't have drunk all that alcohol and made yourself sick. That Flo girl is a bad influence. She has you wrapped around her little finger."

I made an F with my hand and bowed my head.

71

"You are getting too close. You will jeopardise the plan. You must keep away from her. I told them they couldn't come here with us and they are staying at a B&B on the other side of the village."

I nodded.

Bile ran up my throat and the walls of the room spun around my head. My mouth hung open in protest, but I snapped it shut again. I needed Flo.

Grace got up off the chair. "You know what you must do." She reached for a small hand towel which was draped over one of the arms. There was no getting out of what was coming. She had already made up her mind. She shook out her hair and walked towards me. She stood in front of me and gave a sad smile, as though she was doing this for my own good. She placed the towel over my lap. "Three."

She handed me the knife.

I took a deep breath and plunged the blade into my skin. The familiar pressure spread across my arm and I heard a soft tearing before the rip of pain filtered through to the rest of my body. Stinging. Burning.

"Good girl," she said, patting my head as the beads of blood dropped onto the towel. "I'll make us a nice cup of tea while you finish up."

Chapter Eleven

Flo

I woke to the annoying buzz of my phone alarm which grew angrier with each passing second. It was way too early and way too bright; the curtains of the B&B looked like they were made out of fishing nets and speckled sunlight bounced onto my face.

How could Annie even suggest that Dad had something to do with Amelie's death? It was dumb. I mean, that time I'd burst into the classroom and he'd had his arm around Amelie's shoulder – I knew it wasn't a *thing*…

This was all Annie's fault. She was the one who'd slung us out of our own home, but it was weird that Dad wouldn't let us stay the night at Grace's – come to think of it there had been a funny vibe between them long before the shoes were found.

I swiped the noise away and clamped my eyes shut, trying to burrow my way back down into the covers but, as I closed my eyes again, the image of my new super expensive *Triangl* bikini popped into my head. I flung off the duvet – might as well get it over and done with. I had to admit, I was also a bit curious as to why Lily wanted to meet me for a swim at the Bather's Pond. We'd run and cycled around the lake before but had never set foot in its freezing water, plus, I was fairly certain that Lily couldn't swim. The forensics team had swarmed in and Dad and I only had a few minutes to pack our bags, so it was only by chance that I found Lily's scribbled note.

Please meet me for a swim. Bather's Pond, 6.30am.
Don't message me. I don't want Mum to know where I am.

Thank God it wasn't the same stretch of lake where they had found Amelie's dead body. I squeezed myself into my disgusting school swimming costume which pinched the tops of my thighs, there was no way I was getting my new bikini covered with lake slime, and shoved a comfy tracksuit over the top.

Dad's snoring rumbled through the interconnecting door and I was glad that, at last, he'd managed to nod off. We'd stayed up way too late last night, working our way through the coffee sachets and UHT milk pods, winding ourselves into knots thinking about those fucking shoes and how they had got into the pond.

We didn't talk about the knickers.

I didn't mention the hug. It was nothing.

No, the shoes and pants had to be the fish murderer's handiwork; he or she had planted them and then poisoned the carp. But, every time either of us said our theories out loud, they sounded utterly ridiculous and the *why* never got its feeble head off the ground.

I could hear the owners of the B&B clattering around in the kitchen – I really didn't want to have to speak to them; they were super weird; all the shelves in the dining room were covered with dancing china pigs. I crept downstairs, towel tucked under my arm, and opened the front door very quietly. The sky was grey, but the air was warm and fuzzy. Last night I'd tied my bike up against a railing to the left of the house. We'd been forced to cycle here as Annie, in full bitch mode, had decided Tom's car was something which also needed a *thorough investigation.*

Shoving Annie out of my head, I wiped the dew off the saddle, bundled the towel into the basket on the front of my bike and set off.

At this time of morning the roads were eerily quiet although a speedy milkman frightened the tits off me as he appeared out of nowhere and overtook me on his jingling float. It was still far too early for the commuters to be crawling out of their villages. It must have rained a bit last night because the tarmac was shiny and as I pedalled, fine spray coated my ankles. God I was unfit! My legs were already aching as I free wheeled down the hill past the church of St. Terence The Greater. I swerved left and joined the bumpy bridleway which led to the south basin. I liked this side of the lake; it was less touristy. The shore was lined with trees and the dark track leading towards the water was riddled with hoof marks; the potholes semi-filled with puddles despite the boiling weather.

I spotted Lily waiting for me at the water's edge, her gaze focused on the early risers as they sucked in big huffs of breath before launching into the water. I watched as the mist, like something from a zombie movie, rose from the lake and disintegrated into the pale sky. I loved the different way the swimmers dealt with getting into the water; some swaggered along the decking and plunged straight in; others tiptoed over the shingle and waded in until they were nothing but coloured dots bobbing on the surface; only bright caps and goggles visible. I liked how no one gave a shit what anyone else's body looked like – apples on sticks, pears, pencils – it didn't matter.

No one shrieked as their flesh made contact with the murky water. This was hard core swimming; sliders worn down to the water's edge, rolled towel positioned on top of them next to re-usable mugs and small wallets for car keys and loose change. It was far too early for *The Southside Restaurant* to be open, but some clever clogs had taken over a hollowed-out caravan, serving up breakfast for the baptised; filling their bright, neon cups with steaming tea or coffee and handing out breakfast rolls. The smell of bacon and fried sausage mingled with the peaty scent of the lake and made my tongue itch.

I seized Lily around the shoulders and gave her a little shove, before pulling her back.

"Saved your life," I dug her in the ribs. "Now then, Lilster, what's all this about? I thought we agreed, you need your beauty sleep."

Lily didn't respond. Instead, she kicked off her shoes then peeled down her tracksuit bottoms, leaving them in a crumpled heap on the ground.

"Oh, so we really are doing this?" I unzipped my top so that the faded Speedo sign on my costume poked out. Lily took a step into the water, stopped short and clenched her fists. "Aren't you going to take your shirt off first?" Lily ignored me and carried on walking. Soon the water kissed the back of her knees.

"You owe me a bacon butty," I muttered, before breaking the swimmer's code and letting out a huge shriek which sliced through the silence and caused a pair of ducks to quack like mad before scuttling into a heap of reeds. The impact of the cold water knocked the air from my lungs, and I gasped. "You-also-owe-me-an-explanation."

Lily, on a mission, kept her face forward and continued wading into the lake. I stumbled as the pebbles bruised the soles of my feet and soft weed tangled between my toes. I remembered the weed on the floor of the bathroom, the night Lily had gone for a midnight dip. How had it got there?

"Bloody hell," I gasped, my voice a high-pitched squeak. My mottled thighs now resembled two slices of corned beef. I took a couple of giant steps, reached forward and clasped hold of Lily's hand. We were now up to our waists in water and I was grateful for the warmth of my own blood as it pumped around my veins. Lily's shirt ballooned around her middle like a rubber ring. There was no going back. I wriggled free and plunged my shoulders under the surface, gliding through the water, my mouth clamped shut. I kept going until the urge to scream had disappeared.

"Come on." I popped my head up and flipped onto my back, turning my arms into backwards windmill sails.

Face pinched with concentration, Lily lowered her body, her hair fanning out around her.

"*Come on.* See. It's actually not that bad once your shoulders are under."

Lily stayed motionless, her chin resting on the water.

"You can swim, can't you?"

Lily shook her head.

"Shit." I lunged back towards her, grabbing her under the armpits. "Why? I mean *why?*"

"I've got you. Lift your feet up." Lily's varnished toenails emerged from the water and she wiggled them. "Point your feet and kick a bit. Just gently." Lily did what I told her, and I felt the almost magnetic drag of the water pulling around my thighs. Lily twisted her head, a flash of panic wrinkling her forehead.

"It's okay. I'm still here. Now take your arms and flap them in and out, keeping your fingers glued together."

Lily lay on her back, looking up at the sky, her legs frothing the water around the soles of her feet, her arms working against the current. Bit by bit I released my grip.

"You're doing it. You're *sort of* swimming Lily."

After a few minutes Lily lowered her legs and stood up before turning and wading back onto the shore. Satisfied Lily was safely on land, I spent another ten minutes swimming out to one of the buoys and back, determined, after all this effort, to get some exercise.

When, on jelly legs, I wobbled out of the water Lily, now dressed, passed me my towel and a hot sandwich. She'd wedged a polystyrene cup of tea into the stones next to my trainers.

Teeth chattering, I wrapped myself in the towel and then sat down, the shingle digging into my butt cheeks.

We sat, side by side, eating bacon sandwiches, sipping our hot drinks and watching the other swimmers coming and going.

Eventually I turned to her. "What's all this about?" I asked. Lily carried on staring ahead and rolled up the left arm of her tracksuit. I spat out a mouthful of tea. All the way from her elbow to her shoulder were tiny lines; some silver, some pale lilac, others deep violet. The very top of her upper arm was covered in a waterproof plaster.

"You self-harm?" I whispered.

Lily stayed motionless.

"Fucking hell – I'm sorry, Lils. I'm guessing your Mum knows all about it."

Lily lowered her sleeve and bit her lower lip.

"I suppose it explains why she's so protective of you." I stretched my legs out in front of me; cramp was taking hold of my calves. "Is there anything I can do?"

Lily shook her head.

I licked tomato sauce off my fingers, screwed up my sandwich wrapper and, giving my skin a half-hearted rub, clambered back into my tracksuit. I was buying time – I didn't know what to say. I sat back down again and cradled my tea. I decided to change the subject. "Hey, did you notice a bit of an atmosphere between Dad and Grace yesterday?"

Lily reached across for my phone.

A bit. Mum thinks I'm at the gym.

I shrugged. "I suppose it makes sense not to worry her." I turned my head. "But why here? Aren't you a bit sick of the sight of ponds and lakes?"

I needed some space.

"I get you."

I have to tell you something.

My phone started to ring making Lily jump. She dropped it into my lap.

It was Dad. "I've got to get back. That was Dad. He sounded really weird. Do you mind if I scoot?"

Lily's lower lip was trembling. We had our normal goodbye hug, although she hung onto me just a fraction too long. I felt bad – she had just shared a massive thing with me and here I was running away. But Dad had sounded in a right state. I wheeled my bike to the main track but before I got back on, I turned.

"Good luck for the English mock tomorrow," I shouted.

"See you in the library after, yes?"

Lily made a heart with her hands and I left her, tears streaming down her cheeks.

Chapter Twelve

Grace

I was like a jack-in-the-box. My shiny, metal handle was close to being wound tight, to its pinch point, and any moment I was going to spring open, my emotions spilling over the edge and puddling onto the floor. Then, surely, I would slip over in the mess that I had nurtured inside for all these years. Grace could not exist for much longer. The moment Tom refused my offer of a bed for the night, I knew her time was over.

Emily must return while Grace must fade.

It was only now that I could sit back and appreciate how much effort it had taken out of me to exist as Grace. It was far easier to be myself where vindictiveness and hatred sprang naturally from the well. I heard the drip, drip, drip of self-loathing as it filled up the empty corners of my mind whilst self-pity gnawed away at my heart, making it a hollow shell once more.

Grace would have escaped; put on her Hermes headscarf and dark glasses like she was some film icon dashing away to an exotic location, but I knew there was no disguising myself from Frank. I had been conceited; thought I was in charge but, as always, I had screwed things up and now could only sit back and wait for Frank's inevitable wrath. Frank was the only who could see through my pale skin and identify my true being because he was the only one who truly loved me. After all, he was the one who put me back together again. Even when the parts didn't fit, he bashed them up against each other until they did.

I caught a bus to an out of town supermarket and filled my trolley with bottles of cheap vodka and expensive tonic water. My thirst had returned. Just wandering up and down the booze section rekindled my desire for alcohol; the need for its comforting sting seeping into my bones so I could wait no longer. I reached into the chiller cabinet and took out a ready mixed G&T. It was ice cold; the tin smudgy with a cloud of condensation. My fingers were trembling as I cracked it open and took a surreptitious swig. The sensation of the liquid sliding down my throat made my eyes close in rapture and soon the entire contents had disappeared down my gullet. A kid, far too big to be sitting in a trolley, gawped at me whilst his mother chatted to the white-aproned man behind the sliced meat counter. I scowled at him, revelling at the sound of his cries about a nasty lady, as I wheeled towards the check-out.

When I got home, I sank into the armchair in the cosy snug which overlooked the garden. I stared at the butterflies which fluttered around the cone-shaped blossom dangling from the buddleia bush and sipped my vodka, relishing each mouthful and sucking it in through my teeth.

We had featured on the news last night. The lack of any hard facts, apart from that Amelie's body had been found, made the journalists desperate for a story. They had needed an angle and I, like a fool, had handed one to them by standing in front of the camera, scolding the reporter; telling her to leave us alone. *A girl is dead, have you no shame?* So, they had run with 'Community left reeling; emotions running high'. The bulletin appeared at teatime and was the main story for the late news which meant we had received double exposure.

There was no doubt in my mind that Frank would have been watching. He was the sort to turn on the late headlines whilst finishing a large glass of claret and morsel of salty stilton.

Uncle Frank.

I stared at the bottom of my glass and there was his face, looking up at me. I closed my eyes. I wouldn't think about him or how I had let him down. None of this was his fault. All he had ever done was love and protect me. I forced myself to sprint through my memories, searching for something else to dwell upon and it wasn't long before I turned my thoughts towards Tom and the first time we met.

***

It was a hot day; the crowds overwhelming. I slipped through a side door and found myself in the middle of a passageway which smelt of bleach. I scurried along, the soles of my pumps squeaking on the shiny floor tiles. I embraced the coolness which crept over my body. Once more I was in the shade.

My head was spinning with emotions I didn't know how to put into words. I was lonelier than I had ever been in my life and there was no one for me to turn to. Not even my beloved, for surely talking about it with him would make him regard me differently; see me as tainted goods. Perhaps he would think it was my fault – perhaps it was. My heart ached with the burden of carrying around this sense of shame and I didn't know what to do with it. But, then again, maybe I was just being silly? After all it was just a touch – nothing more than a friendly exchange and I knew Frank really did love me and this was just one way for him to show it. And he was a good man. He took care of me; gave me beautiful clothes and gifts. But then why did I feel so sad and confused?

I began to feel dizzy and lunged at the nearest door handle to find a quiet place to sit down.

"Hey!" said a man in a lab coat who was leaning against a wooden counter. "What are you doing in here, kiddo?" There was something in the way the man smiled as he talked which made my body crumple inside. His eyes were bright with energy and his cheeks were smooth and at the same time they glowed. I burst into tears; horrid fat drops which stung my eyes and made me gulp and snort for breath.

"Oh! Hey there, kiddo, I'm sorry. You having a bad day?" The man rushed over and pulled out a stool for me to sit on.

He gave me a bundle of tissues. "Really bad day, from the sounds of it." He made a whistling noise and shook his head.

I nodded several times and dabbed at my hot eyes.

"Well, technically you're not allowed in here, but…" he tapped the side of his nose, "…I guess I won't tell anyone if you don't. The *official* tour group isn't visiting this part of the hospital."

My breath began to fall into its regular pattern. I blew my nose and stared up at the illuminated glass-fronted cabinets that towered behind the man's head. Each shelf was stuffed full of slim white boxes stacked on top of each other like mini building blocks.

He followed my gaze. "This is the part of the clinic where we store all the medicine. I'm doing a stock take. I'm Dr Tom Marchant, by the way," he added pointing to his name badge and giving a wave. "But you can call me Tom." He lifted up a hatch and ducked behind the counter. "Pill counting isn't part of my job description, but we've all got to be here for the grand opening, and I hate all that schmoozing so I'm doing what is known as *making myself useful*." He leaned across and grabbed the clipboard, pulling it to his chest.

He pushed a small stepladder up against one of the cupboards. "I'm actually a children's doctor. So, I guess if you need someone to talk to, I might be your man. I'm a super good listener."

I stared at the backs of my hands and bit the skin off my bottom lip.

Tom pulled a bunch of keys out of his pocket and as he fumbled with the lock, the clipboard fell to the floor.

"Damn!"

I slid off the stool, dipped under the hatch and passed it back up to him.

"Thank you."

I nodded and returned to my seat on the other side of the divide.

"You know, in my experience – not that I'm that old…" he laughed, and his eyes disappeared into a cluster of crow's feet, "…if there's something troubling you, it's always better to get it off your chest. It's as though saying it out loud takes the sting out of it." He fell silent and tapped the tip of his pen against the boxes, whispering under his breath. He scribbled something down on the chart then re-locked the door. He climbed down one rung of the ladder and unfastened the next cabinet. "And because I am a doctor, we actually have lessons on how to listen, would you believe it?"

I swallowed. My stomach was fluttering. Could I really talk to him about what had happened?

Tom's fingertips moved over the cartons and again he scored something on the clipboard. "We're not allowed to talk about what we discuss with a patient. It's all confidential. So, I mean, if you want to talk to me about what's bugging you." He turned and pretended to zip his mouth together.

Would he believe me?

I heard Uncle Frank's booming voice coming from the room next door. I jumped up. He couldn't find me here talking to Tom. What if he thought I had been telling tales? I scarpered towards the door.

"Hey, kiddo," Tom called out. He walked towards me and pushed a card into my hand. It had his phone number on it.

"That's my direct line. You can call me any time, if you need to talk."

Chapter Thirteen

Lily

They found a canvas school bag with a dolly-pink and baby-blue striped handle in Cupid's Wood. It was hidden inside the hollow at the base of a large oak tree, known by the locals as The Tree of Promises. According to Tom, this tree, like the well, was reckoned to date back to the time of King Charles I and as trees went, it was pretty cool. The trunk was squat and wide, and the first branches stuck out horizontally then rose into a series of forks. It was the sort of tree, as a little girl, I would have imagined marked the gateway to an enchanted forest. There was a legend to it which Tom told me about in great detail, but according to Grace, it was utter nonsense and she listened to the entire story with one eyebrow arched.

Apparently, a lady of importance fell in love with a beautiful stable boy and the tree was where they used to meet. Knowing that they would never be allowed to be together, there, in the forest, she made them each a crown of flowers saying that this made them equal in the eyes of the woodland folk and so they declared their undying love to each other. Surprise, surprise, her father found out and set up a false meeting where he killed the stable boy. The lady was devastated and hung herself from the tree – their garlands of snowdrops dangling from the bough next to her. Nowadays, in these parts, if you are truly in love with someone, you must come to this tree and hang a garland of fresh flowers from it.

The really strange thing about the legend though was that I saw Grace hang a posy amongst the branches of the fat old oak. Okay, so I witnessed her putting the bag there too, but that had always been part of her plan.

We'd gone for an early evening stroll and taken Mr Hutton's dog with us because he and Mrs Hutton, she of the tucked-in knickers, were going out for the day to visit a sick relative and wouldn't be back until late. Would we mind popping across to let Barney out every so often and to give him his kibble? Off we went, sliding through the broken panel at the back of the garden, Amelie's bag rolled up inside my rucksack.

Barney was a small, white Yorkshire terrier. He had a cute, teddy-bear shaped face but yapped a bit too much for my liking. The barking, however, was useful because he tended to woof the moment he heard another person or creature. It was like having a personal alarm.

I thought The Tree of Promises was a dangerous choice for hiding Amelie's belongings. On a late summer's evening the tree would be swarming with young lovers/potential witnesses. But Grace explained she needed to put the bag somewhere it would be found and somewhere that would suggest love had played a cruel part in Amelie's death. The tree was the perfect choice.

We arrived at the empty clearing when the fat wood pigeons were flapping and chuntering into their roosting positions; sending dozens of white, fluffy feathers tumbling down to the woodland floor. Barney and I stood on sentry-duty, blocking the path which led from the main bridleway to the tree. I could hear Grace scuffling around the base, overturning moss and clumps of dark leaves, rearranging the woodland debris around the bag.

She was taking too long.

I hooked Barney's lead around the peeling trunk of a silver birch and crept back to the clearing. I could smell damp earth and bruised nettles. Patches of white light shivered on the ground, lighting up a ring of sickly-yellow toadstools and within the pockets of sunshine buzzed clusters of tiny, winged insects.

Grace was standing, gazing up at the underside of the

branches, clutching a garland of tiny sapphire flowers. She appeared to be lost in thought. I was about to step forward, to discover more about this extra detail she was leaving, but something stopped me. Her manner was strange; her ribcage heaved in and out and her lips moved but she made no sound. She bent her head, her auburn hair falling like a curtain over her face and kissed the garland before she looped it on one of the branches. Then she took a step back, her eyes downcast, while a solitary tear ran down her cheek. This was not part of leaving a clue for the police. This was personal and yet, in my entire life, I had never known my sister to have been in love with another person; she simply wasn't capable of such an emotion. I retreated then crunched around in the undergrowth so that, when I re-emerged, she had turned back into a creature hewn from granite.

Grace hadn't asked me any questions when I came back from my early morning dip in the lake which was just as well because my head was whirring with all things Flo.

I was cross with myself for bottling it. I had wanted to explain everything to Flo, but the moment I saw her emerge from the lake, I realised it was impossible. I stood under the showerhead and let the water pummel the back of my neck as I scrubbed the silt from my skin. My body was breaking in half; I was scared of Grace and what she would do to me if I let her and Daddy down, but it was nothing compared to the terror I felt at the thought of losing Flo. There was no doubt that hurting Tom in this way was going to devastate Flo, but if I tried to prevent it now, Grace and I would be ruined. I was part of this, but I was a coward. I wouldn't be able to stand the look of horror on Flo's face as she listened to what I had done. That's what I had been trying to show her down by the lake; that my life was not my own but, instead, all I had done was fill her with pity. She thought I was a freak.

When I came downstairs Grace had a rather pleased expression on her face and when I frowned at her grin, she pointed to something on the table; a cream envelope with my name on it. It was a card with 'nearly there, keep going, you're brilliant' written on it, but, and very out of character, she must have written it in a hurry because all the black ink was smudged. I nodded my thanks and ate my branflakes. That was strange; the little doll from the Lost Property box was sitting upright against a jam jar – her arms and single leg outstretched. All of her hair had been snipped off so that the uneven clump of glue which had stuck it to the doll's head was visible through a thin, orange fuzz.

Grace, like everyone in the county, had the TV permanently tuned into the news channel. The first headline of the day was that they had arrested a man in connection with the murder of Amelie Townsend; the police would be making a statement later that morning.

I stacked my bowl in the dishwasher and put on my blazer then returned to the kitchen for Grace's obligatory kiss on the forehead. Her breath reeked of alcohol.

There was a loud knock. We glanced at each other and then stared into the hallway. More hammering. Grace downed the contents of her mug, wiped her mouth with the back of her hand and went to the front door. I waited in the shadows, trying to regulate my breathing.

"Good morning Mrs Hutton," said Grace, her voice overly bright and cheerful.

I let out a big puff of breath and went to join my sister.

"Have you seen Barney?" asked Mrs Hutton, wringing her hands together. "He's gone missing."

Grace shook her head. "No. Oh, the little monkey. I'm sure he hasn't gone far." I thought I could detect a very faint slur to her speech.

I reached for my phone, but Grace darted out her arm, snatched it from me and flung it into my school bag.

Mrs Hutton dabbed her apple-red nose with a ball of tissue. "It's just that we went out yesterday afternoon and, I simply don't know how, but he seems to have escaped. We've searched absolutely everywhere."

I felt sick.

"You poor thing," said Grace, placing her hands on her hips. "I tell you what, go and get me a photo of him and I'll make you a poster to put up around the village." She turned to me and pushed me out of the house. "Off you get. You can't be late for your exams." Mrs Hutton churned up the gravel behind me as she hurried off to find a photo of her beloved pet. As I left the drive, I looked around and there was Grace standing at the window with a big grin on her face.

I walked to school, tears welling as I remembered poor old Howie Meowie.

Annie and Tom, when they were still together, had adopted a fat, Persian cat which they named Howie Meowie. They fussed over him, lavishing him with Swarovski collars and food fit for human consumption. When Annie and Tom split up, they decided that the cat should stay with Tom and Flo because their home was much more suitable for him, plus she worked shifts which meant Howie would end up spending too much time on his own. But they all agreed Annie should be able to pop over and visit him whenever she liked, and the arrangement was still in place when Tom and Grace became a permanent item.

Then poor old Howie Meowie went missing.

Grace spent all day putting up posters of the lost cat, but he was never found.

***

The number of white vans and sharp-suited journalists in the village had grown overnight. Many of them, for want of somewhere topical, had positioned themselves outside the wrought iron gates with *Mayfield School*, in gold lettering on a wooden board, behind their heads. A group of angry, scarlet-faced parents had come along to give them a piece of their minds and to try and herd them away from the pupils. It was public exam season and the mob presence wasn't helping nerves, although the butterflies in my stomach weren't reserved for English Literature.

I walked into the Great Hall, clear pencil case sliding between my sweaty palms. I tried to remember my Shakespeare quotes, but all I could think about was Flo. I squinted amongst the sea of faces, but couldn't spot her and a cold, jelly feeling vibrated on the back of my knees.

The exam room filled up with students, arms stripped of watches, eyes bright, mouths full of weak smiles. I stood behind my desk, my head whipping around every few seconds, as though it were on an invisible wire. The chair reserved for 'Marchant' remained empty. We were told to sit down. A group of teachers had gathered at the front of the hall, the stage looming behind their heads. They muttered into cupped hands. All of a sudden, the secretary burst through the double doors, pencil skirt swishing as she walked to the front of the room. She hissed something into the Head of Sixth Form's cauliflower ear and he, in turn, gave the command for the papers to be handed out.

As soon as the bell sounded, I went out of the exam hall and hurried across the cobbled courtyard to the library, leaving behind the excited chatter about 'what did you put for question five? *OMG!*' The library, also open to members of the public, was an intimidating Victorian building, set into the walls of the school grounds. It looked like an asylum, at best a prison. Its front was made up of a blanket of small burnt-orange bricks, divided by grey mortar. A large clock with roman numerals and dials resembling a black spider's web sat in the middle of the crenelated tower; like a vast eye, keeping watch on all those who climbed the steps and dared to go through the arched entrance.

I waved my card over the scanner and went through the barrier, ignored by the sniffing librarian who was sucking a menthol lozenge.

When Flo and I studied together we always sat in opposite desks underneath the portrait of William Shakespeare. Flo said, if being next to him didn't inspire you to write well, you ought to pack up and quit. After a time, Flo would get bored and kick me under the desk, pointing at the painting before going cross-eyed and pouting – that was her very own, awful impression of The Bard but it always made me grin.

Our desks were empty.

I turned and went back outside, fear clogging my throat, making it hard for me to swallow. I knew what I had been dreading happening was now, after all these months, unfurling around me and there was nothing I could do to stop it. My feet were treading on quicksand as the world beneath me shifted.

Tom's time was up and mine with it.

As I ran down the steps, my vision clouded by tears, I became caught up in the lead of a small dog; a caramel and cream Jack Russell with long whiskers, one folded ear and dark marbles for eyes.

"I'm terribly sorry," said its owner, his voice deep and wheezy. I blinked up at an enormous rectangle of a man with silver eyes, dark eyebrows and a neat, white beard. "Tiggy. Come here, you little pest." Something stirred in my mind – his voice sounded familiar. I untangled my ankles and stroked Tiggy behind the ears; her fur was coarse and waxy, and she wagged her stumpy tail with delight.

"Are you doing exams?" asked the man, and I nodded.

"Well, good luck," he said tugging at the lead, and I waved and set off towards the main school buildings. As I walked, I reached into my bag for my phone to see if Flo had left me a message, but the screen was empty. My fingertips knocked against a stiff, cream envelope. At first, I thought it was the ridiculous motivational card Grace had given me that morning, but when I looked again it had '*For the attention of Ms Emily B*' written on it in slanting copperplate. I startled.

I should have taken it home and given it to Grace, but a stubborn streak within me decided against it. I took a right turn and headed into the girls' cloakroom, went straight into one of the cubicles and locked the door behind me. I sat on the loo and sliced my finger under the gummed seal, careful not to rip it.

Out slid an old photo. It was of two girls; one a surly teenager with short white hair, the other a young child, with a large gap between her front teeth. I looked again. It was us. I'd never seen a photo of me and Grace as children before. I turned the picture over and on the back, by the same hand as on the envelope, was written: *To my dearest Emily, long time, no see, Uncle Frank.*

Chapter Fourteen

Flo

I tore up the gravel drive, barging past the village idiots who huddled around the gate, pressing their bodies into the blanket of flowers which trailed over the wall. So-called friends, now suddenly ashamed to be caught standing there, were unable to look me in the eye. Although this embarrassment clearly wasn't enough to stop them from spewing out their stupid fucking opinions about Dad to any bugger who asked. One of our next-door neighbours, hoping for an interview, had been out first thing to mow his front lawn and I could smell the sharp scent of cut grass.

Rumour that the police had a suspect in the Amelie Townsend case had been leaked to the national press and I shivered at the scraping sound as the paparazzi pushed their stepladders against the wall. One by one they clambered up, holding their cameras above their heads to get a shot of the police tape around the pond. I prayed that Dad had closed all the curtains.

I side-stepped around the three abandoned police cars in front of the house – grateful that at least they blocked out the view for those lame idiots at the bottom of the drive.

As I reached the front door, it burst open and out came Dad, blinking in the sunlight, his face pale, his eyes red-rimmed. There was a loud surge of noise; bulbs popping, people shouting his name and asking horrid questions.

Although he wasn't handcuffed, two large policemen had their palms pressed on either side of his shoulders as they bundled him to one of the cars. He looked at me and his lower lip quivered.

"Try not to worry, sweetheart," he said, his voice a whisper. "Can you phone my lawyer?"

"Sure," I said although I didn't even know we had a lawyer, unless he was talking about Ollie Rudstock who, as far as I could remember, had dealt with a boundary dispute when we first moved into the area. Ollie, of the floppy hair and mustard cords, often found boozing in the King's Head at lunchtime.

One of the PCs pressed Dad's head into the car and shuffled in after him. There was more hollering and shouting from the onlookers as the car drove away. Chris Gumlin, with his straggly ponytail and pierced nose who had tried to get with me last week at *Dizzy's Nightclub* shouted "Kiddy Murderer," and slapped his fist against the windscreen. It took all my willpower not to launch myself at him and knock his front teeth out. Instead I swallowed it all down and went into the house, slamming the door behind me.

I went into the kitchen, desperate for a packet of Haribos.

Annie was standing by the sink, staring out of the window. She jumped as I walked through the door and turned; her face was puffy and covered in pink blotches. I glared but didn't say anything; it was like the words inside me had shrivelled up and turned to dust. This couldn't be real. I kicked back the chair and sat at the table, burying my head in my hands.

There were officers in Dad's study, and I watched through the open door as people in plastic suits searched through drawers, stopping every so often to stuff things into plastic bags. Someone walked out of the front door carrying his computer in their arms, tangled wires trailing behind. Annie put a finger to her lips and closed the kitchen door then she sat down opposite me and grabbed my wrists.

"Flo," she said, her voice a whisper. "We don't have much time."

I frowned and pulled my hands away.

"Look. Everyone around here knows that Tom and I used to be an item. They aren't going to let me stay in charge of the case now he's been taken in for questioning, in fact, they're appointing a new DCI as we speak."

"But why have they taken Dad in for questioning? I mean, I'm guessing they've discovered that the shoes in the pond did belong to Amelie, but, even so, how does that prove anything? None of us had a clue what they were doing there and if Dad had put them there, then why would he draw attention to them by poisoning the fish?"

Annie put her hands behind her head and rubbed the nape of her neck. "I agree. The whole thing does seem odd, but that's not why they have taken Tom in."

"What?"

Annie glanced towards the door. "I really shouldn't be telling you this at all, but they found Amelie's bag in the woods and there was something inside it which suggests your Dad might have been having a relationship with Amelie."

I laughed; a horrid tinny noise which stayed at the back of my throat. "This is a joke. You *really* think Dad was having a relationship with one of his students? That's *so* not Dad." I paused, remembering the hug. "Why would he, when he's found the love of his life?" I spat the last sentence at her.

"Flo, I think you ought to call your Mum. You need someone to take care of you."

I let out a groan and shoved my forehead back into my sweaty palms. "There's no need for that," I mumbled. "I'm sixteen, nearly seventeen; I can stay here on my own. They'll find out the whole thing is nonsense and then they'll have to let him go. Dad will be back before tea."

Annie shook her head. "Flo, it's best if you don't stay here while they continue to search the house."

I folded my arms. "Fine. I'll go and stay with Grace."

Annie nodded. "That sounds like a good idea, but don't you think you ought to let your Mum know what's happening?"

"What? I take it you *have* met Nina before, haven't you?"

Annie smiled. "Yes."

"Well then, you know she will make an enormous fuss about the whole thing and use it as an excuse to keep me in London forever so she can send me to some god-awful finishing school where they have to wear stupid straw hats in the sixth form."

"But if you don't tell her, she'll see it on the news and then her reaction will be far more extreme. She might even send you to a convent." Annie reached out to squeeze my hand again, but I was too quick for her. "Besides, she might be able to help. Isn't her husband something important in the City and didn't he used to know Tom?"

I scowled. "You mean Fatty Fanshawe? He's a complete dick."

"Cut me some slack Flo. I'm only trying to help. What I'm saying is, surely this Fanshawe bloke will have contacts? I mean anyone's got to be better than Ollie." She paused and then said in a quiet voice. "You know, your parents must have loved each other, once upon a time."

"That's debatable."

"For God's sake, Flo."

"Okay, okay, I'll call her." The back door opened and a plain-clothed officer with large sweat patches under his arms pointed at me and tapped his watch.

Annie nodded. "She's just come back for a few more things." I stood up and Annie copied. "I'll have to come with you."

I shrugged and flounced up the stairs, pretending like I didn't care, but all the time tutting as I bundled more of my stuff into a suitcase.

"I'll take you down to the station to make a statement about what happened with regards to the pond," said Annie. "I expect the new DCI will want to question you about some other matters…" She paused and I swore under my breath as I fiddled with the zip on my overnight bag. "After that's over I'll drop you off at Grace's. In fact, she's already at the station helping the police with their enquiries so she might even hang on and wait for you."

I climbed into the police car and buckled-up, closing my eyes as we drove through the nosy neighbours and reporters, me hoping to knock a few of them over as we went. We wound our way along the country roads towards the police station and I got Mum's number up onto the screen and stared at it. Nina Jackson-Fanshawe. Even the way Mum pronounced her own name made her sound like she was whingeing: *Nee-nah!* Deep down, of course, I loved her, but there was a reason I only stayed with her and Frank at their flat in Chelsea for the occasional weekend; Nina was suffocating, and Frank was like something from the Edwardian era and a little bit creepy.

Mum walked out on me and Dad when I was eight.

Nina Jackson was what Dad called 'a right stunner'. He had met her when she was working in a café around the corner from The John Radcliffe Hospital which was where Dad was based. He was an alright-looking, junior doctor at the beginning of his medical career and Mum, an art student, jumped at the chance to marry him. He could support her and at the same time she could carry on with creating her weird sculptures. But, when Dad realised towards the end of his training that it wasn't for him, they moved from Oxford to Rutland and Dad took a job as a science teacher. Mum wasn't happy – she felt tricked. It was impossible for her to get by on a teacher's salary and her half-hearted attempt at running a café never got off the ground because she was allergic to hard work.

No, Mum wanted to pursue her artistic muse and in order to do this she had to get out of her marriage to Dad and trap someone else while she still had her looks. She left and for the next few years I didn't really fit in with her aspirations to bag herself a rich husband, so I mainly stayed with Dad. Then, before we noticed, it was just the two of us with Mum sweeping in and out of my life when it suited her. Fast forward several disastrous marriages later and Mum was exactly where she wanted to be, married to a super wealthy businessman. And this was the weirdest thing, it turns out she had first met her current husband, Frank, years ago when she was still with Dad. In fact, it had been Frank who had given Dad his first hospital posting – what a coinkydink.

But now that Mum was well and truly settled with several successful exhibitions under her belt, she felt it was time for me to come and live with her; it was her turn to play at being a parent. Plus, Frank didn't have children of his own and, according to Mum, *dearest Frankie* was super keen for me to come and live with them.

There was no way that was ever happening.

"Daaaarling," came Mum's voice on the other end of the line. "How lovely to talk to you."

Unable to help myself, I started sobbing. "Mum," I wailed. "Can I come and stay with you?"

"Goodness! Were your mocks that bad?"

Chapter Fifteen

Grace

The interrogation at the police station took up the whole afternoon. Thankfully, I'd had a chance to sober up first. Of course, they had been delving into their records and discovered our true identities, but my reasons for the fresh start sufficed and I had their guarantee that our real names would remain hidden to all but a few important personnel. I was pleased at how I managed the spikes in my emotions.

For the most part I remained shocked and silent as the allegations about Tom spilled into the room. It was the keeping quiet, however, which was difficult because I was fighting against an uncontrollable urge to dissolve into laughter. I couldn't help finding the whole situation absolutely hilarious.

Just before I was called in, I happened to be in Tom's kitchen to witness a most satisfying exchange. *Imagining* what Tom was feeling was nothing compared to seeing his downfall played out in real time. I had popped over under the pretence of seeing if Tom was alright. He'd checked-out of the B&B that morning thinking that he would be able to return home. He was very quiet. I, however, was full of smiles and reassurance. I avoided all talk about Amelie and, thankfully, just as he cleared his throat and uttered the words: *we need to talk about what happened the other night*, there was a knock at the back door and in popped Annie, clutching a piece of paper in her hand. I trembled with excitement; this was how it felt when an artist finally revealed their masterpiece and tugged the cord to draw the curtain open. *Ta-*

da! That Annie was the one asking the questions was the gilding on the frame.

Annie stared at the sheet of paper and her incessant head-bobbing, which had grown more pronounced these past few days, reminded me of a duck dipping its beak under the surface of the water in search for edible pondlife. Annie held up the page. "I believe this is a photocopy of what you set your class for homework at the beginning of the week, Mr Marchant. Can you confirm it?" *Mr Marchant now.* Tom let out a perplexed sigh and snatched the paper from her hands.

"Yes. Those are the questions I set. What's this about, Annie?"

"You sure?"

He nodded and shrugged. I was at the sink, rinsing out the cafetière, my face out of sight from everyone. I bit my knuckle. Hard.

"Please will you take a careful look at question five," asked Annie.

Tom took a deep breath and stared down at the sheet once more, his messy fringe falling over his eyes. After a couple of seconds, he gasped then spluttered.

"Shit. Shit. I didn't write that." He looked up, pushing his hair out of his face, blinking fast. "What is this? It's filth."

"So, you are saying now that you *didn't* set the homework?" Annie folded her arms.

He thrust the sheet of paper back at her, but she kept her stance, leaving the offending paper shaking in Tom's grasp, mid-air.

"Someone's added that question."

"Hmm! It's funny, but we've checked with the other children in your biology group and it appears that only Amelie got this extra question." Tom's face darkened, his breathing shallow.

"I would never." He looked at me, his eyes growing wider. "I would *never.*"

I sighed and hung my head before muttering something about having to rush off for an appointment at the police station. *Bravo!*

There was a new DCI in charge, a man called Patrick Beaumont with big, cauliflower ears and a face like a balloon with a slow puncture. Thank goodness they had taken Awful Annie and her pointy features off the case; the photos I manufactured were no doubt doing the rounds again. I had to dig my fingernails into my palms to cut off my raging desire to shout out the passwords to Tom's computer; to write down his username for the chat rooms in whose forums I'd spent many evenings spouting forth obscenities.

Like a child, arm in the air, trying to get the attention of a teacher, I fought off my curiosity. Had they found the girl's bra? What about the burner phone in Amelie's locker? Surely they must have found its twin hidden in a false drawer at the back of his desk. Had they gone into the greenhouse and discovered the black lining was missing a couple of sheets? On and on the clues went tumbling through my mind, Amelie's hairs in the back of his car, her key chain, the Rohypnol in the corner of Tom's medicine cabinet, the nude photos.

I thought I would burst with excitement and it was only by using a great amount of willpower I forced myself to focus on my chipped fingernails – standards were slipping! I knew DCI Beaumont wouldn't be fobbed off by any of Grace's feminine wiles so, instead, I spooned some sugar into my tea and took my time stirring it, contemplating my next move.

"I had no idea," I said making my voice as wobbly as possible. "I simply had no idea. That poor child." Were those words really coming from me? I stopped myself short – I had an inkling I was starting to sound like I was performing in a pantomime.

No, I had never stayed at Tom's house before because, unlike some and, *read into that what you want to Annie Harper*, I believed in the sanctity of marriage. That dreadful afternoon when they had discovered Amelie's body by the lake, we'd all felt the need to be together, so we'd gone to Tom's house, whereupon I had slept in the spare room.

The fish? Ah! Well, I said, I didn't really know what to make of that, apart from the fact that Flo was a bit scatty and,

I sucked in my breath, I'd only found out later that evening, when Lily's head was half way down the toilet bowl, that the pair had been drinking. I shook my head and sniffed; of course, I blamed myself. I'd been so shocked by what had happened that I'd been neglectful of my maternal duties. It was certainly possible, although I hated to say it, that Flo, in her inebriated state, had gone out in the middle of the night and fed the fish with weed-killer or whatever it was she'd mistakenly got from the shed. Not on purpose, of course not on purpose, but...

Pat seemed to like that idea a lot and did much scribbling in his notebook, flabby cheeks wobbling as his nib scratched the page.

Was there ever anything, anything at all that might have caused her to suspect her fiancé was having an affair with Amelie or any other schoolgirl for that matter?

I toyed with the idea of fabricating an incident whereby I had caught Tom up to no good, but in the end, I decided that outraged indignation was the best course of action to take. It was more *genuine*.

Oh, just one more thing. Pat tapped his hand on the table and the female detective next to him pushed a clear bag towards me. I wondered what little piece of my puzzle this could be.

"Do you recognise the item in the bag?" asked Pat.

I peered closer. It was an earring, shaped like a teardrop. *Curious*. This wasn't my handiwork. I smoothed out the creased plastic lining which separated the jewellery from my fingertips. I saw a tiny *A* was engraved into its centre. I held Pat's gaze for further explanation.

"The earring was one of a pair which belonged to Amelie. When we examined her body, we found the other identical stud was missing. We're most anxious to locate it. Apparently, she never took them off. Not even at night."

I couldn't swallow and reached for the dregs of my tea to smooth away the knot of anxiety blocking my throat. How could I have been so careless? With enormous effort I managed a shrug, trying to give off an air of nonchalance though all the time my mind was racing. I barely heard the rest of Pat's spiel about the need for keeping in touch and if I thought of anything else, *bla-bla-bla.*

The moment I turned the corner from the police station, I leant against the wall and took a couple of deep breaths. I mustn't panic. I cast my mind back to that Friday afternoon and tried to piece together each frame of the murder as though I was watching it back on a tv screen; desperate to glimpse the missing earring.

***

Rachael and Chloe, the other café workers, were busy clearing up the front of house. The lazy bitches were deep in conversation about whether Chloe should get a fringe cut to hide the wrinkles on her forehead or whether it would be too much effort for her to have to straighten it each morning. I refrained from telling her that a bag over her head was by far the best option and instead mumbled something about signing for a coffee delivery before slipping out the back door of the kitchen. I'd calculated I had approximately one hour before either of them would register her disappearance. I power-walked along the hot pavement and the moment I turned into my drive I sprinted around the side of the house to the back door where my *work clothes* were waiting for me; folded in a neat pile on the utility room sink. I looked at my watch. Amelie would be finishing her coffee; the gang collectively standing up, scraping their chairs across the floor as they dished out endless hugs to keep each other going for the two whole hours they weren't going to be together.

Dark tracksuit on and hood up, I picked up the dog lead and hammer and ran out into the garden. I dived between the thick camellia bushes, my fingers grazing the waxy leaves, flowers knocking into my face like dozens of bowed heads ready for the chopping block. I kicked my way through the bark chippings and stray clumps of grass before reaching the loose fence panel which still smelt of creosote. I shuffled the board across so that there would be a big enough gap for me to squeeze through then crouched on the threshold amongst the dandelions. The wood was quiet, apart from the gentle rustle of the summer breeze in the birch trees and the occasional coo of a wood pigeon. If I pressed my face at a certain angle against the fence, I could see a couple of metres along the dappled path. From out of nowhere a couple of women sprinted past in single file and I shrank back, accidentally pressing my hand down on a patch of nettles. I cursed under my breath. Then I heard more footsteps and Amelie appeared; she was alone. I waited until the girl had gone past and slipped out onto the path. I looked around then called; *Barney! Barney!* Amelie startled and turned her head around.

When she saw it was me she smiled. "Hello," she said pulling out her earphones. "Are you okay?"

I shook my head. "It's Barney, The Huttons' dog. He's escaped again, but this time he's got himself wedged under a tree root and I can't get him out. My hands are too big." I rolled my eyes and waved my palms in the air.

"Oh! The poor little fellow. Do you want me to have a go?"

Bingo! "Oh, you are sweet. Only if you don't mind."

Amelie stooped down and I could hear the tinny music coming from her earphones. "I can't see him." There was a pause. "Is he to my left, or right?"

I took another quick scan of the path before taking the hammer out of my pocket. I came up right behind Amelie and crouched over her body, pretending to follow her gaze. "Left." As soon as the words left my lips, I brought the weapon down on the back of Amelie's head. She slumped to the ground.

I heard laughter in the distance and bile rushed up the back of my throat. Quickly I dragged Amelie's body through the gap.

The voices grew louder; one male, one female.

Without turning, I kicked the panel back into place and turned to check the gap had closed. *Fuck!* The handles of Amelie's school bag were poking out from the base of the fencing and onto the path. Blood rushed around my ears.

"Did you hear that funny noise?" asked the girl. The couple stopped right by the break in the fence; I could see a pair of trainers.

There was a smacking slurping noise and it took a few seconds to realise the couple were kissing. If they looked down, they would see Amelie's bag and if they stooped to examine the loop of fabric further, they might follow it through the gap and see me sitting astride a dead body as plain as Humpty-Dumpty sitting on a wall. By this time, my heart was beating so fast I presumed the young lovers must also be able to hear it. Fingers quivering, I leant forwards and gave the neck of the schoolbag a sharp tug. Suddenly a phone rang. I sucked in my breath; for one terrible minute I thought it was coming from within Amelie's bag.

"Huh," said the male voice. "Yeh." He sighed. "In ten."

There was a shuffling.

"Your Mum?" asked the girl. The boy didn't answer, but the shoes disappeared.

I waited until all was quiet again then hooked Amelie under the armpits and dragged her across the garden into the kitchen. It was while I was changing back into my sundress that I heard groaning. *Shit, I hadn't hit her hard enough.* I rushed back into the kitchen to find Amelie on all fours, mooing like a cow in labour.

"You poor thing. Here, let's get you to your feet." I lifted Amelie onto a kitchen chair.

"What happened?" whispered Amelie.

"You've had a nasty bump to the head."

I fetched her a glass of water and pushed the plate of freshly baked pistachio meringues in front of her. "Perhaps you would like something to eat – a bit of sugar for the shock."

"Where…where am I?"

"You're in my kitchen. Remember? You were helping me to find Barney, the dog, and a piece of masonry from on top of the fence fell onto your head."

Amelie touched the back of her crown and then examined

her bloodied fingertips. "I'll call Mum," she said looking around for her bag.

"No need." I pulled a plastic bag out of my pocket. "She's on her way."

"How—"

I slipped the bag over Amelie's bloodied head and twisted. Amelie began her death roll, thrashing and kicking her feet. The plastic expanded and then contracted with a loud slapping sound. The squealing carried on until all of a sudden it stopped. Beads of sweat rolled down my temples and plopped onto the deflated bag.

I splashed a bit of water on my face to cool down then grabbed my sunglasses and picked up the box of coffee beans which I took back with me to the café. The women had moved onto the virtues of wigs and hair pieces. I hadn't been missed.

***

Somewhere along my murderous route the earring must have come loose. As soon as I got home, I would retrace my steps. I had to find it.

Chapter Sixteen

Lily

I was questioned by a young policewoman who took a good ten minutes getting to grips with the fact that I didn't speak. Most people's first reaction to my silence is to talk slower – it's either that or they start signing. I don't sign, nor do I want to sign and indeed any sympathy flung in my direction is withdrawn once it is discovered I am mute by choice. At one stage Grace thought she could smack the words back into my mouth but then she must've realised it was easier for her if I didn't speak. Lack of any *effort* on my part led to avoidance and then neglect; no one cared how I broke my arm or got bruises across my back: there was something wrong with me 'up top'.

Then I met Flo and she interpreted my words and gave me a different sound. I liked the Lily she projected into the world. Flo became my defender as well as my voice and, bit by bit, her affection for me rubbed off on those around her. I grew a bit braver and dared to wonder if there was a better life out there for me – away from Grace.

I am not stupid. I simply do not speak.

The PC blushed. The crimson glow deepening as she asked me personal information about Tom. Each time she mumbled her question, she looked up at me and had to push her thick-rimmed glasses back up the bridge of her flat nose.

Until that interview, I hadn't realised the extent of Grace's handiwork.

I gave them nothing. Absolutely nothing, but already it was too late.

As I was escorted along a narrow corridor and out of the police station, I caught sight of Annie leaning against a noticeboard. I was surprised when she said in a loud voice to the officer standing next to her that the suspect's daughter was going to be staying at Heartlands Hotel in Chipping Redbury. It was a throw-away comment which she followed up by saying something about how she would love for someone to take her to lunch there, never mind actually staying the night in such luxury. The female officer she was speaking to laughed and said that she thought herself lucky if her husband took her to a MacDonald's.

I let Grace think I was studying in the library and caught the bus to Chipping Redbury. The village, according to my geography teacher, was actually a hamlet made up of a few stone cottages with mossy, thatched rooves. Heartlands Hotel was a famous retreat where the rich and famous dropped in, often by helicopter, for luxury spa breaks.

Nina and her fabulously wealthy husband were in town.

The hotel was a bit of a trek from the bus stop, but it didn't matter; I needed thinking time. I walked along a narrow path which ran parallel to the road. Clouds of custard coloured dust shot out with each step I took. My head was bursting; it was as though I had two voices battling inside my mind; one filling my thoughts with misery, the other frantically trying to search for an escape route.

After quarter of an hour, I stopped at a five-bar gate and stood on the lower rung leaning over the top, the metal cool against my skin. I was pathetic. I had never doubted what Grace relayed to me about my early life and had gone along with whatever she told me to do, after all, she was the only family I had. But, until the very moment I stood over Amelie's dead body, the question had never raised itself: what if everything Grace told me about my childhood was just a pack of lies? After all, Tom was only a faint memory, kept alive by the underwater channel he created.

But it was Barney's death that was the final tipping point.

When I came back from school and saw his poor little lifeless body lying on the patio, I knew this senseless killing was going to continue – Grace had to be stopped.

I knew I could make things right for Flo and Tom. But it wasn't as easy as walking into a police station and confessing. Grace was far too clever for that; out would come Cassie's medical records, the proof I was disturbed and damaged goods. And if Grace caught me in the act of trying to trap her, she'd almost certainly kill me and make it look like suicide; I was a self-harmer, wasn't I?

Or maybe she'd just give me a bloody great overdose of my sleeping tablets.

A grey horse with a pink and white muzzle came over and puffed hot breath at me. I picked a huge clump of grass by my feet and held it out to him on my flattened palm. His lips were velvet against my skin and his whiskers tickled my wrists. A couple of flies danced around his ears and I tried to swat them away.

The only way for Grace to be stopped was for someone else to get to the truth behind who we used to be and that somebody had to be Flo.

The horse nudged me, and I stooped to tear at another handful of grass.

I closed my eyes trying to force my splintered childhood memories to the front of my mind. *What exactly did I remember?* All I knew was what Grace had told me: I had been a terrible, feral child and Dad had sent me to see a doctor. This doctor was Tom and I said something to him which somehow led to my father's death. For some reason, unknown to me, Tom had quit medicine and moved to Rutland and I was left with a recurring nightmare about a mermaid.

The distant rumble of thunder brought me back into the present and I tickled my companion goodbye, promising him more lush grass on my return journey. I had the very sketchy beginnings of a plan and, just knowing that, gave me a sense of calm. The path took a sharp left turn and fanned out into a wide gravel drive at the end of which sat a large, white mansion framed by a broad sweep of parkland. Despite the heavy sky, pockets of sunlight filtered through the clouds and created bright lime patches of grass.

I walked up the wide marble steps and a man in a powder blue jacket laced with gold brocade sprang forward and opened the door. He gave me a quizzical look which swept over my body and finished up following my dusty canvas shoes over the doorstep. Suddenly ashamed of my baggy clothes I slunk into the lobby and almost collided with a narrow plinth; an ebony vase sat atop, bursting with red lilies. Their stamens were loaded with yellow dust and their scent overpowering, like someone had sprinkled them with cheap talcum powder. The reception desk was nowhere in sight. I turned full circle to see a woman with slicked back hair wearing a grey trouser suit and circular glasses, materialise from behind the flowers. I started.

"Good afternoon. My name's Jessica. How can I help?" She held out an iPad as though it were a tea tray.

I patted my back pocket and realised I hadn't brought my emergency notepad with me. Grace had confiscated my phone before I left. Jessica tapped her pencil against the edge of the screen and my ears tingled.

"Hey, Lils. What the hell are you doing here?"

I turned to see Flo walking across the marble tiles and my eyes popped. She was dressed in the most extraordinary outfit; a pinafore dress, white blouse, white knee-high socks and patent buckled shoes. Her hair was tied up with a bow the colour of a pig's snout.

"She's with me," Flo said to Jessica who scuttled back to her hiding place behind the vase. The whites of Flo's eyes were pink, her irises over-bright. She wrapped an arm around me, and I rested my head on her shoulder.

"It's all just a little bit shit, isn't it?" she said before pulling away.

I pointed at her clothes.

"Oh, yes. I know. I look like an absolute prize twat. This outfit is a gift from my stepfather and Mummy dearest insisted I wear it to please the fat git. He's totally old and decrepit – from an era where apparently girls should dress like girls, but I mean – how fucking old does he think I am?"

I held up six fingers.

"Of course, I refused point blank until Mum reminded me that Frank is paying for Dad's legal fees." She pulled at the skirt of her pinafore. "So, you see I didn't have a choice. I'm being blackmailed to look like an extra from *The Famous Five*. I'm just praying I don't bump into anyone else I know."

I squeezed her hand.

"Did Annie tell you I was here?" she asked.

I nodded.

"It's been awful not being able to talk to you. Why can't you use your phone at the moment? Can you believe what they are saying about Dad?" Her voice grew thick. "Did…did they question you and Grace too?"

I mimed writing on my palm.

She pulled my arm. "You'd better come into the garden and say hi to Mum. I'm afraid Frank the Fuckwit is with her but do feel free to completely ignore him. *One* is pretending to be frightfully posh and *one* is having afternoon tea." She laughed. "I must have left my phone out there when I went to the bathroom. Frank's such a fat pig so we've had to order loads of cake so you might as well come and eat some of it."

We went along a dark corridor with wood panelling rising to waist height. Above it hung several portraits of creepy looking men with bulbous eyes, smooth skin and crimson lips. At the end of the passage the door was propped open and the rectangle of carpet next to the doorstep grew bright then dark as the thickening clouds rolled across the sun.

I stepped out onto a terrace. Butterflies fluttered on the breeze and the cream roses, weaving through a trellis next to me, gave out a sweet, vanilla perfume. The tier of patio I was standing on was dotted with circular tables all set with linen cloths and silver cutlery. Women in floral dresses and men in linen suits sat on wicker chairs, sipping tea and nibbling on triangular sandwiches. Flo beckoned and I followed her down a trio of wide steps, ending in a white, gravel path which stopped before a bubbling fountain with two winged cherubs entwined in a passionate embrace at its centre.

"They're over there," said Flo, pointing to a table next to the lawn.

My feet crunched over the gravel path as I skirted the base of the fountain which spat droplets of cold water at me. I rounded the circular pond and was met by a wide expanse of manicured lawn with an orchard at the far side; squat trees covered in glossy leaves and dotted with small, lime-green bullets. I could see hens with feathered legs, like grey snow-boots, pecking around in the meadow. It was beautiful, as though I had stumbled across a remote island, cut off from civilisation.

"Oh, hello you," said Flo, stooping as a little toffee and white Jack Russell came tearing over, wagging its stumpy tail.

I stopped. I recognised the folded down ear and floral collar. I pressed against the stone wall of the pond, keeping myself in line with the cherubs. I grabbed Flo's hand and pulled her back.

"What?"

I pressed a finger to my lips and crouched down. Slowly I peered around the edge of the water feature. There, sitting next to Nina was the man with the snowy beard who I had met on the steps of the library. I pressed the back of my head against the damp bricks.

I made a beard with my hand and pointed.

"I know. Gross isn't he? And Mum actually shags him." She pretended to vomit.

My scalp prickled. This wasn't a coincidence. *Uncle Frank?* I forced myself to look again but this time he saw me – his steely-grey eyes narrowing and a small smile dancing on his wet, mauve lips.

Dizzy, I got to my feet and hurried back the way we came, the soles of my shoes skidding against the gravel. I could hear Flo calling after me, but I didn't turn back. As soon as I was inside the building I headed for the nearest cloakroom, diving into the first cubicle and bolting the door behind me. I sat on the loo with my head buried in my hands, breathing in a nauseating spiced ginger pot pourri.

The door creaked open.

"Lily? Are you in here?" said Flo.

I banged the wall with my foot.

"What's up? You feeling okay?"

I forced myself upright and opened the door. On the other side of the loos ran a shallow, ceramic trough, gold taps placed at regular intervals. I splashed water onto my face, all the time gazing at my reflection in the mirror; my skin now chalky white under the stark neon lighting. Flo had grabbed a handful of paper towels and thrust a pen under my nose.

"What's going on?"

I dried my face with one sheet then unfolded the next, smoothing out the crease with my fingertips.

That man has got something to do with my past.

Flo shook her head. "Who? Fuckwit Frank? You've got to be kidding."

You have to trust me. Grace and I, we used to have a different life. I think he was part of it. Somehow, he's involved with what is happening to your Dad.

"Lily, what the fuck are you talking about?"

Our names haven't always been

The door burst open again and in sashayed Nina. She was groomed to perfection and it was hard not to gawp at her; not an eyelash was out of place, her honeyed skin smooth and flawless.

"Are you alright, Lily?" she asked, her voice stretched and slow.

"She just felt a bit faint," said Flo, screwing up the handtowels and throwing them into the bin.

Nina took out a silver cylinder from her purse and leaned into the mirror, dotting the plum point onto her lips. She continued talking all the time giving her angular face a once over. "I'm not surprised. It's muggy out there today, but with all that's going on…" She grabbed a tissue from a ceramic box and blotted it against her mouth. "Frankie, the dear, sweet man, is very worried about you. He's sent for his chauffeur to take you home."

My eyes bulged and Flo shook her head at me.

"No, Mum, it's fine. Lily's okay now. We're going up to my room to chill."

Nina pinched the tops of her cheeks. "Too late for that. The car is on its way." She turned and put a finger under my chin. "You look ghastly, darling girl. I think the best place for you is at home with your Mum."

I grabbed Flo's hand and ground her fingers together.

She yelped. "Mum, *seriously*. Lils had a funny moment and now it's passed. We're gonna do a bit of English revision together cos it's our last literature exam tomorrow."

Nina flapped her hands around her face. "Florence, you mustn't be embarrassed about accepting help from a friend. Frankie was just about to leave anyway, he's got some business to attend to and then he's heading off to his bolthole, or *man cave*, as I like to call it. Taking all things into account, he was most concerned that Lily should get home safely. I think it's a good idea for him to escort her back. Anyway, you know Frankie, he absolutely won't take no for an answer."

Chapter Seventeen

Flo

I was squashed into a crowd of nosy onlookers; gagging over the disgusting combination of other people's sweat, washing powder and perfume. Mum had offered to come with me, but I didn't want her there; she would've pitched up dressed like a film star, trying to look all mysterious. I knew she was trying her hardest to be supportive, but the presence of the tabloids was too great; she wouldn't be able to stop herself from standing on the stone steps of the court house and making a dumb statement – probably handing out fliers for her next exhibition while she was at it.

Also, to be honest, I wasn't sure whose side Mum was on.

Frank's super expensive lawyer, Clive 'Bungle-Toad' QC, wasn't needed for this bit and though I'd been told a hundred times that Dad wouldn't be getting bail, it didn't stop me hoping.

I knew Grace wouldn't be there. She'd already sent me a flaky message saying she'd finished with Dad. Some self-centred garbage about 'overwhelming evidence' and her need for 'some me-time to process things'. Of course, she hoped I'd understand, but, after all, she had her own daughter's safety to think about too. Bullshit.

I'd hoped Lily might show, but I hadn't heard from her since she'd left in Frank's car which was a bit worrying. As well as needing her support, I'd wanted her to explain what she'd been going on about in the hotel bathroom because it hadn't made any sense.

I was herded into the court room. It was a large, boxy

space, a bit like our school lecture theatre with pale, wooden-framed seating covered with scratchy cushions. There were no windows. White tubes of light lined the ceiling tiles and showed up the grey blobs of chewing gum splattered on the nylon carpet. I slid onto the nearest chair and a fat woman with an ugly pageboy cut elbowed me in the waist.

She gave me a wonky smile. "So sorry. Heavens – it's like being at a wrestling match, isn't it?" She was wearing a dress made of lots of shiny fabric which rustled as she moved, and her jacket puffed at the arms where the excess material had bunched up.

I nodded but said nothing. I was wearing black trousers and a polo neck and had scraped my hair up into a ballet bun, slapping on a thick layer of face powder in the hope that no one would recognise me.

"I just want to look *him* in those evil eyes. Tell him God is on our side," the woman said, wheezing her disgusting coffee breath in my face. "You?"

"My cousin is in for a traffic offence," I blurted out. "I'm here to support him."

The woman clamped her sausage fingers around my upper arm. "May God be with you and him." Then she leaned over and cupped her hand against my ear, her warm breath tickling my neck. "Besides, I'm sure He's got His mind on more important things today."

I opened my mouth, ready to wipe the smirk off the fat bitch's face by declaring that my imaginary *cousin* had ploughed into a mother and toddler group killing everyone in sight but was stopped by a sharp increase of chatter. A man in a charcoal suit was ushered onto a front row seat. It was Amelie's Dad – I'd seen him on the news. He didn't look at anyone and when he sat down, his long body concertinaed into the chair. He leant forward and buried his face in his hands. From my angle all I could see was a bald patch on the top of his head where the neon lights shone through his thin hair and bounced off his scalp.

A few minutes later someone shouted for the courtroom to stand and be silent. Then a door opened and in shuffled a trio of oldies who plonked themselves down on a raised platform.

I held my breath.

The main door burst open and in came Dad, suspended between two tall policemen. I glimpsed his pale face, his sunken eyes and his even more messy than usual hair. He was wearing one of the suits I'd put out for the charity pile. Grace must have given it to his lawyer, the thoughtless cow. Everyone was staring at him, some people standing on tiptoes to get a good gawp. He was led into the dock and stood there, his hands gripping the edge, knuckles turning white. From the back of the courtroom someone shouted 'filthy paedophile' and a murmur of agreement rippled through the auditorium; all the time the usher barking for quiet.

The charge was read out and Clive's spotty minion; his checked suit peeping out from under his gown, entered a not guilty plea which made everyone gasp. The woman next to me tutted and elbowed me again. Then came the matter of bail and although the minion argued all of the reasons Dad should be allowed home, the Prosecution weren't having any of it and the Mags, who'd obviously already made up their minds, announced that Dad was to be remanded in custody.

Before I could figure out what was happening, Dad was out of the dock and back through the double doors. I leapt out of my seat after him, not caring who I banged into or trampled upon. I flattened anyone in my way; spurred on by my disgust and hatred of the mob.

I arrived, just as Dad was being bundled out of the back entrance of the building and into an unmarked white van. I called out, *Dad*, and he turned.

"I love you," I shouted. "I know you had nothing to do with it."

The hug.

He muttered something, but I didn't hear what he said and seconds later a police officer pressed his head down into the car and slammed the door shut.

I leant against the wall. A hand touched my shoulder and I smelt cigarette smoke.

"You okay?" asked Annie.

I couldn't stop the tears from streaming down my face and when I opened my mouth, no words came out.

"Come with me." She led me down the corridor into a small kitchenette; plastic chairs pushed up against the scuffed walls. Annie flicked on the kettle.

"He'll be safer on remand," she called out over the hiss of boiling water.

I blew my nose. "When can I go home?"

Annie held up a teabag and a sachet of coffee. I pointed to the teabag.

"Wouldn't you be better to stay away a bit longer?"

I shook my head.

"You don't take sugar, do you?"

"No. Thanks." I paused. "Grace sent me a text to say she doesn't want to see me anymore." The words came spewing out of my mouth and left me breathless. "She says the evidence against Dad is too much."

"It is, isn't it?" Annie screwed up her eyes as she tried to scrape back the lid of a milk pod with her fingernails.

"I mean why would he put her shoes in the pond then tie them up with her knickers? It's just ridiculous."

"Panic."

Annie handed me the tea and I muttered my thanks. "I want to sleep in my own bed. You've got my prints and DNA samples so it's not going to matter if I'm there or not, right? All my stuff is at the house."

Annie took a sip of her tea and blinked slowly. "Technically, I'm off the case." She darted her gaze towards the door and took a step closer to me. She lowered her voice. "It doesn't mean I'm not still keeping an eye on how things are progressing. But Flo, mate, it's not looking good. There are a lot of things which point to Tom being involved in Amelie's death. I mean, there's Amelie's DNA in the back of his car, he had a burner phone which he used to text her on." She paused and took a deep breath. "That's only the start of it. He visited kiddie chat rooms; he has a web history of looking at pornography."

Hot tears spilled down my cheeks again.

"But…" said Annie.

I hiccupped and glanced up. There was a moment's silence broken by the gurgling of the sink. "You don't buy it, do you?"

"Let's just say, it's a little too neat for my liking."

"There is one thing maybe you could consider looking into on the quiet."

Annie raised an eyebrow.

"Lily was…" I swallowed. "She was really scared of Frank Fanshawe – Mum's husband. I know it sounds weird, but for some reason she thinks he has something to do with what is happening to Tom."

Annie tutted. "Ah! Flo, isn't that just wishful thinking on your part? I mean, I know you don't like the guy, but dragging him into it is kind of…childish. Especially as he's funding Tom's legal fees."

I opened my mouth to argue, but just then a small, female officer poked her head around the door. "Ma'am?" With that Annie drained her tea and shot out of the door, leaving me a tear-stained mess though, at last, I did have something to cling to: Annie was still on our side.

Chapter Eighteen

Grace

I had searched all over for the earring, but it was an impossible task; it could have been anywhere.

What drama! No wonder I was exhausted. I decided to rest for a bit before I resumed my search.

I needed a drink – it would help me to get things into perspective. Losing the earring wasn't the worst thing to have happened so far. I grabbed a vodka bottle, no need for mixer this morning, put on my comfy Juicy Couture tracksuit and went back into the snug.

They would be announcing Tom's incarceration this lunchtime. I raised my glass; *here's to you Tom*. I sank into the armchair, my mind whirring with plans. I knew I would have to keep a very low profile from now on and so had closed the café indefinitely, taking all the money from the business account. In spite of that, I was feeling positive. I don't know if it was helped by the booze, but I'd lost all immediate sense of panic. My reasoning was this; if Frank had seen me, I would have known about it by now.

I sat in the study, laptop resting on my knees, Smirnoff on the coffee table. I was looking at places where Cassie and I could escape to. As long as the police could contact me, it wouldn't matter where in the world we were. Over the next couple of days, I was going to claim public harassment and go into hiding. I had seen nothing and heard nothing – besides which, it wouldn't come to a trial, he'd be forced to make a guilty plea just to avoid being butchered in prison.

I fell asleep and for the first time in what seemed like an age, he came to me in my dreams.

***

I was sitting dangling the tips of my toes in the water while the sun beat down on my forehead. I watched him from behind my dark glasses, drinking in every drop of his being. He was lying on his front, tanned arms hanging over the side of the jetty, fingers trailing to and fro upon the surface of the lake. His long hair tumbled around the tips of his shoulders and I heard his laugh bouncing off the water; saw the muscles in his calves quiver as he shunted himself along the wooden walkway.

He was humming the tune to a folksong; something about going down to a river to pray. He sang it all the time and was trying to teach it to Cassie.

Cassie had lined her jam jars along the very edge of the slats. They were filled with water, but so far were empty of livestock. She began to whine; it was like a mosquito in my ear. There was a splash followed by a scream. He laughed and she stamped her little foot. Suddenly, he pointed and whispered: there, over there. Cassie squeaked with euphoria and seized her net, dunking it into the water. He guided his hand on top of hers and they scooped, lifting the quivering nylon aloft. Something within flapped and wriggled, catching the sunlight and casting a spark into the cloudless sky. Cassie, now screaming with delight, wanted to know what they had caught and he, sitting back on his heels, lowered the mesh into the jar, declaring their prize to be a very fine specimen of minnow.

Cassie held the kilner jar to her eye and oohed and aaahed. Her small, sun-kissed body shivered with delight. Setting the fish down, she lowered herself onto her stomach; heart-shaped face cupped in her hands, dark eyes flashing, curls cascading down the back of her gingham pinafore.

He turned to me and grinned, showing the tiny gap between his front teeth. "What do you think of that, oh ye of little faith?" he asked and I gave a coy smile, one I had been practising in the mirror; forcing a dimple to my left cheek. I fluttered my eyelashes and gazed into the distance.

120

Cassie stated that she was hungry. A ravenous hunger which had hit her that very instant and had to be acted upon immediately. He looked at his watch and said it was a bit early, but why didn't they all have a biscuit and some lemonade to bridge the gap until lunch. Cassie cocked her head on one side then announced that this would do.

I had to bite back my anger when the child came over, chubby fingers splayed around the jar, and plonked herself into my lap. He smiled and folded his arms in approval at our sisterly bond. Cassie demanded I admire her new pet.

Ah! I said, unable to prevent the mischief bubbling up inside me, but have you seen the mermaid yet?

He paused as he took a bite of his biscuit.

The little girl within my arms fell silent, her body tight with the desire to know more.

He finished his biscuit, his dark eyebrow arched, and took a swig of lemonade before handing me the bottle. My mouth trembled as it closed around the rim; how I longed for the taste of him on my lips. The weeping willow became a blur as the lake spun.

He was all smiles and curiosity. Do tell, he said with a nod of his head.

Cassie hopped off my lap and settled herself so she could see my every expression. I shrugged, threw back my head and knowing full well his eyes were upon me I began my tale of Myrtle the mermaid, who lived deep within the belly of the lake. I told the story, stretching and elongating the details until they could expand no more. Lovesick Myrtle, with her crown of forget-me-nots, radiant skin and long flowing hair.

After the story ended Cassie remained silent. She got to her feet then with fairy steps went to the edge of the jetty and peered over.

Cassie was no longer hungry.

The pet fish was no longer wanted.

He told me I was clever then followed it with a touch to my shoulder. He smelt of exotic spices; dark and mysterious. I longed for him to pull me towards him and plant a kiss upon my lips.

Had I put sun cream on? I needed to sit in the shade. Here! He disappeared for a few seconds and returned with his arms full of cushions from the boat house. He arranged them under the eaves of the slanting roof then took my hand and guided me over. He winked then declared he must get back to Cassie duty. He stood in front of me and through his linen shirt I could see his stomach; the gentle channels which separated his muscles.

He patted my head.

The next minute he was alongside Cassie, cajoling her into reading for him, but all that mermaid talk had made Cassie restless.

Tell, her Em, he called, tell her you can only see a mermaid at night, if there is a full moon. I pretended I had fallen asleep.

I started. Cold water was dripping onto my bare skin. He stood over me laughing and dropped something onto my tummy. I sat bolt upright. It was a garland made with water forget-me-nots. *And who shall wear the starry crown, Good Lord, show me the way*, he sang.

He winked. "A crown for the Lady of the Lake," he said, before bowing and returning to Cassie. I held the icy flowers to my palms trying to extinguish the fever which burned underneath my skin.

"Ahoy there," shouted a deep voice from across the water.

His whole body tensed then he turned, eyes wide, voice jagged; *I thought your father wasn't going to be here today.*

Chapter Nineteen

Lily

I sat in the car breathing in a musky, salty aroma which I couldn't place. I leaned my head against the tinted window, its surface cool and hard against my temple. My thighs stuck to the bucket-like, leather seats and the seatbelt sliced into my waist. Tiggy paced around, sniffing each patch of floor to find a comfortable spot. Frank sat to my left with one elbow perched on the rectangular armrest which divided us. His fingers were curled into a fist and a signet ring on his pinky finger blinked at me. It had a tiny, sparkly diamond surrounded by deep grooves which spread out from its central position and were arranged like the sun's rays. Frank was overweight but he was also tall with long limbs and broad shoulders. He was a giant of a man; the sort who spilled over boundaries.

There had been no other option but to get into the jaguar with Frank. He was persuasive and charming; deeply concerned about my health and, in his very humble opinion, I had to go straight back home to bed. Nina had accompanied us to the wide entrance porch of the hotel to shower us with air-kisses and to wave us off with cheery *toodlepips*. Frank's thin lips were stained with red wine which matched the colour of his trousers and before he clambered inside, he had put an arm around Flo and kissed her on the cheek. She wriggled out of his grasp and bolted down the steps to the car.

Flo stared in at me, her eyes wide and unblinking. She couldn't do anything apart from run her fingers through her hair and mouth sorry over and over again. I stared at her and, holding one palm up to the window, I hid my index finger which I was jabbing towards Frank.

Flo nodded.

My window closed.

Frank tapped on the tinted partition which separated us from the chauffeur, and it slid away to reveal the shaven back of a man's capped head. "37 Orchard Close, Far Langton," said Frank with a grin; a ball of spit had gathered at the corner of his mouth. The driver nodded then closed the window and the locks on the doors clicked. I was a prisoner in a moving darkened cell with absolutely nowhere to run. Thank goodness Tiggy was there, her warm body curled up next to my feet, wiry fur tickling my ankles. I thought of poor Barney and shuddered.

"I suppose, by now, you must be wondering who I am?" he asked, and he rubbed his whiskers making a scratchy sound. "I must say, I do find it extraordinary that even after all these years you still choose to play dumb, but then again, you always were a stubborn little bitch." The insult came from nowhere, as though someone had punched me in the back of the knees causing me to fall flat onto my face.

He lifted the lid of the armrest and pulled out a small pad of paper and a silver-lidded pen. I was hit by another whiff of something which conjured up the image of seaweed pasted onto a shiny, wooden groyne; me running along the beach with a bucket full of seashells swinging from my hands. I wrinkled my nose and he snapped the lid shut, placing the pen on top.

He tapped a fat finger onto the paper. "This is for you. I expect you will want to ask me some questions." He winked and then, in a swift movement, he reached over the divide and placed a clammy palm onto the back of my hand. Immediately I peeled it off, throwing it back onto his own lap. Fear and anger churned inside my stomach.

He threw back his head and laughed; a rich, throaty chuckle showing all his tomb-stone teeth. He licked his lips. "Feisty. Just as I expected. Good. I like a challenge."

I twisted my head and looked out of the tinted window as the world whizzed past, all cloaked in midnight blue. Frank repulsed and scared me – I wanted to tear the pad up into little slivers and stuff them into his purple mouth, but I dug my fingernails into my palms and resisted the urge. I had to know who he was and why he had suddenly appeared in our lives.

"I'm very happy to do the talking," he said, guffawing. "But it's hard to know where to begin. You see, once upon a time I knew you, your father and your sister very well. Do tell me, how is dear Emily?"

That name again. He knew who we were. I swallowed and concentrated on interlocking my fingers, one by one. I had to stay calm. He wasn't going to attack me or do anything bad with the chauffeur sitting just behind our heads. I may not have been able to speak, but I could thump my hands against the glass to get his attention. Just then the car jerked and Tiggy jumped up onto the seat, curling herself into my lap. I tickled the underside of her pointed snout and she closed her eyes.

"Tiggy likes you. I wonder if she remembers you after all these years. She's quite an old lady now, you know. I bought her for you when your father went crazy. Do you remember? Poor Tiggy was terribly upset when you both ran away."

Tiggy's breath was warm against my thigh. I would have remembered a puppy, wouldn't I?

Frank clapped his hands together. "Enough of that. Let's talk about *you,* shall we?" He clicked his tongue against the roof of his mouth. "Ah! But you were such a wild little beast. You have a lot of my sister's spirit in you. Your father, bless him, had absolutely no idea what to do with you, but then again, poor old James wasn't exactly cut out for parenthood."

Frank was *my* actual uncle?

He turned to me. I sensed his eyes drilling into my skull. He waited, his breath catching at the back of his throat. Eventually I turned my head and stared back at him.

"Do you remember Daddy Dearest?"

I shook my head. Even if I had wanted to, I wouldn't have

125

been able to unravel my tangled thoughts; to pull out what was a memory and what was a wish.

Sparkly eyes, strong arms lifting me high in the air and spinning me around; laughter; fishing with nets in a big lake.

Frank crawled his fingers along the edge of the window. "I remember how much you loved mermaids. Emily told you there was one in the lake, didn't she?" He sucked in his breath and tapped his index finger on the shiny wood on the inside of the door. "Now, let me see. What was she called?"

I dug my fingers into the soft folds of skin behind the dog's ears.

"Myrtle wasn't it?"

I closed my eyes and willed myself not to think of the mermaid, enticing me down to the deep, but it was too late. She was already there; hair swirling out behind her and tangling itself between the strands of emerald weeds, begging me to help her.

"You caused quite a fuss that night when you clambered out of bed and went down to the lake to try and find her. Quite. A. Fuss." For a few seconds he chewed his lower lip. "You were a wild mouse before that, scampering about the place, doing your own thing, but, after Myrtle-of-the-Lake, you became intolerable." He scuttled his hand through the air, fingers dangling like little crawling paws. "That's when James' addictions spiralled out of control."

I saw St. Terence The Greater's spire flash past the window. I was nearly home.

"Little mice are all very well until they start squeaking," he continued, spitting the words.

I held my breath. It felt as though someone was filling my head with cotton wool. I didn't know what he was talking about. *Bluebells, stinging nettles, dens made of bracken.*

"I always told James he should have been more liberal with his discipline and I think that's why he appointed me to be your guardians in the event of his untimely death."

My body went rigid. Tiggy opened one eye and stared up at me.

"Ah yes," he smiled and shook his head. "Uncle Frank,

caring for his two nieces. I would have loved that chance." The corner of his mouth curled into a snarl. "I was never able to have children," he said, his words dying to a whisper.

"I was heartbroken when you and Emily left, but I knew it would only be a matter of time before you were forced to return." He rubbed his hands together. "But," he snorted, "and here's the funniest thing – I've always known exactly where you were and what you were up to. It was just a question of biding my time and waiting. So, that's what I've been doing. Waiting for your sister to mess up everything so that, once again, she would need me to come to her rescue." He reached out and chucked me under the chin, the skin of his fingertip rough against mine. "You really are the most troublesome pair of girls."

The car came to a stop and the chauffeur opened the door. I nudged Tiggy off my lap, frantically unbuckling my seatbelt.

"Dear Cassie," said Frank, grabbing hold of my arm. My jaw dropped open and blood rushed to the tips of my ears. He reached inside the armrest, pulling out a thin, white, polystyrene box. The sound of his fingernails against the material made the hairs on the back of my neck stand to attention and the smell leaching out of it was overpowering. Even Tiggy whined in protest. Frank scribbled something onto a sheet of notepaper, tearing it off with a flourish before tucking it into the lid of the box. "Give this to Emily. I'll be seeing you soon. Very soon."

I waited until the car was out of sight before ringing the bell.

Grace opened the front door and I took a step back. She looked awful; her make-up was smudged, and she'd scraped back her hair so that her white roots were prominent. She propped herself upright against the door frame.

"Yeeeeessss?" she slurred. "What d'ya want?"

I handed her the box and she stared at it for a few seconds before grabbing it from me and staggering back into the house, her bare feet slapping against the tiles. I followed, closing the door behind me.

She placed the box on the kitchen table, shoving aside the empty bottles.

"What'ss thisss?" she said, her dull amber eyes staring and vacant. "It fucking stinks."

I shrugged.

She pulled at the piece of paper sticking out of the polystyrene, but didn't read it, casting it onto the heap of detritus. When she opened the lid, the stink of rotting fish made me retch.

"Whaaaat...?" Grace gagged and took a step back. She grabbed at the note, unfolding it with trembling fingers, her eyes darting back and forth over the italics. Then she scrunched it into a ball, threw back her head and began to laugh.

Chapter Twenty

Flo

It was our last exam and Lily was a no-show. English Lit was Lily's favourite and I knew she wouldn't have skipped it. There had to be something seriously wrong. For the entire exam I felt like something heavy was pressing down on my shoulders and it wasn't just the whispering or the stares as I walked into the exam hall which triggered it. I could hack all of that shit. Dad was innocent and it was just a matter of time before they found the real murderer and he was released. I wasn't going to think of all the fake stuff being said about him. I wasn't going to think about the hug – I was remembering it wrong – it was nothing. No, what was really bugging me was Lily hinting she had a secret past and that Frank might know stuff which could prove Dad's innocence.

The more I thought about what Lily had written on the paper towel, the more confused I grew. Was Lily really trying to tell me that she had something to do with Amelie's murder? It was dumb – impossible. But ever since Lily pitched up at the hotel, Frank's fat face was stuck in my head. Even while I was writing about the role of witchcraft in Macbeth, he'd been there, on a loop, strawberry juice oozing from his mouth.

After Frank and Lily had gone, me and Mum went back to the garden though I couldn't face eating any more of the scones and jam.

"Mum?"

"Hmm." She didn't glance up from her magazine.

"Frank's such a good bloke…"

"Hmm."

"Remind me how you met." All Dad ever said about Frank was *well, I never, who would have thought it? The Prof of all people!*"

Mum looked up. "Really?"

I nodded.

She shrugged, licked her finger and flicked to the next page of the magazine. "I first met him whilst Daddy and I lived in Oxford. It was just one of those funny coincidences that I happened to bump into him again a couple of years ago."

Her phone rang and she snatched it up. "Cally, sweetheart, are you nearly here? Yes – I know, *hilarious*. How's setting up the exhibition going? Are the Castle staff keeping my little treasure safe?" No talk of Dad. She stood up, rolling her eyes at me as though she really didn't want to have this conversation, then walked across the lawn out of earshot.

That was all I was going to get.

***

Not really giving a shit that my mocks were over, I left Stella and the rest of the gang, swigging cider and vaping. I knew they were only trying to be kind, but I was already pissed off by their fake cheerfulness and clumsy change of subject if anything relating to Dad cropped up. It wasn't taking my mind off the situation – it made me feel even more lonely.

Lily was the only one who I could talk to, but I swung from being worried about her to being pissed off; you didn't just announce that you used to have a different life then vanish.

As I said goodbye, my friends gave me sympathetic smiles and over-long hugs. I left them lying on the scorched grass in the park, giggling about nothing and throwing Stella's cold chips at each other. All the chat moved onto what they were going to wear to Bea's party, and I was relieved to get away. Everything was so fake.

I'd made up my mind. I was going to find Lily. I wished at

the time I'd told Mum she couldn't tell Lily what to do and that Lily could bloody well catch the bus home if she wanted to, but it was too late. As we'd gone back into the hotel to shower and change for supper, the receptionist came over with a telephone message from Frank:

"The girl is home safe. Thanks for a lovely afternoon, my dearest. I'll see you back at the flat in a couple of days. All my love, Frank." Frank didn't know how to text.

But Lily hadn't been in touch with me to say she'd got home safely, and her phone was dead. Worried about that, I'd texted Grace and that's when I found out the bitch had blocked my number.

The only thing I knew about Frank was his surname and that he knew Dad from his time in Oxford.

I bailed on the five-course supper using a banging headache as an excuse, but as soon as Mum went down to the Orangery for prinks with Cally, her agent, I got out my laptop. I did an internet search on Frank Fanshawe, but there wasn't much info. He'd been a professor of psychology at an Oxford College before becoming a director of a big drugs company, Zolis. He no longer worked for Zolis but was still on the board. I typed Zolis into Google, but all I got was the picture of a shining sun and an 0300 telephone number. The address running along the bottom of the page was the registered, not actual, one.

I was getting nowhere.

The next day I got up super early and caught the bus into Far Langton. Walking as fast as I could without breaking into a run, I sped along the narrow, gravel path to the lake, towards the war memorial. Now that Dad was banged up in a remand centre, most of the journalists had gone and all the Mums with pushchairs, MAMILs and oldies, throwing stale bread at the ducks, were back.

Lake View Café was shut. I saw a notice on the back of the door: *Closed due to personal circumstances.* I banged on the window in case Grace was in the kitchen, but there was no one there; the chairs were upside down on the tables, the patisserie shelves empty, the till drawer open.

I carried on along the street and made a sharp turn into a side road which led on to Number 37, Orchard Close. Even if Grace slammed the door shut in my face, I needed to know Lily was inside. Safe.

The house looked weird. All the downstairs curtains were closed, and a bundle of post was sticking out of the door. I peeped through the letterbox and the mail flopped onto the mat below. Then it hit me, and I stepped back, nearly catching my fingers in the brass flap. There was a vile smell coming from inside. I held my breath and looked again, but there was nothing to see apart from bare walls and a couple of angry sounding flies.

I hammered on the door. "Hey!" I shouted. "It's me. Please can you just come to the door if you're there."

A blackbird rootled around in a nearby plant pot.

I followed the path round to the back of the garden, but the gate was closed with a padlock. Then I remembered: one time me and Lils had been late back from a gathering in the park and she was desperate to meet Grace's curfew so rather than taking our usual route around the south side of the lake we'd cut through the woods. Lily had got into her garden through a break in the fence. She texted later to say she'd made it inside with five minutes to spare and no bollocking from Grace.

I went back round to the cut-through for Cupid's Wood which ran the whole stretch of the cul-de-sac. When I reached Lily's fence, I rattled each panel until I came across the loose one. I pushed it to one side and crawled through, putting it back again afterwards.

I crept past the thick bushes until I reached the edge of the lawn. I froze. There straight ahead of me was Grace, her skinny arse in the air. She was on all fours and moving along on her hands and knees stopping every couple of seconds to pat the grass. She was searching for something – had she lost her engagement ring? Thrown it away in a rage and then had second thoughts?

She carried on crawling until she got to the backdoor then stood up, stamped her feet and went back inside, slamming the door behind her.

I didn't know what to do. Five minutes later, me still trying to figure out what next, I heard the sound of tyres on gravel, car doors shutting and more crunching until the noise of the engine had faded.

Maybe Grace had gone somewhere leaving Lily on her own inside.

I sprinted to the back door but it was locked and, as I shook the handle, the bolts rattled. I stepped backwards, the edges of the lawn tickling my ankles, and stared at a freaky flower which climbed up one side of the door; it looked like it was covered with hundreds of unblinking eyes. As I followed the creepy plant along the brickwork, I saw there was a window on the ground floor which was open a tiny slice at the top. I grabbed one of the patio chairs and pressed it up against the wall. Climbing onto the seat I reached up and slid my hands into the gap, pressing down on the frame until it stopped moving.

When I opened the curtains, a couple of flies dive-bombed me, and I squealed and almost lost my footing. Once I'd got my balance again, I looked around the room. It was untidy – not up to Grace's usual standards. There were lots of empty bottles lying on the carpet and a half-eaten tray of iced buns, crawling with fat, noisy flies.

I wriggled through the gap and twisted my arms until I was hanging, like a sloth, onto the thick wooden curtain pole. Slowly I lifted one leg through and balanced on the windowsill, knocking a few ornaments onto the floor. Suddenly the pole gave way and I crashed onto the carpet, banging my arse on the armchair. I lay there for a few seconds wondering how I was going to explain my terrible attempt at breaking-and-entering, but no one came.

I took a deep breath and then wished I hadn't. The house reeked and I'd never seen it looking such a mess. Perhaps the news about Dad had hit Grace harder than I thought. I felt a bit guilty – I hadn't bothered to think of things from Grace's point of view, who, in a couple of days had gone from being dizzy with wedding preparations to being questioned about her reasons for setting up home with a paedo. If only I could sit down and talk with her; make her see sense. But then I remembered what Lily had said back at the hotel and the fuzzy feeling vanished. If she'd been lying to me about who they were, what else had she been lying about?

I ran upstairs across the small landing and into Lily's room which was reasonably tidy; the bed was made. I opened the wardrobe door, and the empty hangers swung about in the draught. Some of Lily's clothes were missing, but not many. As I closed the door, I spotted something poking out from the bottom shelf. *Fuck!* It was Lily's phone and the back was missing – a gap where the sim card should've been. I sank onto the bed; no fucking wonder I couldn't get in touch with her. Lily's silly mermaid doll was sitting on her pillow. That was weird – she usually kept it hidden on a shelf to stop me from teasing her about it.

Without thinking, I shoved the doll into my bag and went for a snoop in Grace's room. The overnight case wasn't lying on the top of her wardrobe.

I carried on; toothbrushes were missing from the bathroom, but when I opened the medicine cabinet, I saw it was full of boxes of Lily's pills – Detra-holzepene – the bright sun logo running along the bottom of each carton. This had to be a good sign. Grace wouldn't have left home without them so maybe they had just disappeared for a few days; left in a hurry because Grace needed time to think things through and get away from the journalists. I put a pack of Lily's pills into my bag, just in case. As I shut the cupboard, I knocked a box of hair dye onto the floor. I picked it up – *Ruby Sunshine* – with a picture of a redhead on the front. I didn't know Grace dyed her hair – I'd always thought she was a natural ginger because of her freckled skin and green eyes.

I went downstairs and crossed through the hall and into the kitchen. The door was shut, but I heard loud buzzing coming from behind it. I opened it and retched – I had never *ever* smelled anything so awful in my entire life and there were flies everywhere.

I wanted to run, but I couldn't ignore the white box, open on the kitchen table. Swatting the flies away, I went closer; inside were seven bloodied fish tails lined up in a row. *This was getting really twisted. I was in someone else's nightmare.*

Gasping for air, I opened the front door and ran outside, glad of the sunshine and grateful that the fat little blackbird was still dancing about in the pot.

The wheelie bin was behind the front gate, ready for the next collection. I didn't want to, but I pinched my nose and forced myself back into house. I didn't know what the fuck was going on, but I couldn't leave those minging fish tails in there a minute longer. I grabbed the carton and ran out again, this time slamming the front door behind me. I sprinted down the drive and chucked the fish tails into the dumpster. But the bin was overflowing, and the lid wouldn't shut so I had to press down on the top black sack to make a bit more room. When I did that the plastic burst and all sorts of yucky shit came spilling out; tissues, baked beans and a white, fluffy tail. *White, fluffy tail!* It took a few seconds to realise that the tail was attached to a small, white, furry body.

I gasped, slammed the lid shut and put my head between my legs. Seconds later I threw up into the hedge.

A car pulled into the drive. I couldn't look up. They were back and it was too late to hide. I couldn't pretend I hadn't just seen a dead dog in their bin.

"There you are darling."

I looked up and there was Mum, stepping out of a taxi, wearing chinos and a silky blouse.

"I thought you might be here," she said, leaning back into the car. "Keep the meter running, won't be a mo."

I'd never been so pleased to see her. I wiped my mouth with the back of my hand. "I think they must have gone away."

"That's understandable. Well, now that Frank has gone back to his countryside bolt hole to sort out a few things–"

"Dad's case?"

Mum shifted from one Leboutin to the other, but didn't say anything.

"Can we go and visit him soon? I really, really have to talk to him."

Mum grabbed hold of my hand. "Of course, of course. But we should really let Clive Trundle-Jones go in there first. He's used to these horrid places thanks to his *delightful* clientele." She put her arm around my shoulder and her silver bangles jingled. She smelt so good. "He'll manufacture a plan to get Tom out of there. They call him Clive the Liar for a reason, you know." For once I didn't care about Mum's backhanded insults – it was just great to hear her voice. "He got one of his criminals off a murder charge even though there was CCTV showing him plunging the knife into the victim."

Okay – she'd gone too far. "But Dad's not a murderer."

Mum sniffed, suddenly very busy with examining the nearest flowerbed. "We can't dwell on it at the moment," she snapped. "I'm here to take your mind off all things unpleasant and to treat you to an end of exam shopping splurge. Where do you fancy? Bicester Village, The Bullring?"

Pushing all the confusing and horrid things I'd just seen to the back of my mind, I made myself a promise: I was going to find out Frank's connection to Lily and I was going to clear Dad's name. I'd been an absolute twat to think that there had been anything going on between him and Amelie and I'd already wasted far too much time by giving it head space. Dad deserved better and it was now very clear to me that I was the only person who was a hundred percent on his side.

"Oxford – I'd like to go to Oxford. Maybe stay the night in that posh hotel you're always banging on about, if that's okay."

Chapter Twenty-One

Grace

I had submerged myself in a delicious pool of memories. It was as though I was floating in dark, tepid water; each thought splashing up against my skin and reminding me of how much I loved him. The wound his departure inflicted upon me had never healed properly – there hadn't been anybody to patch it up apart from me and I'd used too thin a gauze. At the start, I hadn't cared, but over the years, hidden beneath the bandage, the cut had festered and deepened. Now that Emily was re-emerging, I couldn't be bothered to hide the gangrenous tear to my heart. I wanted to recall everything that had happened and re-live it all, right up until its dreadful conclusion because only then could I start back at the beginning and remember it afresh.

One of the things which stuck in my mind was the parties Daddy used to throw; one in particular.

***

Of course, being only fourteen, I wasn't supposed to be there, so I hid myself behind the mahogany cabinet at the edge of the landing and peeped over the edge of the bannisters, staring at the crowd through the twinkling beads of an enormous chandelier. I was dressed in a most seductive gown, one stolen from Mummy's wardrobe which was still bursting with clothes despite her having been dead for almost a decade. The material clung to my skin and revealed every bump and furrow of my body. I had twisted my ponytail into a tight knot and pinned the ends flush against the back of my head. I checked myself in the oval looking glass set into the cabinet and my dark reflection smiled back at me.

I watched as Daddy leant over a small metal tray before lifting his head backwards and pinching his nostrils whilst his eyes, like loose gobstoppers, rolled around the sockets. Then he let out a whinny of delight, threw back his shoulders and tapped the arm of a nearby waitress. A slutty, blonde girl wearing a black skirt, barely covering her buttocks, smiled and handed him a glass tankard filled to the brim with a pale liquid – James Buchanan's classic signature drink; Moet & Chandon served out of pint glasses.

The ballroom was full of men in pale lounge suits, shirts open at the neck. The women wore shimmering cocktail dresses of all shades, but I knew none cut a finer figure than I. Most of the ladies had a pinched look about them; holding their noses a few degrees towards the vaulted ceiling as though they couldn't bear to look at their other halves.

Daddy put his arm around a willowy man with curly, dark hair and champagne slopped over the brim of his glass onto his shirt. The men pressed their scalps together and Daddy's floppy fringe fell like a curtain across his forehead. With his free hand he patted each of his jacket pockets when suddenly Gil appeared and pressed a cigarette between Daddy's lips before striking a match and cupping the flame until the end of his cigarette was glowing.

Daddy gave him a curt nod before slinking over to the French Windows, his arm still thrown around the dark-haired man. Gil, beautiful in chinos and crisp white shirt, stood alone for a few seconds before a skinny woman in a floral jumpsuit pounced. The flowers on the material matched her nails, lipstick and eye shadow. He smiled and tilted his head to one side, and I was absorbed watching her thick lips move. I liked how Gil had smoothed his hair back so that it curled onto his shoulder blades.

It was time for him to notice me.

I took a deep breath and tottered along the corridor. Although I wanted to, I couldn't go down the main staircase because I would have drawn too much attention to myself and risked getting sent back to bed like a little kid. I had to take the servant's passage, the one at the back of the house which cut through the pantry and snaked into the rear of the hall, next to the cloakroom. The needle-heels of Mummy's shoes shortened my stride and my calf muscles tensed under the strain of putting each foot forward.

I held my breath as I hobbled past the slate shelves bursting with the platters of cheese which would be brought out on the stroke of midnight. Then I took a sharp right turn and opened the small, cut-away door into the hall. Standing beneath the portrait of my paternal grandfather, I smoothed myself down and took another deep breath. A slim waitress, tray laden with champagne, walked past and I stopped her to take a glass. The girl, her dark eyes made smaller by a coating of black eyeliner on the inner rim, muttered something about there being a circus in town before stalking away. Uncertain what the waitress was talking about, I took a swig of champagne and spluttered as the sour taste hit my tongue. My ears were burning and my armpits damp with sweat. This was beginning to feel like a mistake.

I couldn't see Gil anymore; he was no longer with the floral lady. All the breath slid from my lungs and the wooden panels around my head wobbled. If I wasn't careful, I was going to faint; my dress was too tight. I had to find somewhere to sit down for five minutes to regain my composure and for the sweat beads across my upper lip to evaporate. I peeled off into a dark side-room; Daddy's second study. This was the one the press office used for publicity shots of James Buchanan MP at work because it had a lovely view of the lake, whereas Daddy's actual study was littered with coffee mugs, overflowing ashtrays and the floor was piled high with complaints from his constituents. The desk in the second study was immaculate, dressed only with a banker's light, leather blotter, silver ink pen and heavy paperweight – a seahorse suspended in clear resin. I used to spend ages holding the glass up to the light to examine the poor little merman. The walls were covered with a fleur-delis wallpaper and two small bookshelves were positioned down one side with a vase of wilting roses sitting upon each.

I didn't turn the light on, but went over to the large, sash window and threw it open, gulping in the faint aroma of wood smoke which emanated from the flaming torches placed at regular intervals along the drive. The full moon cast its shadow into the room, filling it with pearly light.

"Ah," said a gravelly voice. "I thought I saw you disappear into here."

I spun around and grinned at the outline of the towering figure standing in the doorway. "Uncle Frank." There was a large box tucked under his right arm. I ran over and he stooped so I could kiss his whiskery cheek. He smelt of stale tobacco and green peppercorn sauce.

Frank's speckled beard was trimmed to perfection and his linen jacket, done up at the waist, hid his vast gut. He turned on the light switch and his slate eyes rolled up and down my body; his moustaches twitched. "Why! My dearest, you look…very grown up. I swear, each time I see you, you seem more like your poor mother. Dear, *dear* Grace." He sniffed and poked the corners of his eyes with the tip of his thumb. "For my part, though, I think little girls should dress like little girls." He set down the box and I stared at the gaudy paper bow stuck to the top.

Frank smiled, showing stained, horsey teeth. "Go ahead and open it. I bought it for you and Cassie to play with."

I unfolded the cardboard flaps and peered inside. It was a doll's house.

"Do you like it?" he asked rubbing his hands together.

"Oh yes!" I exclaimed, trying to keep the disappointment out of my voice. "Thank you so much." I was far too grown up to play with such a thing, but Frank's enthusiasm was infectious and soon I was cooing and purring as we set it upon the coffee table, Frank pointing out all the intricate furniture within. He had chosen every item himself.

Frank picked up a doll with long orange hair and thrust it under my nose. "She looks like you, doesn't she? A little bit of a naughty girl."

I nodded and he pressed the doll into my hands.

He sank into the leather armchair nearest the fireplace and took a cigar out of his jacket. He stroked the flint of his lighter and waved his other hand in the air. "Play." I cleared my throat but stood still. "Now you don't want to make your dear old uncle sad, do you?" Frank's grey eyes narrowed. "*Play.*"

I knelt down, picked up two of the china figurines and manoeuvred them into positions around the dining room table. I could feel Frank's gaze fixed upon me.

"What are they saying to each other?" he asked. "I can't hear. Perhaps they've been disobedient and are waiting to be punished?"

Heat crept across my cheeks.

The door opened.

"Who the hell are you?" said a male voice. It was Gil. He stomped across the parquet floor until he was standing level with me. I cast aside the dolls and leapt to my feet, hanging my head. That he should have found me in such a compromising position – *playing with dolls.*

"I'm Professor Fanshawe. Who are you?"

"I'm Gil Walton. I'm responsible for the girls."

Frank smirked. "Oh! So, you're the nanny Cookie has been telling me so much about." He took a long drag on his cigar and exhaled a ring of smoke, his lips making a soft popping noise. "You're not doing a very good job," he continued, laughter curdling at the back of his throat. "My niece should be tucked up in bed, not here surrounded by all these villains and wasters."

"I take it James doesn't know you're here." Gil folded his arms across his chest.

"I don't need his permission to visit my darling nieces." Frank waved at me and I gave a coquettish laugh, but Gil wasn't looking at me, he was glaring at Frank.

"Besides which," continued Frank, "as well as seeing my girls, I've a little business proposal to put to James."

Gil seized my hand and pulled me out into the hall.

"What the hell are you doing here?" he asked, his voice

almost a hiss.

I couldn't answer. He still hadn't commented on my appearance.

"Come on Em." He brushed my cheek with his finger. "This isn't the place for you. Let me take you back to your room."

Tears of disappointment started tumbling.

"What the fuck?" said Daddy, appearing behind Gil's head, his speech slurred. "What is going on here?" The whites of his eyes were webbed with tiny lines. He looked at me then turned to Gil. "Well?"

At that moment Frank came out of the room and slapped Daddy on the back. Daddy, on seeing his brother-in-law, shook his head. "Who let you in?"

Frank clapped his hands together. "Good to see you too. Now, I need to have a word with you my dear boy. A little investment I think you might like to help me endorse."

"I told you last time," said Daddy through clenched teeth. "I'm not interested in your dodgy deals."

Frank raised a dark eyebrow. "Ah, but this time I think I might just be able to persuade you." He licked his rubbery lips and gave Gil a sideways glance. "It was *nice* meeting you, Mr Walton."

Daddy opened his mouth then snapped it shut again. He pushed his fringe off his damp forehead. He had taken his jacket off and the back of his shirt stuck to his spine in a V-shape. He smelt like cider vinegar. "Okay, Frank. You can have five minutes. That's all. And then I want you gone. I'll be with you in a second."

Frank winked at me and strode away, plucking a glass of champagne from a nearby waitress.

"What is going on?" hissed Daddy. "Who let that slime-bag in? And why is my daughter dressed like a prostitute? Do your fucking job and take her away."

Gil stared at him. "Seriously? Is that all you have to say to your daughter? What kind of a shit father are you?"

Daddy opened his mouth, but Gil cut him off.

"Don't bother answering. I quit."

It was too much for me and I collapsed to the floor.

When I opened my eyes, I was in my own bed, the covers tight around me. The curtains weren't drawn, and I could see Daddy's elongated shadow by the window. He was sitting in an armchair, head buried in his hands.

Gil stood behind him, one hand on his shoulder. The moonlight pouring in through the window had illuminated the whites of his eyes.

I stayed still and silent. I didn't want them to know I was awake.

"I'm such a fuck up," said Daddy. "I should never have had kids."

"Ah, Jamie, don't take on so." *Jamie!* I had never heard Gil call Daddy that before.

Gil placed his other hand down on Daddy's shoulders and squeezed.

"I dread to think what he's got on me this time or what scam he wants me to endorse." He sighed. "It's relentless. As though Grace's death somehow entitles him to a share of my own inheritance. I can't stand it anymore. This feeling that any minute everything is going to come crashing down about my ears."

There was a noise I hadn't heard before. It was a sort of whimpering which rose into a loud wailing. I could see Gil was kneeling before Daddy, arms around his shoulders, Daddy's head buried in the crook of his neck. Daddy's whole body was shaking. They stayed like this for five minutes, all the time Gil murmuring and patting his back.

Daddy lifted his head and rubbed his eyes with the back of his hand. "And to top it all, my daughter has gone and fallen head over heels in love with you."

Gil got to his feet. "Ah well, she's only human."

They both laughed.

"Come on," said Gil. He held out his hand and Daddy took it, joints clicking as he stood up.

Gil seized Daddy around his upper arms and ducked so that Daddy was forced to look into his face. "You've got work to do. You need to get your backside down there where all your guests are. It's time to schmooze."

Daddy saluted him. "Yes, boss."

Gil pointed to the door and Daddy nodded then strode over. He turned on the threshold.

"You won't go Gil, will you?" said Daddy. "Promise me, you'll stay."

"I promise, Jamie. I promise."

I turned my face to the wall and smiled.

Chapter Twenty-Two

Lily

The hum of raised voices filled my ears and my eyelids snapped open, sending the mermaid spiralling into the gloomiest corners of my mind. I was lying on a scratchy blanket in the corner of a dingy room or shed. My hands were tied together; my body ached, and my clothes were damp. The air smelled musty but familiar and the place was empty apart from an enamel bucket tucked into one corner and a square of threadbare carpet positioned to the left of the door. On the other side of the room, grey light peeped in through the cracks between the wooden panels and lit up the square outline of a smaller door.

I shuffled to where the raised voices were coming from.

"A few days and nights here without her medicine will make her grateful. She'll welcome her new situation with open arms." Frank's deep voice echoed through my chest.

"What about me?" said Grace; her voice slow and slurred. "What situation is there left for me?"

He sighed. "My dearest girl, I cannot pretend how distressing I find this whole incident. At great personal expense, not to mention emotional difficulties, I made your terrible crimes go away." His voice grew louder with each word and it was as though he was speaking through gritted teeth. "And what hurts me the most is that you knew I could only keep the truth at bay if you remained hidden."

"I'm sorry, Uncle. I don't know what got into me." Grace sounded different; younger, confused.

"How could you be so selfish and ungrateful?" There was

the sound of heavy footsteps, as he paced up and down. "Don't forget," he continued, and he was shouting now, "that it was you who looked to me for protection all those years ago. You came to me." There was a pause and the sound of a slap followed by a whimper. "I was the one who made everything disappear. Me. And it was all because I loved you and I wanted you to be happy."

"I know, Uncle. I'm *soooorrrrry*." This snivelling declaration was followed by sobbing.

Frank laughed, a horrid gurgle which sounded as though it was trapped at the back of his throat. "My dearest girl, you have no idea the financial mess your father left me to deal with. Without me, you would have been thrown into prison and your sister into foster care. I had to sell Aldeburgh to pay off his debts."

Grace's cries turned to hiccups then it went silent and I heard water sloshing beneath my feet. It was disorienting.

"Now then, dearest, let's not quarrel," said Frank and his voice softened as though he was talking to a small child. "Every princess trapped in a tower needs someone to watch over them. You can start by writing out exactly what she does when she is having one of her episodes. After I am satisfied she won't cause any further problems, I'll move you both into the lodge. Despite the unfortunate coincidence of her turning up when I was with my wife, I managed to split up the party before Cassie was able to compare notes with Flo."

Cassie. *Emily and Cassie.*

"What I really don't understand is why you went after Tom in the first place."

Grace didn't reply.

Frank sighed. "Ah well. Nina doesn't suspect a thing. She knows nothing of my past, nor is she remotely interested in anything other than her ridiculous art or where the next designer outfit is coming from. Don't get me wrong, I am fond of her and she's great to look at, but we both know the usefulness and limits of our relationship." He paused. "Meanwhile the legal team are so busy fending off the overwhelming evidence against Tom they won't bother to dig deeper let alone go searching for another suspect. Tom was long gone before James killed himself and besides, he never knew it was my niece he treated. If you lay low from now on, I am certain the police will never make the connection." There was more shuffling and creaking of floorboards. "I'll come back tomorrow." He paused. "And don't think about running again or this time you'll regret it."

No one came to give me my pills. When I woke my entire body ached and the sad face of the mermaid was pinned to the back of my eyelids. Grace appeared at the door; her skin apple-white and her clothes dirty. Even from my corner of the room, I could smell the alcohol fumes on her breath. I was desperate for a pee and, fumbling with my constrained wrists, I pulled down my jeans and squatted over the bucket while Grace curled her mouth in disgust and turned her head away.

"You can get rid of your own mess," she said and crossed the room, stumbling from side to side, as though the floor was moving beneath her feet. She opened the small door and the room filled with white sunlight. I crept forwards, the handle of the bucket looped over my wrists, and I saw in front of me a wooden walkway, surrounded each side by water.

"Go on," said Grace. "To the end with it."

The sun warmed my cheeks and my ears filled with birdsong as a pair of swallows flitted in and out of the frothy leaves of a nearby willow. I walked forwards until I reached the end of the jetty then tipped the contents of the bucket over the edge, afterwards kneeling down on the other side to swill it out. The water was cold against my fingers and I set down the pail, cupping a handful and throwing it against my face, willing it to bring me back to the real world.

I turned around and Grace was still there.

I was a prisoner, trapped by the very thing I feared the most – what was hidden beneath the surface of the water.

Grace tossed me a crusty roll; feeding time at the zoo. I tore at the bread, unable to remember the last time I had eaten anything. On one side of the lake a large house poked its head over the top of a row of fir trees. My mind jolted;

147

there was something familiar about the custard colour of the stonework and the neat, rectangular windows which seemed to blink in the sunlight.

I had seen this house before.

I finished my breakfast and brushed myself down, the crumbs falling through the wooden slats and into the water. A tiny shoal of silver minnows came to the surface, making circles with their dark mouths. I closed my eyes, reaching out for the smiling man who was standing next to me, net in one hand, jam jar in the other. *Daddy?* But when I opened my eyes, I saw my fingers were clawing at thin air.

Grace rolled a bottle of water to me.

She sank to the floor and sat cross-legged like a child. "Mermaids. Everything that happened was because of a fucking mermaid."

I frowned.

"Is it here now?" asked Grace, swishing her hand under the surface of the lake. I took a gulp of water and stared into her bloodshot eyes, holding her stony gaze.

Then I heard it; loud, mournful singing, bubbling up from the deep. I scrabbled to my knees and peered into the gloom.

And who shall wear the starry crown?

Good Lord, show me the way.

The singing grew louder. I pinched the soft skin of my forearm.

The wailing trickled into my ears and echoed around the walls of my mind. I plunged my hands into the cool water, trying to catch hold of whatever was hiding below. My body trembled – this was the first time I had heard her outside of my dreams. My stomach somersaulted. She was real.

You must unlock the casket, my darling girl. I loved you so much. Do this for me.

I pressed my body flat against the wooden slats and swirled my arms, willing the unseen creature to swim into my embrace. Pond skaters tickled my nostrils whilst strings of weed slid through my fingers.

I held my breath.

I could hear her so why couldn't I see her?

Her unbearable wailing spilt into my soul causing a sharp pain which sliced across my stomach. The noise was deafening and pressed against my temples. Unable to resist any longer I slid my body into the water.

Immediately the singing stopped and all I could hear was the march of blood drumming around my ears.

I was sinking and my hair swirled around my head.

Then I heard screaming and I realised it was coming from above me. Water seeped into my nostrils and my chest tightened. When I looked up, there was Grace's face, as though melting behind a sheet of glass. She was shrieking but the sound was muted.

Blind panic coursed through my body. I kicked my feet, but my bound arms were like lead weights pulling me down and strangling me. I was swept under the wooden bridge and plunged headlong into a tangle of olive weeds.

I was going to die. Bubbles like glass beads danced about my head, growing smaller with each second.

There was a loud splash and I felt a vice like grip under my arms and then all went black.

The next thing I remember was lying on the decking, coughing up water and undigested clumps of bread.

Grace was on her back, propped up on her elbows, panting. Rivulets of water trickled down her face and her clothing clung to her body and made a damp border around her frame.

"What the fuck?" she said. "You don't get to choose. D'ya hear me? You don't get to choose." She rolled onto her side and then heaved herself onto all fours.

Her body froze and a noise came from within her which made my skin prickle.

I followed her gaze and there, amongst the bundle of dislodged blackened weeds, I saw the unmistakable shape of a human skull.

Chapter Twenty-Three

Flo

Mum and I sat in a café which was tucked into a corner of The Covered Market. I had chosen it mainly because Mum had turned her nose up at its sticky wooden floorboards and the limp flowers dangling out of their milk bottle vases. But it also had a huge selection of crazy sounding milkshakes and I was enjoying sucking pink froth off the top of my *nutty butter n' thimbleberry* mix. My eyes were fixed on the shop opposite which had loads of bright coloured, old-school satchels stacked up in the window – they were ugly and cost a fortune; I really couldn't figure out who would buy one.

Mum pinched the handle of her teacup and sipped her herbal tea as though she thought someone might have poisoned it. A great tragedy had occurred on our way over; one of her gel nails had torn and every so often, when she wasn't giving a running commentary on the state of the locals, she picked at it.

"I think you should see if that fancy salon can fit you in," I said, pointing at the peeling mauve husk dangling from her thumb.

"But, darling, I don't want to spoil our shopping expedition. Maybe you could come with me and get your nails done too?" She cleared her throat. "Someone could tidy up your brows while they were at it."

I snorted and pink milk splattered onto the table. That was such a classic Nina move. Mum tutted and wiped up the spillage with her napkin.

"Thanks, Mum. If it's alright with you, I might just poke

my head into a couple of the colleges."

Mum's mouth twitched. "But I thought Oxford was *far too elitist* for you."

"Ah. That was when I didn't think I stood any chance of getting in." I sat up straight-backed. "Ms Phibbs thinks I have *potential*."

Mum arched an immaculately plucked eyebrow.

"Seriously, you go and get those nails seen to. I'm going to take a few photos of any colleges that I like the look of. Maybe see if I can find a couple of students hanging around and ask them what it's like to study here."

"Well, if you're sure."

When we walked through the door of the salon, the temptations proved too much for Mum and, as well as having her nails done, she decided on having a seaweed skin wrap. It bought me at least a couple of extra hours to myself which was perfect.

As I was about to leave Mum in reception, filling in forms and drinking more herbal tea, I had a final go at getting some more info about Frank. "Mum, do you have any suggestions about which colleges I should visit?"

Mum remained focused on her questionnaire, repeatedly clicking the end of her biro. "They all look the same to me. Straight after the wedding your father and I had our drinks reception at one of them."

"I didn't know that. How lovely." Any photos taken on that special day had either been destroyed or boxed up and shoved in the loft.

Mum set the clipboard down on the coffee table. "As you well know, my disastrous marriage to your father isn't something I really like to talk about." I bit my lip, resisting the urge to point out that I was the by-product of that *disastrous marriage*. A woman in a white coat came over and took the paperwork away.

"The Dark Ages," I said under my breath.

"What did you say?" Mum was now engrossed by the varnishes on the shelf behind her.

"I said it's going to take ages, looking around the colleges.

151

It would be nice to have a starting point. A connection. I mean, you always said you were a couple of weeks pregnant before you married Dad so, *technically,* I have been to one of them before."

Mum laughed and picked up *paparazzi pink*. "Well, if I remember correctly, it was dear Frankie who sorted the venue for us. It was such short notice, but I think he managed to pull a few strings because he was one of the resident tutors and friends with the Provost."

"That was kind of him," I said, my heart beating a bit faster. "Can you remember the name?"

Mum shrugged. "Sadly, it wasn't one of the one's that's always on Inspector Morse, but I seem to remember it has some connection to Alice in Wonderland. Yes, that's it! We had our photos taken at the end of a long stone corridor which is meant to be the inspiration for the rabbit hole Alice fell down or some such nonsense. Your father, of course, thought the whole thing was marvellous."

The woman in the lab-coat returned with a folded dressing gown which she handed to Mum. "We'll meet at *The Duke of Norfolk* at five for a cocktail," she said, leaning over and kissing my cheek. "That's the one at the top end of the shopping street just over the road from our hotel." The double doors behind the reception desk opened, filling the room with a minty lavender smell. Mum was shunted into the hidden bit, and I tried my hardest not to sneeze.

I went back onto the High Street, now rammed with tourists, and took a sharp right turn down a cobbled passageway. I leant my back against the wall, took out my phone, and googled *Alice in Wonderland in Oxford*. Fuck; almost every college claimed a link to this Lewis Carrol guy and even with the extra seaweed hours, I didn't have enough time to go into every one of them.

I came out of the side street and ahead of me was a weird round, yellow stone building with a domed roof. I sat down on the steps in front of the main door, not giving a shit that I'd stuck myself right in the middle of an Asian trio's super complex photo shoot. I rested my chin on my knees and swept my hand over the dusty ground next to my feet. This was a total waste of time – I'd have been better browsing on the internet back at the hotel.

When I looked up again, I was staring at a bloke wearing a velvet tailcoat with a frothy cravat around his neck and a wonky top hat. The woman standing next to him was in a floaty linen dress, a pair of fluffy rabbit ears on her head and a large, cardboard cut-out of a fob watch pinned to her waist. She held a wooden placard with the Queen of Hearts playing card pasted onto it and *Alice Tours* painted in black italics underneath.

I went over. "Excuse me."

The girl turned and stared down her pointy nose at me.

"I don't suppose you could tell me which of the colleges have a special connection with Lewis Carrol."

She waved a fistful of pamphlets at me. "Join the tour and you can find out for yourself. Thirty pounds for an hour's guided tour."

"I'll just take a flyer, thanks."

"One pound fifty," said the girl. What a rip off. I handed the money over and sat back on the steps to read the info. It was the last one on the list, Gloucester College, which claimed the tunnel link.

From a distance, the college looked like a Lego castle and I kept expecting a knight on horseback to come charging out of the large wooden gates. I walked across a small courtyard and through a cut-out door in the gate and then I found myself standing on a large stone patio, looking between fat, circular pillars at a stripy lawn. One side of the quad looked like it was part of a magnificent Georgian town house, but the other side was made up of little cottages with diamond windows and low rooves.

A door behind opened and a man in a hoody came out. He held it open for me.

"Thanks," I mumbled, ducking under his arm. I stood inside a rectangular hall with a high ceiling, wood panelled walls and large windows. Benches ran up either side of the room leading to a table set on a raised platform at the end.

There were a few people sitting at one of the benches, chattering away and eating salad off china plates, but no one turned to look at me.

I spotted a load of group photos which ran the length of one of the walls. Each frame was full of dorky students wearing black gowns and silly square hats. The name of each student was written underneath in italics and the year was drawn in metallic pen at the very bottom of the frame.

Mum and Dad had been married sixteen years ago.

I counted back on my fingers and stopped in front of what I reckoned was the right time Mr and Mrs Marchant would have been hanging around Oxford. One photo stood out – it was more colourful than the rest – the people in it were wearing bright gowns with fluffy edges. Their faces were wrinkly, there was more grey hair, or no hair, plus there were a lot of men with beards. The professors. I ran my finger along the names and found F.J.P. Fanshawe with a load of random initials after his name. There he was; big round face and neatly trimmed beard. He hadn't changed much over the years; he'd just got a bit fatter and his facial hair had turned whiter.

So what? So, he had taught here and met Dad. That didn't prove anything.

I went back outside and walked down the steps towards the lawn which was covered in *keep off the grass* signs. Though I was pissed off I decided I ought to at least see the tunnel but it didn't make me feel any better. I didn't feel the magic flowing through my veins. *Alice in Fucking Wonderland.*

I returned to the lodge and was nearly flattened by two students running up the stairs with folders under their arm. I followed them up the spiral staircase and as they swiped their cards against the magnetic reader, I snuck in. I had found the library.

I remembered how pleased Frank had been last year when someone asked him to write an article for one of the big newspapers and Mum had gone out and bought loads of copies to send to her friends. I didn't see the big deal, you could have got it online, but Dad said that academics always liked to see their name in *actual* print.

I went into the medical area and found Frank's name in the psychology section. I hopped from book to book searching every index. Time and again his name came up under the heading "Fanshawe's Safe Housing theory."

I tried to read some of the entries but didn't understand the language – it was too complicated. A huge medical dictionary had a more basic summary:

Once considered pioneering treatment for trauma: Fanshawe's Safe Housing theory relies on creating a safe place within the patient's mind then storing the memory and unpacking it at a later stage when the patient is able to deal with it. Trials have had limited success, with doctors preferring other forms of cognitive therapy. Fanshawe himself has said his therapy is no longer necessary thanks to the emergence of Detra-holzepene, a drug which he claims to be a much more effective method of trauma management. See article 2008 in Harper's Medical Journal for further examples.

Fuck! I searched along the row of paperback journals and picked up the one with 2008 on its skinny spine. I flicked through, expecting to see another dull essay, but then I spotted the initials *PTM* at the end: Phineus Thomas Marchant. It had been written by Dad. I slipped the journal into my bag.

I went back to my hotel room, ordered tea and chocolate cake then sat in a comfy chair by the window and went through the article. It was very Dad – all facts and no detail.

"Girl X. Eight-years-old. She has behaviour issues, is disruptive and suffers from night terrors. Together we created a safe place for her to retreat. She chose an aquarium as her favourite place and we have buried her bad memories there inside a treasure chest. She has a key, something I picked up from a charity shop, and with which she seems taken. The prop is effective in making her take control and will act as a trigger to unlock her thoughts at a later date. After two weeks, with the memory safely stored, her family note that there has been an improvement in behaviour."

That was it. I poured a second cup of tea and continued flicking through. There were a few photographs in the middle of the book; one was a child's drawing done in thick crayon. Underneath the picture was the title: *Girl X's drawing of her Safe House*. I smoothed the page and looked closer, trying to make out what the shapes were meant to be. The girl had drawn a rectangular tank with a treasure-chest at the bottom and dotted all around were coloured triangles – fish, I guessed.

I spilt tea onto my lap.

There, at the bottom of the tank was a tiny creature; it had a fish's tail but a human body with hair swirling around her face. *Murtle* had been scribbled next to her head.

It was Lily's mermaid.

Chapter Twenty-Four

Grace

I loitered at the foot of the drive and leant my head against the first in line of the army of redwoods which guarded the mile-long sweeping entrance to Aldeburgh House, now Alpha Apartments. I was relieved that the Wellingtonians hadn't been carved up along with my home. I shut my eyes and imagined the gravel beneath my feet, refusing to acknowledge the tarmac which had been laid to appease the Porsche owners. I pressed my palm against the tree's rough surface and gulped in the evening air which mingled with the sweet scent of resin and damp bark.

The taxi driver revved his engine.

I veered off to the left and unlatched the gate to a bridleway which was peppered with dandelions. I glimpsed the slate roof of the gatekeeper's lodge through the leafy treetops and beckoned for the car to carry on. I wanted to walk the last bit.

There! There is Emily delighting in her mother's gowns, ringing a bell to summons Cookie into the drawing room with a pot of Earl Grey.

I laughed at the irony; the Grace I had created was born to be the new Lady of the manor and I almost felt guilty that I'd got rid of her.

I always knew I would have to return to Frank at some stage. After all, we had made a deal; he would make everything go away as long as I kept myself hidden. But I couldn't keep my promise and now that I had allowed myself to be found I must go along with the consequences, whatever they might be.

The branches of the firs whispered 'welcome home' over the top of my head as their needles rippled in the soft evening breeze. They told me I must carry on with my journey; they would keep me company. I mustn't be frightened.

I walked along, my shadow lengthening, and as I walked, I remembered.

***

It was morning and Cassie couldn't find her mermaid doll. Despite it being there last night, Myrtle had vanished from her bed. From the sound she was making, you would have thought her world was coming to an end.

Gil's blonde hair was ruffled and there was a soft glow at the tips of his hollow cheekbones. He was simultaneously begging the girl to eat toast and marmite soldiers whilst tying her soft hair into a French plait.

Gil closed his eyes and took a deep breath in through his nose. "Em, would you be a sweetheart and have another scout around to see if you can find it? I'm never going to get her to school at this rate."

I sipped my coffee. I had sacrificed my spoonful of cream and sugar to show Gil how cosmopolitan I was, but without them, the drink tasted of liquid charcoal and was making my empty stomach recoil. Gil opened his eyes wide, his soft mouth downturned at the sides. He was beautiful even when pushed to the edge of his patience. Cassie batted another piece of toast onto the floor. "Pretty please."

I got to my feet and stretched, my spine giving a satisfactory click. "Cassie – you know what?"

The little girl immediately stopped her wailing and looked at me. Direct conversation with me was unusual; a novelty worth quietening down for.

"Do you know what day it is today?" I asked.

Cassie hiccupped and sniffed in rapid succession. Her big eyes were bright, her dark lashes glistening with tears. Cassie gave a small shake of her head. Behind her, I saw the tip of

158

Gil's tongue poking out whilst his brow furrowed as he ducked down to wrestle with the hair at the nape of her neck.

I folded my arms. "It's a full moon tonight and, if you don't shut up and do what Gil tells you to, the *real* Myrtle will hear about it." I tapped my foot against the polished oak floor. Cassie's full lips were parted. "And," I continued, "if she does, she will be sure to stay on the bottom of the lake to avoid having to listen to your horrid caterwauling. Mermaids hate loud noises."

"Is the real mermaid going to be on top of the lake tonight?" asked Cassie, her voice a whisper.

Gil's expression turned into a quizzical rebuke, but I knew he was relieved that the noise had stopped. He smiled to himself as he managed to tighten the elastic around his neat braiding.

I shrugged. "Maybe, maybe not, but right now just you concentrate on helping Gil get you ready for school. Mermaids also like good behaviour."

Gil winked at me. "Thanks, Em." He turned to Cassie. "Right, pickle. Your super kind sister is going to have another search for Mini Myrtle whilst you get some of these toast soldiers inside your tummy. Okay?"

Cassie nodded, her eyes now locked onto the slice of lake visible through the window.

I went into the kitchen where Cookie, real name Marigold Mogford, was busy sweeping the slate floor tiles. She whistled a tuneless melody under her breath. The faint whiff of smoked fish hung in the air despite a large pot of chicken stock bubbling on the stove. Daddy must have caught the early train to London – no one else ate kippers for breakfast except him. Cookie smiled at me, momentarily erasing the criss-cross lines which grooved the puckered skin above her wide upper lip. After the breakfast shift was over, Cookie was free to go. It was her day off and she didn't have to be back until eleven o' clock the next morning. Her routine was the same every week. She went into town to get her hair rinsed then set into fat, sausage roll curls. After that she met up with her friends, Clara and Maud for a pasty and a half pint of stout before catching the number 22 bus to the bingo hall on the outskirts of town.

"Gilbert's in charge of heating up the supper tonight," said Cookie. "You're having beef and ale pie followed by, your favourite, Bakewell Tart and custard." I groaned. Since falling in love, I had been trying to lose a bit of puppy fat in order to fit into more of Mummy's designer clothes. But Cookie didn't see the point of having five a day unless boiled or stewed until all the nutrients had seeped out of them. She had cooked for the Buchanan family for several generations and her repertoire consisted of good, hearty English fare all doused with lashings of lard and blankets of salt.

The only good thing about supper was that I was allowed to eat it in the dining room with the grown-ups rather than with Cassie at four o'clock in the kitchen. That had been Gil's idea.

"Thanks, Cookie," I said. "By the way, I don't suppose you've seen Myrtle."

She shook her head. "Already had a good search. Have you had enough toast?" she added pointing at the slabs of thick-crusted bread stepping out of the bread bin. I nodded, hoping Cookie couldn't hear the coffee sloshing around my empty insides.

I wandered along the dark corridor and into the playroom. In a former life this was the reception room for visiting merchants to stand and wait until they were summonsed into the master's study. It was long and narrow, dominated by a huge mullioned window; a pot of gerberas wilting in the centre of the sill. There was a bookshelf in one corner with a bright, miniature oven positioned in front of it, plastic food spilling from its surface. At the other end of the room there was a whiteboard set on an easel with scatter cushions underneath.

And there, as clear as anything, was Myrtle, sitting on the ledge next to the marker pens and a block eraser.

I grinned and went over to get her; Gil would be pleased. Above Myrtle's head, in an enormous black ink love heart, was written:

"Be at the boat house ten o'clock sharp."

I traced the words with my finger, picked up the doll, and stalked out of the playroom. I was floating. This was the day my life would change forever.

"You star," said Gil as I put the doll onto Cassie's lap. The little girl buried her face in the mermaid's woollen hair.

"Where was it?" he asked.

I couldn't look at him; the wave of emotion rushing through me was too much and I thought I would faint. "In the playroom. Next to the notice board."

Gil slapped his forehead. "So obvious. Why didn't I look there?"

He knew I had seen his command to me and he knew I would obey. He turned to Cassie. "Right – teeth, then we're done."

A quarter of an hour later Cassie and her mermaid backpack were bundled into the rear of his VW Golf. "Do you want a lift to school?" he asked, strapping Cassie into her booster seat. She kicked her feet and tiny L.E.D. lights on the bottom of her shoes flashed. "I've got to go to the shops to pick up a few bits for later so it's no problem."

"No," I said, smiling. "I'm going to cycle. It's such a beautiful morning."

"Oh! Okay. Good for you. It's certainly shaping up to be a gorgeous day. Have you got much going on at school?"

I couldn't stop grinning. I shook my head.

"Well, have a good one and I'll see you later."

I waved them off. Cassie held up Myrtle's velvety arm and flapped it at me. After the car had disappeared from sight, I ran around to the side of the house into a brick courtyard. This part of the grounds was a mishmash of sheds, lean-tos and cars. In the old days it had been used as the tradesman's entrance. I pushed open the door of a small, stone building and sat on the wide shelf, next to a sack of potatoes. I kicked my toes against the chest freezer and waited. After about ten minutes I heard Cookie slam the back door shut and start up the engine on her Mini.

I was left with nothing but birdsong and the gentle hum of

161

the freezer.

I was alone.

I went into the house and straight up to Mummy's dressing-room wondering what one wore to a romantic coffee morning. I chose a tweed pencil skirt which wouldn't quite meet at the top, silk blouse and patent court shoes. I threw a string of pearls around my neck, put on a thick layer of make-up and sprayed myself with a perfume which smelt of chocolate and freesias.

It was only half past eight. I had acres of time to spare.

I decided that I may as well take a book and go and wait for him at the agreed rendezvous point.

The boat house was situated to the left of the mansion. To get there I had to pick my way between the neat rows of vegetables, taking a right turn through a gravelled, privet corridor until I reached the edge of a meadow which led down to the lake. I marvelled how the colour of the water matched my mood; dark and mysterious.

The wooden building was perched upon a timber shelf and it reminded me of something plucked from a folk story; the ideal place for the huntsman to take Snow White. I climbed up the steep, creosote-soaked steps and opened the door to the building. I glanced around to check no one was watching then shut myself inside, my nostrils filling with the aroma of churned mud and pondweed.

The boat house consisted of a ground floor leading up to an open mezzanine layer. The lower deck was furnished with a couple of fold-up chairs and upon a dusty shelf, which ran along one wall, there sat a couple of cobweb-crusted, candle lanterns. A circular table draped with a white linen cloth stood in the middle of the room and a bottle of wine, two glasses and a carton of strawberries rested upon it. A vase had been positioned alongside and it overflowed with forget-me-nots; my favourite.

I lifted my gaze towards the mezzanine floor and spied that the mattress had been covered with a couple of soft, fleece blankets. Petals were dotted upon the pillows.

My body was glowing. He must have been up very early

to get all of this ready for me.

I imagined myself lying on top of the covers. Naked. My head thrown back to reveal the soft scoop of my neckline.

I flushed with embarrassment.

There was a loud creak as the door in the far corner of the room swung open. Surely he wasn't here already, hiding in the store cupboard. I hurried over and peeked my head inside, but there was nothing there apart from a multitude of engines, broken rudders and old cushions. I wrinkled my nose as I spied Daddy's extensive fishing equipment all nailed to a warped wooden board; sharp scissors, hooks and feathers hanging from it. A patch of sunlight filtered through a gap at the bottom of the small door which led from the store cupboard and out onto the jetty. It was the place where Cassie had spent many an hour, lying on the blistered planks staring into the water for a glimpse of Myrtle.

Now that we were officially lovers I began the task of planning his first sighting of me in this new guise. Should I be sitting at the table reading or perhaps lying under the covers of the bed waiting for him? Once again, I blushed at the thought of my awakened desires. It must be wine and conversation first. I rehearsed what I was going to say in my head. First, I would ask him something about his journey into school before bringing up the topic of Myrtle. Next, I would laugh and tell him how clever he was to contrive for me to go into the playroom and read his message. Then, unable to contain his desires any longer, he would sweep me into his arms and carry me up to bed.

I heard someone on the steps. I scuttled off into the room at the back with a mind to surprise him. I decided I would slink out of the shadows and put my palms over his eyes. He would startle, laugh then turn and kiss me. The pit of my stomach was churning, and my body quivered with the anticipation of his lips upon mine. I flattened myself against the wooden panels and listened to the lapping of water against the stilts and the knocking of the rowing boats beneath my feet. Later, after he had ravished me, I would suggest we take a turn around the lake. I would ask him to make me a crown of forget-me-nots, after all, I was his Lady of the Lake and he must do as I commanded.

His footsteps were heavy. Swift. There was loud creaking as he ran up the stairs to the bedroom. This was followed by a flurry of activity and the thump of shoes being flung to the ground, the jingle of a discarded belt.

I was holding my breath. I thought I would melt into the floorboards. I hadn't realised his passion for me was so strong. I knew I had to go to him and give him what he desired.

Suddenly the front door slammed shut again. My palm froze around the door handle. We had been caught. But instead of a cry of indignation I heard a whoop of laughter followed by feet stampeding up the stairs.

I tried to shut out the declarations of love and the moans of ecstasy, but it was no good and within minutes my entire world dissolved into a puddle of tears around my feet.

Chapter Twenty-Five

Lily

Frank pulled me up by my armpits and dragged me back into my wooden prison, hurling me like a rag doll into the corner of the empty room. He slammed the door which led out onto the jetty, muffling Grace's lament.

My head was buzzing with questions about the skeleton from the lake.

Grace's extraordinary distress coupled with Frank's lack of surprise suggested they knew exactly who the bones belonged to. There was no mention of calling the police. I shifted my bedraggled body into a sitting position and lifted my bound wrists over my knees, hugging them towards my chest. Water puddled around me and my clothes stuck to my skin, chilling my flesh and making my teeth chatter.

Frank stood in the opposite corner of the room and leant against the wall, staring down at me with his silver eyes now set alight by streaks of rosy light which pierced the panelling. A sheen of sweat glistened at his temples and damp patches had spread under his arms. He was ruffled. After his breath regained its regular wheeze, he tipped his head on one side and his mouth twitched as though he was unable to get the words out.

That's when I realised; we weren't alone.

Out of the corner of my eye I could see another person; a tall man with long blonde hair and golden skin, but the moment I turned to look, he vanished. My body flooded with warmth and calm.

"Why are you grinning like a lunatic?" Frank clapped his fat hands together to get my attention. "Cassie. Look at me and understand this: you belong to me. From now on you will answer to me and *only* me." He took a step forwards and smiled, showing his horrible coffee-stained teeth.

"And…" he paused, "…if you are a good little girl and do as I say, I will let you come and live with me in my cottage. How would you like that?" His voice had softened to a whisper, but it carried an icy undertone which made me shiver. He took yet another stride closer and with much grunting sat down opposite me, his joints clicking. "I didn't want to keep you here." His stale breath flooded my cheeks and made me recoil. He paused and picked at a sliver of skin next to his thumbnail. "Nothing like a bit of tough love to make one more pliable, hey?" He expelled another great puff of sour breath. "But I needed to be sure you weren't going to make any fuss about your new circumstances. You see, unless you remain hidden here, away from the real world, people will soon discover who you are and unfortunately, they will also realise what you have done." He shook his head. "You will go to prison for a very long time and, as for your sister, well, she will end up in the loony bin for the rest of her life. But," he held up a hand, "as long as you are quiet and stay within the grounds of my cottage, we won't have any problems and I will be able to take care of you once more." He smiled and chucked me under my chin. "How's about I put you back on your meds? Would you like that? We could even double the dose."

Say no, said a voice inside my mind.

I shook my head.

"No!" He gave a throaty chuckle. "But don't they make you feel numb? Don't they shut out all the horrors of your pathetic world? Be kind to yourself, Cassie. They make you forget and that's what I want you to do – forget." He reached into his pocket and picked out a silvery packet of pills which he clawed. He leaned over so that his face was level with mine; speckles of saliva glistened on his lips.

Frank's breathing deepened as the air whistled from his nostrils. With a swift movement he reached out and grabbed my finger, squeezing it between his index finger and thumb.

166

The skin on the back of my hands puckered and my mouth went dry. "Dearest, you must be a good girl for your Uncle Frank."

I turned my head away.

"What's this insolent behaviour?" he spat, his fingers pressing down on mine, squeezing my bones together. Suddenly he pulled his hand away.

I kept my gaze upon the wall.

There was a rustling sound as he pushed a couple of pills through their foil backing. Then he grabbed hold of my chin and tilted my head, so I was forced to stare straight into his eyes. With a grin, he pinched my nose and forced my mouth open, placing the tablets onto my tongue. I pushed them above my top front teeth, tucking them behind my upper lip and then gave a theatrical gulp. A loud shriek from outside made Frank curse and get back to his feet. Immediately his face was turned I spat the pills out and watched them tumble between the slats of wood into the dark water below.

The strange sensation that I wasn't alone rushed through my body and filled me with confidence. A new thought rang inside my mind like a tolling bell. The words settled on my tongue and, before I knew it, they had emerged from my mouth; broken and stilted, but all mine.

"I - know - what - you - did."

Frank, his palm around the door handle, stood still for a few seconds then turned back to me. A snarl curled at one corner of his mouth. "Well, well, well. So, it appears you have got a voice after all. That certainly makes things more interesting. We'll let that be our little secret for the time being." He blew me a kiss. "Sweet dreams."

I curled myself into a foetal position and faced the wall, keeping my eyes shut tight as I feigned a deep sleep. In half an hour they both entered the room and there was the shuffle and scrape of something being dragged along the floor. A blanket was thrown over me. "Don't want her catching a chill," muttered Frank. "Think of the inconvenience another dead body would cause."

Just as the russet sky turned to indigo, I fell into a deep, natural and dreamless sleep with not a mermaid in sight.

It was Grace who woke me the next morning. She had dirt ingrained under her fingernails and there were dark bags hanging under her eyes, but, despite her haggard appearance, she was grinning. She untied my hands and pulled me to my feet.

"Time to get you home," she said, her voice too cheerful. I glimpsed the steel in her amber eyes and an ache of dread seeped into my stomach. She was up to something.

"It's just the three of us now." She linked arms with me. "Oh!" she giggled. "That's obviously not including our four-legged friend, Tiggy."

She led me through a storage room, the walls of which bulged with fishing equipment, and into what appeared to be summer hut set on two levels. On the upper mezzanine floor lay an old mattress and a sleeping bag and on the lower deck sat an armchair and next to it a small table littered with empty crisp packets and crumpled cans of beer. This must have been Grace's home for the past few days.

She opened the front door of my prison and the bitter scent of algae filled my lungs whilst tiny flies tickled my face. As we descended the steep steps onto the gravel bank, I heard sloshing and tapping. I turned and, peeping through the rungs, I spied a wooden rowing boat bobbing up and down on the surface of the dark water, its snout knocking against the stilts as though bursting to get out of its pen.

Grace was in a hurry and marched me along a tangled dirt track which fanned out into an overgrown lawn dotted with tall poppies. At the far end of the garden, beneath a cluster of fir trees, stood a tumbledown cottage which was cloaked in shadow.

"This is our new home." Grace squeezed my arm. "What do you think?"

I stared at the crumbling bricks, crooked chimney and moss-carpeted roof.

It was dismal.

I blinked and forced my mouth into a smile.

"We knew you would love it."

We. My heart sank into my stomach and Frank's face simultaneously popped into my thoughts. *Frank*. Was the reason for Grace's happy mood the prospect of us all playing happy families together?

We made a path through the dewy grass and went into the cottage through the back door and straight into a boot room. The smell of hoof oil made my nose twitch. Grace ushered me past the rows of Barbour jackets and wellington boots before pushing me across a narrow corridor and into the downstairs bathroom.

"Give me a shout when you've cleaned up and I'll show you to our bedroom."

I turned around and almost jumped two foot in the air – there ahead of me was a glass container and inside it a stuffed fox – its mouth open, as though mid-scream; yellow marbles instead of eyes. I shuddered and peeled off my damp clothes, discarding them across the linoleum. I turned on the shower and stepped behind the curtain, trying to prevent its mildewed hem from grazing my ankles. As the hot water pounded against my skin, I scrubbed the dirt away with soapy lather until my flesh was pink.

There was a loud knock on the door. I held my breath. *Please don't let it be Frank.*

"Come on dearest," said Grace in a sing-song voice.

I wrapped myself in the fresh towel laid out for me and when I emerged from the steamy sanctuary Grace took me past another cabinet, containing a dead owl perched on a stick, and showed me into a bedroom.

"This is where we are all going to sleep. Now, hurry and get dressed then join us outside for tea on the lawn."

All the inner warmth from yesterday had disappeared

There had never been a guardian angel. I was simply losing my mind.

I stared at the double bed and my stomach bubbled.

On top of the patchwork quilt was laid out a selection of strange, old-fashioned clothes: underwear, a navy gymslip, white blouse, white socks and shiny patent black shoes.

My fingers trembling, I put on the clothes and turned to

stare at myself in the mirror on the wardrobe. "You're okay," I whispered, surprised to find my voice was still there and hadn't vanished along with my protector. Maybe I could make a run for it. Shout for help. But if they caught me, that would be the end – I'd never be able to help Flo clear her father's name.

I re-traced my steps through the boot room and stood on the threshold looking out. Grace was busy arranging furniture and crockery at the bottom of the garden. As soon as she saw me, she beckoned me over. I forced my body forwards and she greeted me with an air kiss before pointing to a plastic chair with a scarlet cushion on top.

"Do be seated." She sat down on the opposite chair. On top of the cushion on the third chair sat a rectangular chocolate biscuit tin. I went to move it onto the table with the rest of the pastries, but Grace smacked my hands away.

There was a loud woofing and from out of the undergrowth scampered Tiggy. I squinted into the woods behind her, fully expecting to see Frank lumbering into sight, but he didn't emerge.

"I went to get all of these goodies this morning." She pointed to a bike leaning up against a gate in the fence then turned her face to the box. "We were just saying how lucky I am to have transport. Isn't that right, dearest?"

I stared at her bright cheeks and then at the tin of biscuits.

I needed to know where Frank was but wasn't ready to share my voice with her yet.

As if she could see into my mind she said, "Uncle Frank has gone. We won't be seeing him again."

Relief flooded my body, but was swiftly replaced by an uneasy prickling at the back of my mind. If there was no Frank then what was with the three chairs? I held up three fingers.

Grace leaned across to the biscuit box on the cushion and patted its lid. Perhaps there was a small creature inside; a tortoise or hamster. Butterflies started to flap their limp wings inside my belly. There was something very wrong going on here.

"Darjeeling?" I nodded. Grace made a fuss of lifting the teapot high and pouring the golden liquid into the china from a great height. "We like it with lemon, don't we?" she said to the biscuit tin and nodded her head several times. "But Cassandra takes it with milk."

She passed me a cup and saucer and pointed to the plate of cakes – Bakewell Tarts with thick icing and half a glacé cherry stuck in the middle like a clown's nose. "I got them for you. I know you like them."

I didn't. She didn't know what I liked, but I picked one up and took a small bite, icing instantly gluing itself behind my front teeth.

My mind felt as though someone had tipped a cloud of fog into it. This person in front of me wasn't recognisable.

A loud 'hello' from the far end of the garden made Grace spill tea over the rim of her cup. Her eyes narrowed and her mouth followed suit.

"Stay here," she hissed through clenched teeth. I wasn't sure if she was talking to me or Tiggy.

She marched across the lawn and I strained my eyes to see who our visitor was.

It was a slim woman wearing smart jeans and a fitted jacket. I couldn't make out her features because she had on a baseball cap and dark glasses, but there was something familiar about the way our caller carried herself. The woman appeared to be upset about something; she was waving her arms about her head and pointing.

Aware that Grace's attention was elsewhere, my curiosity got the better of me and I snatched up the tin and lifted the lid.

Inside was a skull, nestled on a navy velvet cushion.

In my fright, I dropped the box and the skull tumbled onto the grass. Tiggy yapped with delight and sank her teeth around the nasal cavity. I tried to seize it back from her, but the silly creature thought I was engaging in a game of tug-of-war and clamped hold of it tighter.

Before I knew what was happening, Tiggy, now victorious, went tearing across the lawn to show off her prize.

Chapter Twenty-Six

Flo

"For God's sake, Mum," I said, holding the phone away from my ear. "Would you calm down a sec and tell me what you just said again." I sat up and downed the glass of water by my bed – my mouth tasted disgusting after last night's jalfrezi.

"I just bumped into Cookie." She sounded like she was walking somewhere fast and air crackled through the receiver making it hard to work out what she was saying.

"Who's Cookie?" I forced myself out from under the duvet. I padded barefoot into the kitchen and squinted at the clock on the far wall. It was eight thirty in the morning and, until my phone had rung a few minutes ago, I'd thought Mum was still in the flat.

Maybe she'd gone to that lovely deli two streets down for croissants.

"Cookie is Frank's housekeeper at Toad Bungalow. Well, I say housekeeper," continued Mum, "even though she doesn't seem to do anything more than rinse a few teacups and shake a mop across the floor."

I switched my phone onto loud-speaker and stuck it on the draining board. I reached up to the super shiny coffee machine set into one of the overhead cupboards and flipped out the water jug.

"So," said Mum, "it turns out that Frank has got his *relatives* staying with him in his horrible little shack."

"And that's bad because?" I clattered around, searching the fridge for a packet of coffee. Last night's leftovers smiled at me from their Tupperware box. It wasn't a good idea. I knew I shouldn't...

"It's bad because I didn't even know he had relatives."

I grabbed a teaspoon and dived into a heap of pea paneer. It was even more delicious cold.

"Florence? Can you hear me?"

"Hmmm. Well, it could be worse, they could be staying with us here in Chelsea. At least he's bundled them off to the country."

I heard a bell ring followed by chattering. "Soya latte double shot."

"Mum what's going on?" I swallowed another spoonful of last night's take-away and flicked on the coffee machine. I would start my healthy eating routine tomorrow. I wondered what Lily would say if she could see me eating curry for breakfast. If only she would get in touch. Let me know she was okay.

"But why didn't he tell me about them? *Yes, double shot.* I mean, he's always said he's completely alone in the world. Why lie? I mean, if he's lied about that what else has he lied about? *Contactless.*" More scuffles and a pinging sound. "Apparently they're the daughters of Frank's dead sister."

"Hang on." I repeated the connection in my head. Something didn't sit right. Grace and Lily had lied about their pasts too – was that just a coincidence? "Know anything else about them?"

"She died when the youngest one was only two and then the father died twelve years ago." She whispered something, but I couldn't make it out.

"What?" I squashed coffee powder into the handle and wedged it under the head.

"Suicide," said Mum in a loud whisper. "Frank's brother-in-law had been caught up in some sort of scandal. His name was James Buchanan and he was an MP – I vaguely remember the name. According to Cookie his death was all hushed up for the sake of the children, but she says there was a history of mental illness which ran in the family and unfortunately Buchanan seems to have passed the loopy gene

173

down to the girls."

"Muuuum. Seriously?" The light on the machine blinked green and I hunted around in the cupboards for a mug. All the crockery in the apartment was snow white – not a cheesy slogan to be seen. I wondered where the mug I'd bought her for Christmas had ended up: the one with Keep Calm and Carry On Shopping printed on it in capital letters.

"Maybe he didn't tell you out of embarrassment," I said. "I mean his generation are pretty shit at talking about mental health stuff."

"But where have they been all these years? Cookie said she thought they may have been in a special school. Perhaps they are *transitioning*."

"Oh my God. Did you really just say that out loud? That's really not the right word, Mum." I pulled the lever so the coffee trickled out, filling the room with a gorgeous nutty smell.

"You know what I mean though. Perhaps they are using Toad Cottage as a half-way house."

Thankfully the phone went dead.

I went into the sitting room and curled up on the massive sofa. I took a sip of coffee and scrolled though my music until I found *Friday I'm In Love.* Then I sat back and gazed out of the French window at the treetops; a narrow branch wobbled as a couple of grey squirrels bounced across it.

Where the fuck was Lily?

I decided to scribble down some of my thoughts. I grabbed my bag and pulled out a notebook and, as I did, Lily's toy mermaid fell out too. I held it in front of my face and its shimmering tail crackled. As I moved my hands over it, I felt something hard wedged down the back of its body. I flipped the doll over and slid my fingers behind the join where the mermaid's velvet tummy changed into a sequinned tail. I pulled out a faded photo and my fingernail caught on a large clump of fluffy Blu Tac squashed onto the back, I guess where it had been tacked up on a wall. Two girls; one a plump teenager with short white hair, the other a much younger child with gaps between her front teeth. *Shit!* It was

Grace and Lily – but how could that be – Grace was far too young-looking in this picture to be a mother. I turned the picture over and on the back was written: *To my dearest Emily, long time, no see, Uncle Frank.*

My heart pounded against my rib cage. Were they the nieces staying at Frank's cottage? Mum always rolled her eyes at the mention of Toad Cottage and was very quick to moan about the state of it. In fact, Mum had only ever stayed there once because it was close to a dinner party both of them were going to. Never again. According to her, the cottage, actually a bungalow, wasn't one of those chocolate-box thatched ones with roses around the door. It was damp and full of stuffed animals and all the furniture looked like it had been bought from an old people's home. It smelt of cabbages and wee.

Mum told me that one of the rooms in Toad Cottage was piled high with boxes of Frank's memorabilia and, apparently, he'd gone ballistic when he found her poking around in it. I wondered what he'd do if he found out she'd used some of his crap in a couple of her sculptures. With a bit of luck, he'd have a heart attack.

But Mum wasn't a fool. Both Frank Fanshawe and Nina Jackson had pasts they would rather not drag up. Mum was always banging on about how a marriage only worked if a husband and wife had loads of time apart and she often went away for weekends with her girlfriends. Mum's favourite catchphrase was *past lives have no business in the present.* This kind of pissed me off because I was very much a part of her past life, although she swore it didn't include me. Since she and Frank had got hitched, she'd been bugging me to come and live with them and kept banging on about how Frank had never got the chance to have a family of his own and how delighted he was to have a stepdaughter. So, I suppose I had to agree with Mum; hiding young, female relatives was an odd thing to do.

My phone rang again.

"So, Frank has nieces, Mum," I said, trying to sound bright and cheerful even though I was feeling on edge.

"Maybe they're nice. Do you… er, know anything else about them?"

"Well, they certainly aren't nice. Cookie said that the older niece gave her the sack. Just like that. No warning or anything."

"Surely only Frank can do that?"

"That's exactly what I said. I told her that it wasn't up to them, but Cookie said Frank had gone abroad and left them in charge and the older girl said she didn't have any need for her. And, get this, she told Cookie that the cottage actually belonged to her and her sister." Ah! That's why Mum was so pissed off.

I remembered Lil's message in the hotel bathroom. We used to have a different life.

I closed my eyes, desperately trying to get my thoughts straight in my head. "Wait! Frank's gone abroad? But he wouldn't go away without telling you first, would he?"

"Of course not. It's absurd and I'm on my way there now to get to the bottom of this whole thing. Maybe Cookie has got herself muddled up about what they actually said. Either way, I shall remind them who is really in charge."

Lily's pale and anxious face sprung into my mind. "Be careful though, Mum. Don't go barging in and upset them."

Mum tutted. "Right. I've arrived at the gate." I heard a car door slam. *"Keep the meter running. This won't take long.* Good God this place is revolting. Everything is overgrown with weeds – even the air smells of decay. Why he didn't cherry-pick the penthouse for himself simply beggars belief. The signal will give out in a minute, Frank has no understanding about the need for broadband so be warned. I'll see you later, right?"

"No, Mum. Remember, I'm meeting a friend today and I'm not sure when I'll be getting back."

The line went dead.

I was relieved. Okay, so I wasn't lying about the friend, but I wasn't telling the truth either. A bit more probing by Mum and I might have blurted out that I was meeting Annie at Redding Station. We were going together to see Dad and just the thought of going inside a prison was making me jumpy – I had no idea what to expect. Also, Dad had no idea I was coming because, so far, he had refused to see me. Annie had only managed to get me a visiting slot because of her police status; they were under the impression she was asking Dad a few questions and that I needed to be present to clarify things. My conversation with Annie to get me inside had consisted of me crying, then begging, then crying again. In the end, Annie, although it 'was against her better judgement' told a white lie to get Tom to agree. But I really did need to see him now. I had to ask him what he knew about *Uncle* Frank and his estranged nieces and why had he never thought to mention that Lily used to be his patient.

I tried Mum again, but there was no answer. I put it out of my mind; the taxi driver was waiting for her; what was the worst that could happen? Most likely no one would answer the door.

After I showered and dressed, I still had an hour spare before I needed to get to the station. I made myself another mug of coffee which I took into the sitting room. I sat back on the sofa, opened up my laptop and typed James Buchanan MP into the search engine. Nothing much came up on him apart from one article about his retirement from public life. At the bottom of the paragraph was a headshot of James wearing a pinstriped suit with a perfectly knotted silk tie. I'm ashamed to admit, I thought he was quite fit – if a little boring looking with wavy black hair, dark brown eyes and chiselled cheekbones.

I finished my coffee. The door to Frank's study was ajar. Now Mum was out of the way, I decided I may as well have a proper snoop. I went in and was hit by a strong citrus smell coming from a large Jo Malone candle. At either end of the mantel piece sat silver block initials; N and F. *Naff.* The room was bright and airy, like the rest of the flat. Everything was so neat and tidy – even the plaid dog basket was free from Tiggy's hair – the room had been Nina-ed. The desk was clutter free with only a hardbacked diary and shiny ink pen on it and the books in the shelves behind were arranged in, of all things, rainbow order. The cream walls were covered with photos of Frank meeting famous people – a sort of grotesque Frank wallpaper – his fat face leering from inside every silver frame.

I sat on the edge of his desk and picked up the diary. There was a picture of a small sun shining in the corner – the logo from his pharmaceutical company, Zolis. I went back into the sitting room, grabbed my bag and pulled out the box of Lily's pills. There was the exact same sun. Lily's drugs were made by Frank's company. Was that just a coincidence?

I put the pills back and returned to his study. I flicked through the diary, but there was nothing interesting there. The few lunch dates and drinks dos had all been written in by Mum. I slammed it shut and stared at the far wall which was taken up by one of Mum's exhibits.

Mum's art was more sculpture than drawing. She had made a name for herself by taking random objects and putting them together to make a 3-D picture. The one which spread across Frank's study wall was called: *Freedom*. It was part of a triptych which together formed a wider work: *What is Love?* The other sections were being displayed in various galleries around the country.

I'd seen the piece lots of times before, but I liked it and went over for a closer look. In the far left-hand corner was a flattened birdcage with its door swinging open. Threading through the wires of the cage was a man's watch with its face smashed in and the hands missing. From the bird's perch hung an engagement ring with the precious stones taken out of their setting. Outside of the cage, a bird made up of brightly coloured feathers was suspended mid-air and appeared to be flying towards a huge moon made up of hundreds of painted wine corks. I was fairly sure these, if added up, made the number of bottles of sauvignon blanc Mum had consumed during the course of her many divorces.

When I turned back again I was faced with yet another wall of photographs. How many times could Frank be snapped smiling and shaking hands? Someone should tell him he needed to shake up the pose – maybe go for a high five or even a headlock next time. I turned away but then whipped back around. There, in the photo straight ahead, was a face I now recognised; it was James Buchanan. I lifted the frame down from the wall and examined the faded print. Frank was shaking James' hand and the pair were standing in front of a large sign which said *The Fanshawe Clinic* with a large red ribbon lying around their feet. On one side of the camera was a bunch of white-coated, fresh-faced medics, one of whom was Dad. That in itself wasn't so strange, but on the other side of Frank stood two young girls; one a teenager with a sulky expression, hair in a messy ginger bob, the other a small, dark-haired child with big brown eyes and an elfin face. The same girls as in the mermaid photo.

Lily and Grace.

Frank's nieces.

Chapter Twenty-Seven

Grace

The dead of night. It's what Gil used to call the witching hour. My heart was overflowing with happiness.

After all these solitary years, we were reunited at last.

Frank, dressed in a trilby hat and thick woollen overcoat with the collar turned up, leaned against a tree. He shone a torch at me and each time I looked up from my task I saw his gargantuan outline animated by dozens of fluttering moths. I thought of poor, dear Tiggy who assumed we were going for a night-time stroll. Instead he left my little dog whining inside the poky kitchen, claws scrabbling at the door to get out. I vowed to give her an extra treat when I returned.

"Put your back into it," he shouted as I ground the shovel into the hardened soil. I was digging a shallow grave in a section of woodland which fell under the jurisdiction of the gatekeeper's property. How clever of Frank to keep all the tainted bits of Aldeburgh to himself and surround them with electric fences and spirals of barbed wire, daubed at intervals with large 'Keep Out' signs.

Apparently, Uncle Frank heard the commotion from his postage-stamp of a lawn where I imagined he was wedged into a deck chair sipping his first Pimms of the evening. I heard him thundering down the overgrown track and when he arrived on the scene his cheeks were ruddy with exertion and rage. This was certainly not his idea of *lying low*. He slapped me around the face until I fell silent then dragged Cassie back inside the boat house.

All the while I cradled my beloved.

After twenty minutes he emerged, panting, with a crumpled Ikea bag tucked under his arm. He forced me back into the lake to retrieve what little of him I could find.

I hit the spade into the hard ground and every aftershock, as the metal made contact with the earth, ran through my body and made me quiver.

***

I remembered their tangled limbs poking out from under the pastel blanket.

I remembered screaming at them and the noise was inhuman; a vixen howling in the night. Immediately all movement ceased, and the men turned to gawp at me. I foamed with rage; how could they, how could they? Daddy moved towards me, his arms outstretched. He was tousled and out of breath with rose petals clinging to his hair. It was a ludicrous sight. I turned and, eyes cloudy with tears, I ran down the steps and out onto the decking, gulping in so much air I began to hiccup.

I sank onto the hot, wooden planks and curled myself into a ball. Soon I heard footsteps and without opening my eyes I knew that it was Gil sitting next to me; I could tell from how he breathed and the warmth his body radiated. I heard him swallowing; unsure what to say. I unfurled myself and stretched out my legs, staring into the distance, only allowing my eyes to rest upon the matted hair of the old willow. I took a deep breath in and spluttered – his skin was tainted by my father's aftershave and it repulsed me. I dangled my legs into the lake and kicked. The coolness of the water and the gentle drag against my feet soothed my fluttering heart into a steady rhythm. I had run out of sobs. Gil put an arm around me to try and pull me close, but I shook it off and shuffled a few inches further away from him, splinters scraping my legs.

"I'm sorry you–"

"Don't."

He was staring at my profile and I tilted my nose towards the sky. "Why are you even here, Em?" He combed his fingers through his hair. "You should be at school."

My scalp prickled and my cheeks burned. I remembered the note on the whiteboard and recalled the scribbled words. How could I have been so stupid to believe the message was for me? If I hadn't got so carried away with my imagined love affair, I would have seen straight away that it was Daddy's handwriting. I contemplated sliding my body into the water, would that I could dissolve or turn into the wretched mermaid I'd invented for Cassie. There were worse things I could think of than remaining in an underwater prison for the rest of my life.

I heard more footsteps. Daddy sank down on the other side of me and plunged his bare feet in the water. At least he'd had the decency to put his shirt back on. Here I was; flanked either side by the two lovers.

"Darling, I'm so sorry you had to see that," said Daddy. He gave a soft cough and threw his head back. "A bit of a shock, hey?" He kicked his foot hard, flicking water onto Gil's calves and Gil shouted hey and splashed him back. I, meanwhile, was caught in the crossfire.

Fuck off with the flirting.

Gil shrieked with delight and pointed at something in the lake. S-shaped ripples came rolling across the water. I shielded my eyes from the glare of the sun and could now make out a snake swimming towards us, its tiny head raised a few centimetres above the surface. Daddy murmured with appreciation at its elegance, but I saw it for what it was; a sea serpent. I knew it had no venom but as it swam past me, I felt its poison seep into me through the soles of my feet. And just like that, Gil and Daddy were leaning over me and chatting about the creature, marvelling at the speckles of brown on its pale skin. It was as though what I'd witnessed five minutes ago didn't matter. This was their world and I was the intruder – to be chastised for momentarily spoiling their fun.

"Cassie would love that," said Gil. "Wouldn't she, Em?" He dragged his gaze away from Daddy and once again stared into my eyes. His own so clear, the colour of a forget-me-not. I returned his gaze and my distorted face shone back at me. It was as though I was seeing myself for the first time. This must be how he viewed me; nothing but a stupid, plain, naïve girl.

I didn't remember plucking the scissors from the storeroom, but there they were, in my hands.

"My Lady of the Lake, forgive me," whispered Gil.

I pressed the tip of the blade into my palm. It was sharp.

"You know I love you Em," said Gil. "But not in that way. I love your father, and we're just waiting until–"

"Until we can find a way for us all to live together," chimed in Daddy. His voice was laden with childish excitement and the words tumbled out. They must have spoken to each other about this many a time, but I imagined this was the first instance they had uttered these words outside of their own private bubble. I really should have been honoured. "Obviously, with my job, it's not going to be easy."

Bla-bla-bla.

I tuned him out and flexed my fingers, allowing the poison to course through my veins. Meanwhile, the scissors burnt a hole in my palms.

I moved quickly, surprising even myself. Gil looked down and saw the blade sticking out from between his ribcage. The expression of astonishment dissolved into slack-jawed horror as his heartbeat began to fade with every second. The world slowed down and all I heard was my own breathing. Daddy wrestled Gil into in his arms, his chest darkening while the deck grew slippery with blood.

I watched as a nest of pondweed floated towards me. How ironic – for they were the very flowers he crowned me with all those days ago when our love was embryonic.

***

Loud tutting interrupted my thoughts. "Get a bloody move on, Emily," barked Frank.

I leaned on the spade's wooden handle and reached up to wipe my forehead which was blistering with sweat.

Something rustled overhead and I looked up through the trees and glimpsed a couple of bats flying across the sky.

"You have too much of his tainted blood in you." Frank wagged a fat finger at me. "James bloody Buchanan. What a weak-willed disgrace of a man, no, *creature* he was. And as for that disgusting nanny he cavorted around with." His body trembled with rage. "Both of them perverted in the ways of the flesh. You know, everything that man touched he ruined." Frank shook his head and gave out a small volley of laughter; his chin wobbled. "The poor fellow couldn't even make a decent job of killing himself."

I froze, my ears tingling.

"Hey! Why have you stopped?" Frank took a step forwards, torch now shining directly into my face, so I was forced to cover my eyes.

I muttered under my breath. "You told me I killed him."

"What? *I said, what?*" He came closer and I continued my faint mumbling. "You made me believe that I killed him."

"Now come along Emily, dearest. Enough silliness. Let's get this job over and done with then we can get back to the cottage for a nice cup of tea with an extra spoonful of sugar to help with the shock."

I cackled – half laugh half cry.

"What's so funny?" He bent over me and as he did so, I brought the spade down on his head with all the pent-up rage I had inside me.

Again and again and again.

184

Chapter Twenty-Eight

Lily

Grace said she wouldn't be long. Then she locked the front door of Toad Cottage and took the key with her. I stood in the hall and watched my sister fight her way along the overgrown path at the right-hand side of the house. The grass was long, and its pale tips spilled onto the windowsills. Her hazel eyes rolled around her head as she commanded me to wait for her in the sitting room where she had left me out a glass of fluorescent-orange squash and a few books 'to occupy my time'. There was a doll's house in the corner of the room, but I absolutely wasn't to touch it.

She tapped on the window and pointed to the sitting room. I nodded and collapsed onto the worn leather sofa. I was tired, but my body wouldn't stop trembling, besides, I simply couldn't allow myself to fall asleep.

Grace had been breathless when she had given me my instructions, but I guessed that was down to the woman at the gate's sudden arrival. It had given her a shock. And then, of course, Tiggy had trotted over with a human skull wedged into her jaws. After Tiggy's surprise appearance, Grace ushered the woman through the gate and then they both disappeared. I heard the woman's car drive off so Grace must have smoothed things over. Tiggy, on the other hand, had disappeared into the undergrowth with her treasure.

For a while I had stayed glued to my seat in the garden, trying to breathe in through my nose and out of my mouth until the rhythm of my heart steadied. Then, after what seemed like an age, Grace beckoned me into the house.

The books she had given me to while away my time in the sitting-room were hard-backed picture books for young children. They smelled musty, and the corners of the brittle pages were dog-eared. They were full of fairy stories written in simple English. I flicked to the front cover and in the top left-hand corner the words 'Cassandra Buchanan' were scribbled in felt-tipped pen. I snapped the book shut.

So many thoughts rushed around my head and I couldn't begin to process what was going on, although one thing was certain – Grace terrified me. Just the thought of being in the same room as her paralysed me with fear. The fact that the 'we' she referred to was a human skull made pulses twitch at the sides of my head. And who the hell did it belong to in the first place?

That Frank had vanished should have been a small comfort, but the mysterious circumstances left an uncomfortable shadow at the back of my mind. How could Grace be so certain Frank wouldn't return? What had happened to give her the upper hand? I glanced around for any evidence of him, but there was nothing there; no overcoat; no overflowing ashtray and no trace of his musky cologne lingered in the stuffy air.

Grace wheeled her bike past the side of the house and the gate creaked open and then slammed shut. She had gone.

I took a sip of squash, so concentrated it stung the back of my throat and made my nose run. I set it back onto the side table and pinched my wrists to check I wasn't dreaming. Surely the guardian angel from yesterday was a symptom of the simple fact that I was descending into madness. A side-effect from not taking my pills. It wouldn't be long before I too was referring to inanimate objects as intimate friends. I glanced through the dingy hall at the empty hat stand by the front door. "How do you do?" I whispered.

I could see the doll's house out of the corner of my eye. The colour of the roof tiles struck a familiar chord in my mind; their shape and texture similar to a bourbon biscuit. I went over, crouched in front of it; my fingers instinctively moving to the small, metal latch at the hinge. I opened the

186

doll's house and immediately recognised the tiny rooms within. A memory came tumbling into my thoughts; me sitting in front of a fire, the heat from the flames warming my cheeks while its orange light cast half of the miniature mansion in shadow. My heart pounded as I recalled the deep voice of the man sitting in the gloom, telling me to put the little people to bed. Grace smacking my hands away as I tried to move the figurines around. She had got everything just so and didn't want me spoiling things.

I looked inside and the air vanished from my lungs. All of the matchbox beds had been broken – smashed. My gaze moved to the family sitting at the dining table and I blinked; each one was missing a limb which now sat staring up at them on a tiny china plate.

I leapt to my feet as though stung and hugged my elbows. Pull yourself together, I scolded. Grace may have locked the door, but I could smash a window and climb out. I could run away. But where would I go? Who would help me? Maybe Flo had already unearthed our past and figured out what we'd done to Amelie and Tom.

The house was empty, and my ears prickled in the silence. From somewhere within the bungalow there was the sound of a tap dripping and the gentle whir of a washing machine. I went into the pokey kitchen, crossing the sticky linoleum to reach the kettle. The cream Formica units in the kitchen were scuffed and the stainless-steel handles were smudged with dirt – the entire room had the faint whiff of blocked drains. I opened the nearest cupboard to discover a meagre selection of beige crockery and I pulled out a cup, its rim stained with a thick tannin ring. The teabags were spilling out onto the work surface along with the empty box of Kipling cakes. A quick scout of the rest of the cupboards revealed nothing more than a half-empty jar of Mellow Bird coffee and an out of date packet of fig rolls. The milk in the fridge was fresh but there was nothing else inside apart from a sweaty block of cheese and a half-drunk bottle of tonic which lacked bubbles. As I waited for the kettle to boil, I stared out of the window allowing my gaze to soften, making the poppies, buttercups and cornflowers dance across my vision; their colours blurring into a rainbow wheel.

I took my tea into the utility room which was little more than a glorified cupboard. The washing machine under the window bobbed up and down on its final spin and filled the humid air with the scent of talcum powder. An upright hoover stood in one corner and next to that was a rusty ironing board with a wonky clothes horse leaning up against it. At last I had discovered where the dripping sound was coming from and I crossed the room to the metal sink and gave the tap a sharp right twist. The dripping continued.

I drank my tea in the hall under the watchful gaze of the stuffed owl. As I drained my cup, I became aware that there was one other room I hadn't yet explored. The door was shut. My heart thudded, perhaps Frank was lying in there waiting for Grace to leave so he could pounce. I counted to ten and taking a deep breath, I reached out and turned the circular handle. It was locked. I tried again with more force. Nothing. I rattled it. I stooped down to see if I could force the lock out of its cavity, but it was no good. Either Grace or Frank must have taken the key. Adrenalin spiked through my body and for a moment my tremors subsided. I had to see what was inside.

I decided I might be able to climb in through the window and get to the chamber from the outside in, but how to get out of the bungalow in the first place was my next challenge. I'd have to find another window to climb out of. One by one I went around the windows, but they were painted shut – no wonder the house smelt rotten. The beep of the washing machine made me start. My autopilot activated, I went into the utility room to hang up the clothes, but when I stooped to the door of the machine I glanced up at the window. It was a new addition with a PVC frame. My heart skipped a beat – there was a visible lock.

Every house on the planet has a drawer-of-shame with random keys and cables wedged inside. I rushed back into the kitchen and pulled out every unit until I found it. Hidden amongst a few out-of-date guarantees, a ball of string and pair of blunt scissors was a small, shiny key. I grabbed it and ran back to the utility room, clambering on top of the still beeping washing machine. The key fitted in the lock and I opened the window sucking in the air which was tinged with the faint smell of bonfire smoke. I teetered out onto the sill and dropped to the mossy grass below.

A few strides later and I was standing outside the locked room.

I rattled the window, but discovered it was also glued together with paint. I glanced around and my eye fell upon a statue of a frog – or perhaps it was a meant to be a toad, all things considered. I ran over and without thinking picked it up. The frog-toad stared back at me with blank eyes, its mouth half open in a leer. I closed my eyes and hurled it with all my strength at the window. It made a loud thud then bounced back from the glass and dropped onto the ground. In slow motion, a small white circle appeared at the centre of the pane and then the glass splintered all around, like ice cracking on a frozen pond. I picked up the statue again and hurled it once more; this time the weakened glass shattered. I grabbed a stick from the hedgerow and used it to clear the spikes from the wooden frame.

When I was confident it was clear, I scrabbled up onto the sill and with tiny movements I manoeuvred my body through the open frame and onto the other side of the ledge. I pulled aside the thick curtains which had prevented most of the glass from flying into the room and brushed the remaining fragments onto the carpet below. Around the edges of the room were stacks of boxes, piled on top of each other so they almost reached the ceiling. At the centre of this cardboard wall was an armchair, small coffee table and angle-poised lamp. I leapt as far as I could into the centre of the room, landing with a thump.

I turned around the gloomy chamber and stepped forwards to the nearest box, letting my fingers trail along the cardboard. Each one had a description of what was within, written neatly in black permanent marker: *Grace; fur coats and hunting dress*, *Grace; vintage tea service*, *Grace and*

James; Wedding memorabilia. So that's the reason Grace had chosen it for herself. My eyes prickled with tears. Why didn't I know that was my mother's name? Then I saw a crate marked: *Cassie; playroom.* My tongue stuck to the roof of my mouth. This was mine. I shifted a couple of the boxes and pulled my one out, ripping off the crusty packing tape which sealed the joins. Holding my breath, I peered inside. There were a couple of puzzles and soft toys which I didn't recognise. I delved deeper and pulled out a Speak and Spell which I turned on and the green letters on the screen blinked at me. The American male voice cut through the silence: "Spell Tortoise." I turned it off and put it back in the box. There was no time for games.

I looked at the other labels. One of the boxes, labelled E & C documents, had been left open. It contained bank statements, birth certificates and immunisation records. Poking up from a bundle of utility statements was a passport. I opened the cover and there, staring back at me, was my face. *My face!* I peered closer. That didn't make sense – it was me, as I looked now. I flicked to the personal details. This passport was in date and it gave my current address as Toad Cottage and my next of kin as Frank Fanshawe. My breathing rattled around my chest as I riffled through more papers and discovered several bank accounts in my name. Cassandra Tabitha Buchanan. One of them had over £1,000,000 in it. Spots danced before my eyes; I had money? Did that mean Grace had money too? I searched for her passport, but it wasn't there.

I glanced at my watch. Time was slipping away, and I decided to go back into the sitting room and wait for Grace's return. For the time being, I'd pretend I knew nothing about the broken window and with a bit of luck, what with it being on the far side of the house, she wouldn't notice it until I'd come to a decision about what to do next.

On my way out, I passed another box with "family photos" written on the side and my fingers tingled. I couldn't resist. This box wasn't sealed, so I lifted the flaps and came face to face with hundreds of old snapshots. I picked up a handful and sifted through them. There was a picture of my sister as a toddler holding hands with a slim, auburn haired woman and a tall man with dark, wavy hair and big smile. I didn't recognise her, but I thought I recognised the man. On the back it said 'me with James and Emily walking through the meadow'. I flipped the picture around again. They were my parents. My fingers trembled. How was it I didn't know what they looked like? I ran my finger over James' face then cast the picture aside, hungry for more.

I found one of me wrapped in a long white shawl with Frank cradling me in his arms and laughing. Me on Dad's lap at the top of a slide with my sister sitting at the bottom holding a green balloon. Mum certainly liked to take a photo, but it appeared that, after Mum died, Dad didn't. But then I saw a picture which made me gasp. It was of a sullen looking teenage Grace; chubby, plain and scowling at the camera and there I was, holding up a jam jar with something blurry inside. Standing next to me, head thrown back in laughter, was a tall man with long blond hair and bright blue eyes. My heart stopped and, once again, a warm rush of contentment flowed through my veins. I recognised him.

I looked at my watch once again, my throat drying with worry at the speed with which time was slipping away. The walls of cardboard were closing in on me. I needed to process all of this without the worry of Grace's return hanging over me. I put the photo back and as I did my fingers touched a large folder with *Hospital Records* written on it. I opened it and there was a typed report with my name at the top right-hand corner. There were stacks of initials and printed tables scribbled with more initials and abbreviations I couldn't comprehend. I continued to flick through and came to a clear wallet containing a large, ornate key. I took it out of the plastic case and turned it over in my hands, pressing my fingers through the metallic weave. It was familiar in touch and smell. It was mine, I was sure of it and, instinctively, I put it inside my pocket. I carried on leafing through the folder, skimming over reports about my diagnosis but then I stopped short and it took a few seconds for my mind to catch up with what my eyes were seeing. I was no longer looking through my report but was now looking through someone else's hospital records; those belonging to James Buchanan.

The air shot from my lungs and I bent double. Horror spread like a lit touch paper through my body and blood whooshed inside my ear drums.

According to these papers, James Buchanan was still alive and currently residing in a secure psychiatric hospital in the next county; *The Fanshawe Clinic*.

The knot in my chest tightened. I had to get out of this room and this place. To hell with the plan to stay put and wait for Grace. I needed to get as far away from there as possible. I'd find Flo. I'd tell her everything and deal with whatever the consequences. Grace needed professional help and I'd surely be safer in prison where Frank couldn't get to me.

In my panic to leave the room I caught my hand on a jagged piece of glass sticking up on the frame and blood trickled all over the sill turning the white paint crimson. Grace would know I'd been in there. This was all getting out of control.

I took the lace-edged handkerchief out of my tunic pocket and wrapped it around my hand.

Suddenly Tiggy came trotting across the lawn and just for a few seconds I was glad. I screwed up my eyes as she approached. The white of her fur was pink and her muzzle was crusted with a dark brown film. I crouched, holding my arms out to caress her, but it was only when I pressed my hand onto her body, I realised she too was covered in blood.

Chapter Twenty-Nine

Flo

HMP Rainsford was a Victorian red-brick building set into the old city walls. I glanced up at the windows which overlooked the pavement below; the small panes of glass were frosted and set back behind thick iron bars. If Dad was on the other side, he wouldn't be able to see anything apart from a block of striped light.

"Right," said Annie. "Try not to worry. You've had a text from your Mum to say she's fine and on her way home. Grace has no idea we've got our suspicions about her. Frank's their only relative – it stands to reason she's turned to him for refuge. For the moment, things are fine as they are until we know for certain what actually happened."

"But Lily's frightened of him."

Annie locked the car. "Because he knows their real identity. Come on. We don't want to miss our appointment."

The visitor's block was a boxy building right by the main entrance of the prison. They'd tried to hide the barbed wire fence, which went all the way around it, with a thick hedge, but it was still really obvious. We had to go through a door with a time-lock, then our bags were searched as we passed through a scanner. Two huge sniffer dogs sat at either end of the room. It was a bit like being at an airport, but without the excitement of a holiday at the end. Annie, used to all this, made me leave most of my stuff in the car so all I had on me were notebooks and pens – it didn't stop me feeling guilty though, like they were going to find a bag of coke in my back pocket.

A fat officer with gelled brown hair showed us into a cubby hole off the main hall.

He grinned. "Bit more cosy." The walkie talkie hanging from his belt beeped and a stream of babble crackled over the airwaves. "Right. Take a seat and I'll bring Mr Marchant through." I sat on the orange plastic chair and drummed my fingers on the table. Annie, sensing how nervous I was started jabbering on about the new Nepalese restaurant on Main Street which she was going to try tonight. She thought I might want to go with her. But the thought of food made me want to heave so I ignored her and fiddled around with my pad of paper.

The door opened and in came Dad. I think I screamed. His cheekbones were hollow, his lips were puffy and the skin around his right eye was bruised. The moment Dad saw me he turned back to face the officer and pointed to the door.

The officer folded his arms. "What's this. An ambush?"

"I want to go back to my cell," said Dad.

"Dad. Please."

Annie stood up; chair legs screeching across the floor tiles. "Tom. I'm sorry I lied, but this is important. Flo really needs to talk to you. It's about your court case."

Dad paused, then turned back into the room. The officer nodded at Annie. "Alright DS Harper – you've got half an hour."

"Don't suppose we could get some coffees?" asked Annie.

"What do you think this is? A bleeding hotel?" He smiled. "I'll see what I can do, but don't hold your breath. I think the machine is on the blink." The moment the door shut, I ran over and threw myself at Dad. He winced at bit, then pulled me towards him. He still smelt like Dad.

"I didn't want you to see me like this," he whispered into my hair.

"I know."

"Come on," said Annie, her voice bossy. "We've got to get a move on."

I tore myself away from Dad and pointed to the nearest chair. I sat down opposite him and held out my hands which he took in his. The knuckles on his right hand were bruised too. Good – maybe he'd fought back.

Annie opened her notebook. "I'm not meant to be here. If this gets out, I'll be in all sorts of shit. I've put on the form I'm here to examine evidence, but that's totally out of my remit – I'm off the case altogether." She ran her fist down the crease of the empty page. "This was the only way we could think of to get you to see Flo. Us."

Dad squeezed my fingers and I'm ashamed to say I started sobbing.

"Don't." Dad's voice was shaky. "If you start, you'll set me off and I really don't want to go there."

"Absolutely," said Annie. "Pack it in, Flo."

I sniffed and pulled my hands away, pinching the skin under my eyes to try to stop the tears. Annie was right – this was no help to anyone.

"So, Tom, lovely to see you and all that, but we're really here to ask you some questions," said Annie.

Dad sat up. "Okay."

The door opened and in came the officer with three plastic cups of coffee balanced on a tray. He set them onto the table and threw a few sachets of sugar down next to them. "Courtesy of Her Majesty."

Annie grinned. "Thanks. Much appreciated."

The officer nodded then left the room.

"They've told me to plead guilty." Dad hung his head. "They said the judge will be more lenient in his sentencing if I do."

"No way," I said. "That's fucking ridiculous. Don't you dare. What the fuck do they think–?"

Annie clicked her fingers at me. "Enough. That's irrelevant for now. Tom, what can you tell us about Frank Fanshawe?"

Dad frowned. "What? Why?" He turned to me. "Wouldn't your mother be a better person to talk to about him?"

I shook my head. "It's important we hear it from you."

Tom sat back in his chair and tilted his chin upwards. "A long time ago, eleven years to be precise, Frank was my boss.

He ran a mind clinic within one of the main hospitals in Oxford – and asked me to come and work for him. They were trialling some new drugs and he wanted me, as a junior, to take notes and record my clinical findings."

Annie scribbled into her notebook, her tongue sticking out. "Why did you leave?" she asked without looking up.

Dad was staring at the grey tiles on the ceiling. "I guess, it just didn't work out."

Annie stared at him. "Liar."

Dad did a double take and I shifted in my seat.

Annie smiled. "You always do that when you are telling a fib."

"What?" asked Dad.

"Jut your chin out at the end of the sentence." I couldn't believe I'd never noticed that before.

Dad folded his arms and sulked.

I tugged on his sleeve. "Look, Dad, we haven't got time for all this bullshit. Why didn't it work out?"

Dad's mouth twitched and he laid his arms on the table, staring at his wrists. "There was an allegation made about me."

Annie's pen hovered over her notebook. "What sort of allegation?"

"A sexual one."

I swallowed and tried to keep my expression even.

"Go on," said Annie.

Dad looked up and stared into my eyes. "Someone said I touched them inappropriately. I mean it was utter nonsense – a complaint made by a nurse I don't recall ever having spoken to, let alone…" His words trailed off. He took a sip of coffee. "Good old Frank said he'd make it go away, but that I would need to lie low while he went about sorting it."

"So the allegation didn't come in front of a proper panel?" asked Annie.

Dad shook his head. "Frank said it would be better if it didn't. *Mud sticks* and all that. He said it would harm my career."

Annie stared at him. "Did he sort it?"

Dad shrugged. "I took a teaching job and then before I knew it, Nina had walked out on me and it just didn't make any sense to go back to medicine. Life with a small child is so much easier when you have fixed working hours." He gave a dry laugh. "I never for one second thought she'd end up with Frank though. He seemed old even then."

I had to bite my lip to stop blurting anything out. We needed to hear it from him.

"Do you remember James Buchanan?" asked Annie.

Dad sighed and screwed up his eyes. "James Buchanan," he repeated. "Yes. You're talking about Frank's brother-in-law? I've often wondered what became of him."

I nodded. "Did you ever meet him?"

Dad sat back in the chair and stretched his legs out. "No. I didn't ever meet him, but I was there when he opened the new hospital wing."

"So, you didn't speak to him?" asked Annie. Dad shook his head.

"And, Dad, did you ever meet James' daughters?"

Dad shook his head again. "Didn't know he had any daughters."

Okay. We were getting somewhere. I pulled out the article I'd photocopied and handed it to him. He stared at it. "Jesus! I wrote this a long time ago. Where did you get it?"

"Tell me about the girl," said Annie.

Dad shrugged. "I can't tell you any more than what's in there. It's confidential."

"You're not a fucking doctor anymore," snapped Annie. "You're a man who's very close to being locked up for the rest of his life. This is important. Who was she?"

Dad rubbed his eyes. "I was treating a young girl, eight years old, whose behaviour was out of control. She was excluded from school and her father simply couldn't cope. I spent some time with her and discovered her behaviour stemmed from something horrific she had witnessed. Something she couldn't make sense but which at the same time troubled her."

"Did you help her make sense of what she saw?" said

Annie.

Dad hung his head. "No," he muttered. "The gravity of the situation demanded I report it to someone senior. It just so happens that, at the same time, the allegation was made about me and I had to go."

"Who did you leave to sort things out?" asked Annie.

"Why Frank, of course."

"Ah!" said Annie, her eyes narrowing. "So, you left Frank to sort out the allegation and deal with the traumatised patient." She paused. "And did he?"

"Did he what?"

"Sort out your patient."

"I wouldn't know. It wasn't my business. I handed over all the notes, but I believe it became a matter for the police."

"Only it never did become a matter for the police because Frank kept it within the family," said Annie.

Dad frowned. Annie jerked her head at me, and I took out the photo of the girls from my folder and pushed it towards Dad.

"What am I looking at?" he asked.

I tapped the corner of the picture. "Do you recognise the girl?"

"Yes. It's the girl I treated. It's Mary."

"Look closer Dad," I said pushing the photo right under his nose. The blob of Blu Tac fell off the back and onto the table.

"It's not Mary, Dad," I said. "It's Lily and that's her *sister*, Grace."

Dad's jaw fell open.

"You treated Lily, Dad, and after she told you what she saw, her father killed himself. Grace thinks you are responsible for her Dad's death. Nine years later Lily and Grace came into your – our – lives. It's not a coincidence."

"You...you can't possibly think they had something to do with Amelie's death?" said Dad, his voice cracking.

"What did Lily see?" asked Annie.

Dad paused. "She saw a body in a lake. She thought it was a dead mermaid. She called the creature Myrtle."

"Shit," I said. "Shit, shit, shit."

"It sounds like Frank wanted you out of the way to avoid a family scandal," said Annie. "Perhaps he confronted James who then killed himself, either way, it would appear that Grace and, by default, Lily, hold you responsible for his death and all this time Grace has been out for revenge."

"But…but why kill Amelie?" Dad couldn't stop shaking his head. "Why not me or why not have a go at Flo? It's so… calculated. Grace just isn't like that."

"I think Grace's behaviour is all an act," said Annie. "I've had my suspicions about her for a while. There were a couple of things she did which don't match her public persona although they aren't enough to prove anything. Think. Did you have any misgivings about her?"

Dad put his hands together like he was praying. "We had sex the night before all the fish died. She started off very keen," he wriggled in his seat and cleared his throat a couple of times, "but quite soon, it got a bit weird."

"What do you mean weird?" asked Annie.

I stared at the floor.

"She wanted me to, er…be forceful. Smack her, that kind of thing." He paused and took a sip of coffee. "And after it was over, she lay there crying and calling out for someone named Gil. I was angry and a bit disgusted. A bit jealous too – I suppose. I wanted to know who this Gil person was." He drained the rest of his coffee. "We had a massive row and I asked her to sleep in the spare room. I couldn't figure out what had just happened. It was weird. The next day I was going to talk to her about it, but then everything started crashing down around me and the chance never arose. In the end she finished with me."

"She killed the fish, I know it," I said. "She was breathless when she came running into the bedroom and her clothes were already wet. And, now I come to think of it, there was pondweed on the floor. Lily wanted to tell me. I know she did." I couldn't stop the tears rolling down my face. "But I didn't listen and now it's too late. Grace drugs her to the point where she sometimes doesn't know if it's day or night."

Dad sighed. "Lily didn't need medication. She needed therapy. My treatment of her involved a type of hypnotism which allowed her to bury her bad memories until she was ready to confront them. I passed on all my notes to Frank, but I guess he never acted on them." He shuddered. "I dread to think what impact these supressed thoughts have done to Mary's, I mean, Lily's mind."

"Is there anything we can do to help her?" I asked.

Dad shook his head. "I set a physical trigger and there's no way you can get to her hidden memories without it."

"What do you mean? What trigger?" asked Annie.

"We hid her bad thoughts in a lockable casket, and I was in charge of the key which I handed over to Frank along with her notes. It was an ornate, old-fashioned key – its head shaped like a spider's web. God knows what he's done with it."

I picked up the ball of Blu Tac on the table and rolled it between my fingers. Something sharp jabbed into my skin. I pulled at the stretchy material – there was something inside.

It was a gold, tear-shaped earring with the letter A in its centre.

Chapter Thirty

Grace

My mind was churning as I pedalled along the dirt track. Nina's Mulberry bag dangled from the handlebars of my bike, scratching my left knee as it swung back and forth. I would dispose of it when I got to town; throw it into one of those huge steel dustbins which sat in the back alley behind the fish and chip shop. I decided to spend every last penny from Nina's purse – the revolting woman's untimely arrival had forced a change of plan and we would need provisions if we were going to survive the next few weeks.

A soft breeze whistled past my ears as though trying to sweep the thoughts from my mind, but now that I had found him, the events of my youth shone clearer with each passing second. They sat side by side with the here and now, so I was no longer sure what was real and what was wishful thinking.

***

We never spoke about what happened on the jetty almost a decade ago.

I remembered hearing Cassie screaming and screaming. We dashed out towards the lake and saw the little girl lying on the decking, peering down at Gil's bloated face which stared up at her from beneath the surface of the water. Uncle Frank, who happened to be staying for supper, told me to take my sister back into the house, lock her in her bedroom then hurry back with an axe from the shed. When I returned, Daddy and Frank were standing next to an empty tea chest.

Daddy was trembling.

I remembered the thud as the axe fell and how the moonlight danced on top of the puddles of black blood. After the first blow Daddy crumpled into a heap on the floor and Frank snorted at him, rolled up his sleeves, wrestled the axe out of Daddy's grip and finished the job.

It took all three of us to lift the trunk and drop it into the lake.

The next morning when I looked in the mirror, my hair had turned white.

Cassie became my responsibility and I encouraged her to return to her feral ways; and soon she was spending every waking moment in the woods with nothing but her imaginary friends for company. As for what she had seen down by the lake – we told her it was just a bad dream.

Daddy took refuge in drink and drugs, but no one really noticed a change. Cookie, having grown up serving the aristocracy, took his behaviour as quite the norm. Somehow, he managed to muddle through his day job thanks to Frank and a great team of admin staff who worked better when he wasn't at Whitehall.

Before long Frank had taken complete charge of the estate and moved into Aldeburgh House and we were coping but then social services came calling about Cassie's exclusion from school, and Frank had to act. Desperate to avoid a public scandal, Frank assessed Cassie himself and decided to hand her over to one of his junior doctors who was working at his new psychiatric clinic. Courtesy of pharmaceutical giant Zolis, they were trialling a new brand of sedative which he figured would be just the thing to numb Cassie's wilful spirit.

One early autumn evening, I tiptoed down the back staircase. I was on my way to the pantry to steal a slice of Cookie's Bakewell Tart, my favourite, and take it back to eat in my bedroom. I had to cross the hall and as I crept past the study, breathing in the vanilla scented smoke of Frank's cigar, I heard raised voices coming from within. Something in the frantic tone of Daddy's speech made me stop.

"You're trying to tell me that Cassie actually told someone she saw a dead body in the lake?" Daddy's voice had an almost operatic edge to it.

"James, James. Just calm down," replied Frank. There was a squeak as chair legs scraped across the parquet floor accompanied by the gentle hiss and crackle of new wood burning on the open fire.

I moved closer to the door and peered in through a slender gap. Daddy had his arms around an empty wing-backed chair whilst Frank sat on the opposite side of the hearth rug, legs outstretched, sipping dark liquid from a small crystal glass. "Cassie told the doctor that she saw a dead *mermaid* floating in your lake." Frank smacked his lips together then laughed.

"Fuck!" said Daddy, leaning his brow onto the edge of the chair. He looked up at Frank, his cheeks flushed. "What am I going to do?"

Frank took a long drag of his cigar and tapped the side of his glass with his long fingernail. "I will take care of the doctor. Tom Marchant is a newbie; a bright young thing. In fact, he was one of the few students who took it upon himself to try a different mode of treatment not sponsored by Zolis. Ha! Ha!" Frank's laugh rattled around the back of his throat and morphed into a cough. "Who would have thought my safe-housing theory actually worked." His laughter continued and he stared at the fireplace; irises gleaming white as he watched the flames dance. "What is it with these doctors who want to look outside the candy store when there is so much already available to them? With the dose they've put her on Cassie will quieten down and most likely forget about the mermaid altogether. Or else it will be confined to her lost thoughts, only available in her darkest moments." He grunted. "Either way, she will become pliable. It's a shame about Tom really. He showed promise, but it's clear he can't follow instructions. I'll see to it that a *complaint* comes his way and warn him that he needs to disappear for the time being."

Daddy sniffed and wiped his eyes with the back of his hand. "Won't...won't he say something to the police?"

"No. I'll tell him I've got things in hand. In the meantime, he doesn't know anything about Cassie – her real name or that she's related to you." He paused then lowered his voice. "I'll make it go away, James. I always do."

Daddy got to his feet and perched on the edge of the armchair, spreading his hands across his knees. "Will Cassie have to stay on this medication for the rest of her life?"

Frank drained his glass. "For the foreseeable future, I suppose. Otherwise the image might resurface. Tom said he only partially recovered the memory, so goodness knows what else she's got hidden in there." He tapped the side of his temple.

Daddy opened his mouth then closed it again. The grandfather clock in the corner of the room chimed ten times, filling the room with loud clanging. For a few seconds afterwards the residual note lingered in the air. "It's no good Frank. I can't go on like this. I've got to get out of the mess I'm in. I think I should resign."

"What?" said Frank, his voice sharp.

Daddy gulped. "I think, considering what you've just told me, I should quit. I should take Cassie away from here and move on, go abroad, try to make a fresh start."

"Now, just one minute," snapped Frank. "It's no good having a parenting crisis now. Moving to the South of France won't miraculously make you a better father. You've damaged those kids for good. You have to stay and face the consequences of your actions." Daddy hung his head, his floppy fringe falling into his eyes. Frank stood up and pointed his index finger. His body quivered. "I've worked very hard on forging a relationship with your government and Zolis. They provided very nicely for us and I don't intend to let you walk out on this until the final deal is struck and all because you couldn't control your sexual urges."

Daddy sank onto his knees and buried his head in his hands. "I'm sorry, Frank, I know you are only trying to help, it's just…"

Frank's silver eyes narrowed as he looked down on James' crumpled body; a sneer at the corner of his mouth. "There,

there, dear boy. Maybe there is something more I can do to shoulder the burden for you. For instance, if you were to temporarily sign over the estate–"

I stumbled forwards and the door made a loud creak.

"Come in, dearest one," said Frank without turning his head. Daddy's body went rigid and he stared down at the rug, refusing to catch my eye. I walked into the centre of the room and bowed my head. "Daddy's just off to bed, aren't you?" continued Frank in a sing-song voice. "There's a good fellow. I tell you what, I'll get Emily to bring you up a nice cup of sweet tea in a minute. How about that?"

Daddy didn't answer and crept out of the room.

Frank pointed at the doll's house which had been placed next to the bookcase. I sank into a cross-legged position and began my usual job of rearranging the little figures within.

He took a drag of his cigar and exhaled slowly. "That's my girl. You sit down and have a little game. What are you playing this time?"

"Hospitals."

After a few minutes Frank knocked a block of ash into a heavy glass bowl which was already overflowing with Daddy's half smoked cigarettes. "Were you standing at the door for long?" he asked, giving me a sidelong glance.

I didn't reply.

Frank's tongue darted out and swept over his front teeth. "It's alright dear, you're not in trouble, but you know you must always tell me the truth. You know how much I love you." He flexed his fingers and flattened his palm – a gentle reminder of his method of administering justice.

I gulped and gave a quick nod.

"So, you heard that your father wants to run away with Cassie?"

"Yes."

"That is a terrible blow, isn't it? That he wants to leave us, well specifically you, behind and make a fresh start."

The room went fuzzy.

"No need for tears, dearest. Uncle Frank won't let it happen. It's just that your father…" He gave out a great sigh.

"It's just that he blames you for what happened." Frank rose to his feet and reached for the decanter sitting on the sideboard. "I don't. If anything, he is the one to blame, carrying on in that disgusting manner." He sloshed the port into his glass and raised it to eye level, swirling the liquid around the glass. "But technically you *were* the one who killed his lover... so you can understand why he might not want to be around you anymore. You see, you have become a daily reminder of what happened that terrible day. You are a sort of human punishment for him." Frank took a sip of port and smacked his lips together.

The tears were rolling down my cheeks and they splashed onto the polished floorboards.

"Now, don't you fret, my dearest, because clever Uncle Frank has a plan to win him around. We – specifically you, are going to make it so he never wants to leave." Frank rubbed his hands together and chuckled. "Now off you go into the kitchen and take him up a nice cup of tea and make sure you put plenty of sugar in it. It's good for the nerves. But first a special hug."

As I left the room, Frank took a peek inside the doll's house.

"Heavens child," he gasped. "What in God's name has happened to all the dolls?"

***

My phone pinged, snapping me out of my daydream; a burst of texts and emails. I scrolled through them, deleting as I went. None of them were important but then I noticed a couple of messages from that bitch Annie Harper telling me there was something wrong with my statement. Either she could come to me or I could meet her at a convenient location. Fuck – I couldn't ignore this.

Chapter Thirty-One

Lily

I stared at my fingers, now tacky and crimson. Tiggy had her tail between her legs and was whimpering, her ribcage quivering like crested waves on a patch of open sea. My head was spinning – I didn't know what to do – my flight instincts had been turned upside down. A few minutes ago, I had resolved to sprint to the nearest police station and turn myself in. Get the hell away from this horrible place, but now my feet stayed planted in the garden of Toad Cottage. Tiggy's appearance brought with it the suggestion that something terrible was waiting for me in the shadows and I had no alternative but to face it, or as Flo would put it – 'grow a pair.'

But Grace could return at any moment and each rustle, snap or chirp of a bird burned onto the tops of my ears. My body was screaming out for sleep, but the blood couldn't be ignored. *Could it?* The little creature was daubed with the stuff and a swift fingertip investigation had proved it wasn't hers. I tried to convince myself Tiggy had come across some sort of wild animal and fought with it, but it was too much of a stretch even for my imagination – there wasn't a scratch on her. If she had been devouring a dead pheasant or a rabbit carcass, she wouldn't be shaken. I scratched the underside of her toffee coloured ear and whispered, *it's okay.*

In the end, Tiggy took the matter out of my hands and forced the decision. She shook her head and trotted back to the undergrowth then she stopped, one of her front paws suspended mid-air, and turned her head towards me. She barked and the sound, like a volley of machine gun fire, was sucked into the gaps between the swaying ash trees.

My flight instincts were now piqued by a morbid curiosity which wouldn't disappear until I had seen the source of the blood. The wood itself ran parallel to the track which I figured must lead onto a road. Although drugged at the time, I had been driven here by car and the mystery female visitor had also arrived by a vehicle of some sort. So, I consoled myself with the knowledge that if I were running away, this would be the direction I needed to take.

To get to the side of the woods Tiggy was entering, I had to walk past a dustbin incinerator. A trickle of smoke circled its way out of the funnel and disintegrated into the slate sky. I tapped the metal with my fingers; it was hot, but not unbearable. I knocked the lid onto the lawn and the movement sent a cloud of ash mushrooming into the air. I picked up a stick and poked around in the soft grey heap, my movement stirring up a brief tangerine glow, but all that I uncovered were a few melting buttons and a zip. I turned to go when something caught my eye; not a button but a tiny face. A china head – the hair sizzled off, but nevertheless an impish face, grinning up at me.

Tiggy barked again and jolted me from my paralysis.

She was already disappearing into the undergrowth. I followed and the brambles clung onto my body, catching the sleeve of my blouse. I paused to unhook myself, flinging the springy branches back into place and my feet kicked against browning bracken and soggy stinging nettles which spilt large droplets onto my patent shoes. The air around me was laden with the scent of moss and wild garlic and, as the atmosphere grew heavier, so the tree trunks thickened.

Tiggy scampered along, kicking up clumps of fallen bark in her wake. As she gathered speed so every instinct in my body warned me to slow down. A pigeon in a branch overhead gave a mournful coo, but apart from that the wood was still – the only sound my footsteps and Tiggy's scuffling paws. After a few minutes of brushing away overhanging boughs, I arrived at a circular clearing with a heap of earth at its centre. Pink worms straddled the soil whilst white roots combed their way through the rich chestnut wall, guarding what was behind it.

My eyes smarted with tears.

I didn't want to look.

Tiggy's whimpering was trapped at the back of her throat and I winced as the sound grated against my eardrums. I clenched my fists, willing her to stop. Then the pigeon chimed in and I put my hands over my ears, hearing the beat of my panicking heart pulsing through my veins. I saw a flash out of the corner of my eye and whipped my head around to see a shovel leaning against a lichen-crusted trunk. The blade was streaked with crimson lines.

When I looked back Tiggy had disappeared, her whimpering now muffled. She was behind the soil partition.

My knees trembled, but I dragged myself forwards until I was standing at the edge of a long, rectangular hole.

I looked down. It took a few seconds to make sense of what was in front of me.

Frank was lying there. A bundle of crumpled material had been flung on top of him leaving only the top of his torso exposed. Tiggy sat on his barrel chest whilst Frank stared up at the sky, his eyes wide open.

The top of his head was missing.

I retched, steadied myself and then promptly threw up all over my sandals. My body convulsed, like I was twitching on the end of a noose in my final death dance. I closed my eyes and as my memory splayed the image across my mind, I realised my mistake. It wasn't a bundle of material which lay on top of him, but another body.

I tried to catch my breath; sucking in the air through my nose and holding it within my lungs for as long as I could.

Who was the other figure? Could it be Grace? The world was spinning. I sat down with a bump and hugged my knees to my chest.

Tiggy hopped out of the grave again with a fresh coating of redness glued to her fur; amethyst pearls decorating the tips of her white underbelly.

I held out my hand, overwhelmed with the need to make contact with the living. She came and stuck her body into the crook of my arm. I kissed her head and her coarse, warm fur tickled my nostrils.

More thoughts cannoned around my head. Had Grace killed Frank? Had it been like one of those cheap horror movies; that just when she thought she was safe, he, in his death throes, rose up from the grave and killed her.

I screwed up my eyes, but it didn't stop the thoughts from tumbling into my mind. The voice inside my head whispered that it wasn't Grace; that wasn't what she left the house wearing. But the clothes were familiar. I was so frightened I was sure I could taste the metallic bitterness of my own blood upon my tongue.

I had to run for it. Run and get help. Tiggy would be okay – she was a dog. I had to run to the nearest road, flag down a car and throw myself on the driver's mercy.

I was a child. I could use my voice and ask for help.

Suddenly I heard a soft moaning and I lifted my head, pulling at my earlobes.

I got to my feet. The moaning grew louder.

My whole body trembling, I peered back into the hollow. The person on top of Frank was alive. I stared at the clothes; taking in the diamante buckle, Burberry cap and sunglasses, caught in the clutches of a snaking tree root. I gasped. It was the woman who had come to the gate when we were having our tea on the lawn.

What had Grace done?

I scrambled down into the pit and my shoes made a gentle thud on the earth floor. It was a shallow grave. Did its lack of depth indicate it was unfinished or was Grace simply not bothered? Was she waiting for more bodies before she filled it in? Was this the fate she had in store for me?

I stooped down.

I touched the woman's soft, powdered cheek. "It's okay." A sentence more for myself than her. I slipped my fingers under her chin, scanning her body whilst I felt for her pulse. The nape of her neck was wet; it was as if someone had

210

tipped a tablespoon of damson jelly onto the top of her spine. The strands of her jet-black ponytail were clumped together. Her pulse was faint, but she was alive. I slid my palms under her stomach and rolled her towards me. Her eyelashes quivered then she opened her dark eyes and stared at me.

"Where…where?" she croaked.

My mouth fell open. "Nina?"

She groaned.

"Who did this to you?"

"Frank's niece, Emily." Nina sat up and yelped, placing her hands across her forehead and screwing her eyes shut. "You can talk?"

"It would seem so." I put my hands on her shoulders, steadying her in case she collapsed again. Sweat shimmered on her forehead and a sudden burst of white light shone down through a canopy of leaves giving her olive skin a grey hue. She looked so fragile. Like one of the broken china figurines from the doll's house.

I looked up. I could see the sun's rays, filtering through the branches, creating a path of flimsy light. We were in the pit of hell, staring up towards heaven.

"Do you think you can stand?" I asked.

She coughed then all of a sudden, she yelped. "Frank."

She leaned forwards and pressed her face onto his chest, her long fingers reaching up to stroke his beard. Her bright pink shellac nails were chipped and crusted with black soil.

Sadness sat upon my tongue and blocked the back of my throat. Here was Nina's husband lying in front of her with half a head. She didn't know the secrets he had been keeping, and I certainly wasn't going to tell her. Not now. I touched her arm and gave it a gentle shake.

She sobbed; the noise stuck in her throat, grating – like a grasshopper rubbing its legs together.

"We have to go," I said, my voice firm. "Gra– Emily will be back soon. We have to get out of here."

Nina grabbed Frank's lapels, mauve veins on the back of her knuckles rising to the surface of her skin. "No," she growled.

"Nina – think of Flo. She needs you. Frank is dead, you can't do anything for him. Come on. Now. Think about Flo."

Nina drew in a large breath and shuddered. Meanwhile Tiggy had leapt out of the hole and was running around the perimeter of the grave, scuffing up the soil with her paws. She no longer wanted to be with Frank, perhaps the scent of decay was beginning to repulse her. His inky blue lips protruded from his ruby splattered beard. Those unblinking silver eyes. I shivered. I would have closed them if I had a shred of courage, not least because they seemed to be watching my every move.

I hooked myself under Nina's arm and pulled her to her feet. She stood up then stumbled, crashing back down onto Frank's stomach. I almost toppled onto her.

"You've hurt your leg." I pointed to a large rusty-stained tear in her jeans.

"I don't think I can walk."

She was struggling to catch her breath and her skin grew a deeper shade of ash. She spluttered and a maroon trickle ran from her ear canal and down the side of her neck.

Then I heard it and my heart stopped. In the distance – the faint whir and click of a rusty bicycle chain going around. I shot a glance at Tiggy, who was lying with her head on her front paws, her eyebrows twitching. I put a finger to my lips as though the dog would be able to understand. Nina opened her mouth and I clamped my sweaty palm in front of it. I pushed her down and flattened myself into the grave, snuggling my body into the cavity between Frank's body and the soil wall. My head was aligned to his shoulder and blobs of gelatinous gloop burst against my cheek.

I held my breath.

The cycling slowed down. Was she going to stop? Tiggy stayed where she was, eyebrows still twitching from side to side.

There was the squeak of brakes and the clatter of the bike being lowered onto its side. Then there were footsteps. Grace was chuntering to herself. I couldn't make out the words, but the tone sounded angry. I heard the rattle of metal being shaken, heavy breathing then the creak and clank of the bicycle disappearing into the distance.

I gulped.

She would be home very soon.

She would find I wasn't there.

She would find the blood and broken glass.

She would begin her search, probably starting with the woods...

I put my head under Nina's armpit and with all my strength heaved her up to her feet. By now she was barely conscious, spit collecting at the corner of her mouth. I dragged her out of the hole, hooked my elbows underneath her armpits and pulled her through the undergrowth causing a jumble of muddy leaves to ride up the legs of her designer jeans.

After a few minutes, my back bounced against something, forcing me to stop. I turned and was faced with a large meshed-wire fence which stretched both ways as far as I could see. This was why Grace hadn't come any further – she couldn't. I stuck my fingers through the holes and rattled it. The track on the other side led to the road, I was certain of it and I wanted to be on it. I could follow the bridleway, keeping parallel to the fencing, but there was no way of knowing if, when we reached the exit, I would be able to find a break in the fence – it seemed fairly impenetrable.

There was nothing for it, we'd have to go back to the boat house and barricade ourselves in there.

"Is there any chance you can get to your feet?" I asked. Nina gritted her teeth and nodded. I draped her body around my shoulders and dug my shoulder blades in. My breath was ragged with exertion whilst hers rattled with frailty. Tiggy danced around our feet, as though we were playing a game, the rules of which we hadn't made clear.

After ten minutes I could see the lake glistening through the thinning undergrowth. We came out into the open and I stood there, my face burning and sweat trickling down my spine. About a hundred metres to our left was the boat house. My former prison. I saw a flash of gold underneath the wooden structure which dissolved into the dark water behind the steps, like a star twinkling in the night sky.

I began to sing through gritted teeth; one of Flo's favourites; *So wonderfully, wonderfully, wonderfully, wonderfully pretty, You know that I'd do anything for you.* Nina coughed a smile of recognition onto her face and I felt my neck moisten with her blood. I clenched my fists. I had to do this for Flo. I had to get her mother to safety. Shingle crunched under my feet whilst Tiggy dipped in and out of the water, still curious as to the game we were playing.

"Flo," whispered Nina.

"Yes – that Flo's song. You're going to see her really soon."

It felt like there was steel band circling my stomach, forcing an inner strength to expand into my tired limbs – dredging up energy from my body's reserves.

I heard a scream. An angry scream followed my name.

"Cassandra," came the roar.

Tiggy barked.

"Tiggy," I hissed. "Be quiet."

Then there was silence on the airwaves, apart from grating shingle and the gentle lap of water.

We reached the boat house and I paused for a few seconds, my back flat against the soggy wooden stilts which the structure sat upon.

Grace's voice was now full of melody. "Tiiiiiiiigy, Tiiiiiiigy, where are you? I've got bic-bics." That was it. Tiggy gave a giant woof and scuttled away, back to the path which led to the cottage.

I shut my eyes. This wasn't going to work – Grace would be able to break down the door. Then I heard it; a gentle knocking sound; tap, tap, tap.

I peered into the underbelly of the boat house and there, nudging against the panelling bobbed a small rowing boat. My heart soared.

I sat Nina down against the steps and she slumped forwards onto her lap.

"Don't worry, I won't be long," I said, wading into the

water. I gave a sharp gasp as the freezing water hit my shins and within seconds my pinafore skirt had ballooned up around my waist. The air was putrid and, as the blanket of dark water moved, a sheen of algae lolloped towards me, draping my midriff with a coating of bright green. In the corner was a rectangle of golden light – the narrow corridor leading out towards the lake. Is this what I had seen? Not my guardian angel but an optical illusion? What the heck was I doing? There was no going back now. Soon I had reached the boat and I clapped my hands with delight to see that the oars were inside. My fingers shaking, I undid the knot which tethered the nose of the vessel to a rusting metal hook on the wall.

Then I heard barking. Joyous barking. A reunion.

"Cassaaaaandra. Cassaaaaandra. Where are you?"

Breath hissed from my lungs and the splash of water echoed around the wooden planks. I pulled the boat towards the steps, ignoring the carcass of a decaying rat which came floating towards me.

"Nina," I hissed. "You have to help me." She groaned and opened one eye. "You've got to get in here and lie down." I pointed at the boat and she nodded.

My name was growing louder and louder.

She was coming.

I almost threw Nina into the boat. I heard her joints knock and slap against the inner shell. I pictured the colour of the bruises she would get, if we were lucky enough to survive.

I pushed the boat back into the dark water towards the golden passage.

Grace's voice was upon me; she was screaming with rage. I waited for her to grab hold of me, but she didn't stop and thundered up the steps into the building, making the walls shudder. There was still a chance. Ever so slowly, I pushed a path through the water.

I sensed her.

I looked up and there she was, standing above me, her breathing shallow. Tiggy woofed and pawed at the floorboards; certain this was a game of hide-and-seek.

Grace knelt down and pressed her face to the floor.

Our eyes met.

"And where," she said, her voice silken with laughter, "the fuck do you think you're going?"

Chapter Thirty-Two

Flo

I checked my watch again – it felt like it had been almost two o'clock for ever. Why did time drag when you were waiting for something? The sky had gone dark and big black clouds were stacked on the horizon. I was in the courtyard of Paget Castle, pressed up against the cobbled wall, waiting for Annie's signal.

We had a plan.

As soon as we'd left Dad, Annie tried Grace's phone again and this time the status next to her message showed she'd read it. Annie kept the tone breezy. Said she simply wanted to tie up a few loose ends. It was all her fault, *bla bla bla*, and she was terribly sorry for the inconvenience, but she really did need a signature. Annie let Grace come up with the meeting place and she had picked The Reading Rooms in Great Morton, which was some sort of museum. I'd found Toad Cottage on google maps – it was only a twenty-minute drive from the town centre.

So far so good.

The plan was sound. We would split, but both watch Grace arrive. Annie was going to get inside The Reading Rooms early and wait for Grace while I hid in the entrance over the road. Plan A: if Grace had Lily with her then I would go inside too and hide behind the stone pillars in the hall. Annie would pass Lily a note telling her to pretend she needed the loo and then, as soon as I saw her, we'd run to the nearest police station. Plan B: if Grace showed up alone then I would get a taxi from the market square and go straight to Toad

Cottage to find Lily while Annie stalled Grace for as long as she could.

Annie wasn't massively happy with the plan. She had wanted to go straight to Toad Cottage with police back-up and confront Grace there, but I knew we had to find a way to get Lily on her own. We didn't have any proper evidence to connect all the bits and what we did have – the earring, didn't exactly make things look good for Lily. Even Annie agreed that there was no way the police or CPS could take action until the photos had been verified and even then, what did it prove? Annie said the police already knew that Grace and Lily had changed their names because of an incident in their past. So what? No one had made the connection between Dad, James and Frank – the time lapse between James' suicide and Dad's treatment of Lily was too long plus Lily had been treated under a false name. Add to that the fact the police had closed the case because of all the solid evidence against Dad.

We needed to hear the truth from Lily. If the police went crashing in now with our theories, then Grace would be spooked and still have plenty enough time to snatch Lily and do a runner. This way, though a bit risky, meant we could get Lily to safety, figure out what exactly was going on and then act.

Annie drove us from the train station to Great Morton. She wasn't concentrating on what she was doing, and I kept getting jerked from side to side along with all the tonnes of empty coke cans and crisp wrappers she'd chucked onto the floor by my feet. She was chewing gum as though her teeth had been sewn together with elastic, going over the plan again and again.

I really wished I hadn't eaten curry for breakfast.

When we turned into the main car park, Annie's phone beeped, and she grabbed it from the pocket behind the gear stick and handed it to me.

"What does it say?"

I entered the code for the lock screen, which was still set as Dad's birthday, and scrolled down. "She's changing the meeting place. She says The Reading Rooms are hosting an event and it'll be too noisy."

"Oh! Right."

"She's typing something else. Okay. She suggests meeting at Castle Café."

"Where the fuck is that?" asked Annie.

"I'm guessing over there." I pointed straight ahead at the huge grey building in front of us.

We followed the brown road signs to Paget Castle and Annie parked on the road, half-way down a busy side street.

"Pull your hood up," said Annie. "Follow me at a distance." We went through an alley which opened out onto a cobbled courtyard, full of market traders. The air was thick with the smell of frying onions and burnt sugar. Paget Castle stood in the far corner, towering over the wooden barrows and their striped awnings.

I heard a distant rumble of thunder.

Annie pointed to a large map nailed on the wall and I tapped my finger on the picture of the castle. "Okay," I said. "It looks as though the café is inside the castle walls, so you'll have to walk up that slope to get there."

We turned our heads and squinted. I could see the gravel path which twisted its way up the hill and stopped at a glass-fronted building with automatic sliding doors. "If Grace is already there, she'll see me approaching with you," I said. "That's not going to work."

"You'll just have to stay here and mingle. I'll text you. Remember, Y is go, N is stay where you are and I'll send Lily to you. Maybe get as close to the path as possible but keep under the canopies with your hood up."

I leaned against the wall and watched Annie go up the path. I waited until she'd disappeared inside the café and then decided to have a look around the stalls. It was getting colder and I shoved my hands into my pockets, finding a bit of loose change. I went over to a stall selling honeyed cashew nuts and the man filled a paper bag to the brim and handed it over with a big smile. The grease soaked through the paper and made my palms warm and sticky. As I chomped my way through the *authentic Elizabethan snack*, I riffled through a handful of leaflets telling me how I should be spending my time in Great Morton.

Paget Castle was the star attraction, closely followed by The Reading Rooms and St. Mathilda's Well, both of which were located in the town's central square.

I picked up a shiny brochure entitled 'Castle News' and started to skim read.

Paget Castle was originally built on the remains of an Anglo-Saxon burial site. This fortress had been held by descendants of William The Conqueror for a century before being destroyed and it was left in ruins until the time of Richard The Lionheart when there was a complete rebuild. Since that time, the castle passed down the Paget family line until the civil war when The Royalist supporters were betrayed, and it fell into the hands of the Roundheads. After the Restoration it was bequeathed to the loyal Hopkinsons of Beauchamp who resided there until the last family member passed away and gifted it to the National Trust in their will.

I stared at the jutting turrets which looked like a row of witches' hats. I re-folded the pamphlet and spotted a sticker on the back which apologised for the temporary closure of The Reading Rooms. That was weird. I read on: *The National Trust are converting the upper rooms of the library back to their original state which means the doors won't be opening again until early Spring. Sorry for any inconvenience.* I tucked the flyer into my pocket. Why had Grace said the library was hosting an event? That was a lie. Why didn't she just say it was closed?

There was another rumble of thunder and a raindrop splashed onto my nose.

I stepped back under cover of a posh coffee stall. The smell of the freshly ground beans made my tongue tingle. I checked my change; I still had enough money for a macchiato – the caffeine hit but without all the liquid – the last thing I needed right now was to be hunting around for a public loo. I drank my coffee, staring up at the castle as the rain pelted down all around me, drumming onto the canvas.

My phone pinged. I took it out of my back pocket.

No sign. Remember - keep yourself out of sight.

Ok, I texted with my thumb. I finished my thimble of coffee and pulled my hood tight around my face. I needed to stop fannying around and focus on keeping an eye out for Grace. I really hoped Lily would be there too. I'd missed her so much. God – if only I'd paid attention to what she was trying to get at down by the lake then maybe none of this would have happened.

Ten minutes passed.

Her phone's dead, texted Annie.

The rain was now coming down in sheets and splashed off the cobbles, soaking my trainers. I took another step under the covers and wiggled my damp toes.

"Hey!"

I turned around. The fat, grey-haired woman behind the counter was waving her tongs at me. She put a cookie into a paper bag and handed it over.

"On the house, pet," she said. "You look a bit lost. Not a good day to be seeing Great Morton."

I smiled. "Thanks, so much. You know, it still looks pretty in the rain." I took a bite of shortbread.

She wiped her hands down her apron. "Are you waiting for someone?"

"Um," I said, crumbs spilling out of my mouth. "Kind of."

"Well, pet, I'd get myself up into the Castle Café if I were you and wait it out there in the warm. They've got a great exhibition going on in the back room – it's all about the time when the Paget family were betrayed by Cromwell's sour-faced lot." She smiled. "Plus, it's free."

"Aren't you just sending me straight into the hands of your competitors?" I asked, tossing the bag into the dustbin.

The woman winked and held up her palms, silver ring on each finger. "You've caught me out. We sell our coffee beans direct to them so actually it's a win-win situation. There's a lovely art display there too by one of our local painters – she's quite famous in *those* circles, you know. The details are in here," she said, tapping her fingernails on a pile of flyers next to the sachets of sugar. They were the same as the one in my pocket. Just then a young couple came over to the counter and she moved away to serve them.

I took out the pamphlet again. How had I missed this? *For a limited time only, Nina Jackson will be loaning us one part of her famous triptych. Chosen for its extraordinary interpretation of this season's theme.*

I felt sick.

I phoned Annie who picked up straight away.

"Yes?" she hissed.

"The art exhibition. Can you see it from where you are sitting?"

"Um, yes," said Annie, her voice muffled.

"Take a closer look."

I heard her chair scrape across the floor. "Okay. I'm taking a closer look. It's a bit weird if you ask me. Right now I'm staring at a knife sticking out of." She paused. "I think it's meant to be the pages of a diary. Crazy."

"It's by my Mum."

"Oh!" Annie coughed. "It's…well it's interesting."

"Never mind giving me your artistic interpretation," I snapped. "What's it called?"

"Hang on." I could hear her breathing. "What's with the shredded shirts, covered in lipstick? Ah! Here we are. It's called *Betrayal*. Oh! That kind of makes sense."

"Shit! Shit! She's seen us. Seen we're both here. Don't you get it – betrayal? It's a message. She must have been watching us the moment we hit the main road into town. That's why she made that decision to change the meeting place without making sure her story checked out. She knew we were up to something and now she's bought herself some more time. She knows we're coming for her."

Chapter Thirty-Three

Grace

I sat on the jetty clasping the handle of Frank's umbrella between my knees. My clothes clung to my body as though I had grown an extra layer of skin. The sky had become a sheet of jaundiced steel which cast an eerily bright glow onto my pale skin, turning my flesh luminous. The peculiar lighting made the boat in the centre of the lake appear as if it was nothing more than a cut-out silhouette, something Gil and Cassie had made out of black sugar paper whilst cosied up together in the playroom. The thunder and lightning had melted away, leaving only the loud splosh of water against water which churned the surface of the lake into a hem of white froth.

The pelting of the raindrops onto the brolly skin was hypnotising me; drumming its way into my soul and stirring up the remaining embers of hatred, blowing on them until they glowed once more.

I knew Cassie would have to return to me, or they would both perish on the water.

I wondered how long it would be before Flo and that stupid bitch Annie arrived. Their appearance would force my hand one way or another. I took a swig of gin and let the juniper firewater rinse through the gaps in my teeth. The liquid numbed my throat and stoked the fire inside my stomach. I kept my gaze on my sister's hunched figure and reached my hand onto the decking, stroking the rifle lying next to me.

This would all end soon.

I cast my mind back to the events which led up to Daddy's death.

***

It was dark outside. Although it is was technically afternoon, the October nights had begun to make their presence felt along with the withering leaves.

Daddy didn't do much else now apart from sleep, cry or write feverishly; filling pages and pages of thick cream paper with his spidery handwriting. If it weren't for Frank, Daddy would have remained unshaven and dirty. Frank took care of his brother-in-law as though he was caring for a mewling infant.

I helped.

I held the soapy bucket of water steady while Frank shaved Daddy's face and I pulled him out of his armchair so that he went out to use the bathroom. I cut his apple into small squares and took it away again when the cubes turned brown. Before he went to bed, I brought him up his tea. I always made sure there was a spoonful of sugar stirred into it and exactly the right amount of his sleeping draught which Frank had shown me how to administer.

I did basic housework and managed Cassie. There was no way of knowing what was happening inside her head now; she hadn't uttered a word for over a month – from the exact moment she came back from the clinic. It prompted Frank to buy her a therapy puppy; a tiny Jack Russell with toffee coloured ears called Tiggy but, though Cassie spent every waking minute with the creature, her speech remained locked inside.

If a passer-by had stopped outside on that dingy, blustery night and stared in through the window, they would have thought they were peeping in on a scene of blissful harmony: a father absorbed in writing his memoirs, a jovial uncle drinking a glass of port whilst his two nieces, dressed in pinafores, played at his feet; one with a puppy, the other a doll's house.

That same evening, I took Cassie for her bath as usual. She dipped her toe into the water and then shot it out again, biting her lip. I put my finger in but was unable to gauge the temperature. I was numb. I turned the taps off.

"Too hot?"

Cassie nodded.

I turned the cold tap on fully and the water streamed onto an iceberg of bubbles, forcing a clump of froth to break off into the air which in turn flew onto Cassie's nose. There was a time when the girl would have been beside herself with giggles at such an event; now she simply wiped the foam away with the back of her hand; mouth turned down at the corners.

Frank said Cassie's lack of speech was due to delayed shock and that it would eventually return, but my hair remained colourless so maybe Cassie's words would stay away too. I couldn't have cared less. I preferred it that way and without my sister's endless torrent of chatter I was able to retreat further into my own thoughts. At times it was as if I was going through life viewing events from a distance. I saw myself reading the child a story before tucking her into bed, ignoring her longing glances. I heard the kiss I planted on Cassie's forehead, but didn't feel my lips pressing against the little girl's skin. I watched my sister shrink into herself all the time avoiding the portrait of Mummy which hung in the stairwell at Aldeburgh House.

Numb.

My body was turning into stone. The only thing that kept me alive was the memory of falling in love with Gil and each day I tried to rekindle the surge of euphoria which filled every corner of my body when I had been in his presence.

Between Daddy's prolonged bouts of staring into space there were short bursts of frantic activity. Then he sat at a desk in the drawing room and scribbled words onto pages, humming Gil's folksong under his breath. When the clock struck ten, Frank gave him a five-minute warning and he sighed then stuffed the papers into an envelope, begging Frank to take them to the post box immediately. Frank always agreed but the moment Daddy left the room, Frank tossed the thick envelope onto the fire. I was curious to know what he wrote about with such a sense of urgency. One time when Frank disappeared, almost tripping over Daddy's shadow, I plucked the bundle off the fire and read the smouldering manuscript – it was a love letter to Gil.

At night, Frank locked Daddy in his room.

That terrible evening, after I'd been a good girl for Frank, he told me to tidy up before I went to make Daddy's tea. I cleared away the newspapers and stacked the empty plates and cups to take into the kitchen. I removed the saucer of shrivelled clementine segments from Daddy's bureau and there, tucked under the paperweight I saw two tickets; one for James and one for Cassandra. One-way tickets to Toulouse. I searched the desk for another ticket, but it wasn't there. I felt sick. I went into the kitchen to make the tea, all the time my stomach churning. There must have been a mistake. He wouldn't go without me. I took up the tea. Frank was in the room, standing at the window, looking out onto the moonlit lake. I set down the cup and saucer on the bedside table. Daddy was sitting up in bed, staring at the ceiling rose.

I stepped back from the bed and folded my arms across my chest. "Uncle, please may I talk to you for a moment?"

"Not now dearest." I saw his pale reflection in the pane of glass and his skin glowed white under the shadow of the moon.

"But–"

"I said not now." His voice was harsh sounding and I knew not to press him further. It would keep until the morning. The date of travel wasn't until next month.

I was woken by Frank the next morning. He burst into my bedroom, calling my name. He pulled back the curtains so that the slow rising dawn lit up a rectangle of the floorboards. I sat up and Cassie, lying next to me, stirred. As usual the brat had woken early and crept into my bed for warmth and company. I blinked back my confusion at the serious expression on Frank's face.

"Dearest," he said. "Last night..." He swallowed and

226

rubbed his hands together. "You brought James his tea last night, didn't you?"

I pulled my dressing gown about my shoulders, watching my breath rise in a cloud before my face.

"Yes, Uncle. Of course. You saw me. Why?" I shivered.

"Dearest one." He shook his head. "Terrible news. I'm afraid you have killed him."

"What?" I had misheard.

"You killed him. You must have put too much of the sedative in his tea."

"No," I gasped. "No, I know I didn't."

Frank drew himself up to his full height and folded his arms across his chest. "I'm telling you, dearest, you must have put too much of the sedative in his tea. There is no other explanation for it."

"But..." I screwed my eyes shut and tried to remember. In my head I heard the kettle shriek. I tipped the water into the mug, squashed the teabag for a few seconds removed it and added the milk; then the sugar, next the powder – a level teaspoon just as Frank had shown me. I shook my head again.

"Dearest, it is perfectly understandable. You have felt pushed out and neglected. To be honest, I blame myself," he hung his head, "I blame myself." He pinched the skin under his eyes and sniffed. There was silence apart from Cassie's soft breathing, she had curled herself into a ball and her spine pressed against my thigh.

"No, Uncle. You are not to blame."

Frank dabbed his eyes with a handkerchief and sat down on the edge of the bed; the springs groaned in protest. "I should have seen it coming. Your father blamed you for what happened to Gil and–" he gasped, shooting a hand to his head. "The tickets. Oh! My dear child, you saw the tickets."

"Yes."

Frank leaned across and pulled me to his chest; the brass buttons on his jacket pressed against my cheek. His breath smelt of coffee. "You poor dear thing. You weren't meant to see them. I was going to tell James that it was impossible –

that he simply couldn't abandon you." He rocked my head back and forth, squeezing my temples with each movement.

Cassie peeped out from under the duvet then slid from the bed. She trotted across the room and disappeared.

"But I didn't do anything." Loud woofing rose up through the floorboards.

His eyes narrowed. "Dearest, you have killed before. You have an unfortunate condition which means that when you are angry, emotion takes over your whole body and makes you oblivious to your actions. I know exactly what happened – it is obvious." He rose from the bed.

I hugged my knees to my chest. Now that Cassie had gone, I wondered if he was going to want our special time, to show me how much he loved me.

He stood at the foot of the bed. "You saw the tickets, were livid with hurt and disappointment and you went straight into the kitchen and put an extra spoonful of sleeping draught into James' tea. On top of all the other chemicals that he puts – *put* – into his body it wouldn't have taken much to finish him off. It was a moment of blind panic, dearest."

I couldn't think straight. I ran through the events of last night again. This time I saw myself heap spoonful after spoonful of powder into the tea. Uncle was right. I must have done it.

I sobbed.

"You aren't to blame, dearest."

"What will I do, Uncle?"

Frank was pacing up and down, clicking his knuckles. "Dear, dear. What's to be done, indeed?"

He took a deep breath then clasped his hands together. "One thing for certain is this; we don't want the police coming around here and questioning you. You might confess what you did and then go on to mention Gil and what a mess that would create. I know you didn't mean to do it, dearest, but the law will take a much dimmer view of these events."

I was shaking. Frank pulled out a hipflask from his jacket pocket, unscrewed the lid, and pressed it to my lips. "There, dearest, you've had a shock. Take a swig." I obeyed him, like

I always did, and he tipped the liquid down my throat; it tasted of burnt cherries and made me catch my breath. The burning sensation continued circling my belly long after I had swallowed. I liked it.

"I think the best thing is for you to take Cassie and go somewhere far away. Don't tell me where so that if I am questioned, I simply will not be able to answer. I will give you money to start you off with, but then you must fend for yourselves. Change your names, become different people but, whatever you do, you must stay in the shadows. Do you hear me?"

I nodded.

"You are old enough to take care of yourself and your sister now. Old enough to make a new life for the both of you."

"But what about you, Uncle?"

He shook his head. "I will stay here and smooth things over. If I can, that is." He sighed. "But don't worry about me. There is no time to lose. You must pack a few necessities and I will take you to the station."

"May I say goodbye to him?"

Frank started. "No!" he snapped. His eyes widened and he coughed. "No dearest. I don't think that would be the right thing to do."

We went to the train station and he left us on the platform with our luggage. He didn't wait to see us catch the train. I clutched hold of my sister's hand; if Cassie was surprised or distraught, I wouldn't have known or cared. Frank had been generous. We had enough money to get by for a year and it was stuffed into envelopes inside my suitcase – we were lucky that Frank happened to have so much cash in the safe.

I sat on the train and imagined what the funeral would be like. Cookie would over-cater, and I knew there would be a tray of untouched egg sandwiches whose corners would curl in on themselves thanks to the oppressive heat of the drawing room. People liked to observe other people's grief and I imagined the dozens of pairs of eyes focusing upon Frank, wanting to feed off his sadness. They would be disappointed that *the girls* weren't there – Frank would have to explain that we were too traumatised by the event and had gone to stay with relatives.

I imagined throwing a posy into the coffin and let out a loud sob. Cassie glanced up from her book then quickly returned her gaze to the page. Tears were flowing down my face as I thought of Gil. He would never be buried; his body was assigned to the bottom of the lake for eternity. The rattle of the carriage dug into my bones and my sorrow faded, replaced by an emerging sound.

The voice went by the name of Blame.

It was Blame that chose to go back to Tom Marchant and punish him. After all, he was the one who set off the chain of events which had led me to the here and now. Blame was kind to me and never once considered that my involvement also made me culpable; it ignored my misreading of Gil's affection; my creation of the mermaid; my administering of the overdose.

No! Tom Marchant. It could all be traced back to him. He had promised me the chance of a normal life, but it was all a lie. I would never be able to experience what it was to have a loving relationship with a man. So instead, I dreamt of how I would get my revenge and the cruelty dished out to me, I passed down the line to my sister.

Things were different in our new Norfolk flat. I chose bedtime stories with unhappy endings – the Brothers Grimm or Hilaire Belloc. If I had to suffer then so did Cassie. At the start, I never did anything tangibly cruel apart from to starve the child of the hugs and cuddles she desperately wanted. The cutting came at a later stage when Grace had been created and I needed Cassie to appreciate the seriousness of what I was trying to achieve.

The self-harm reminded me of the blood that had been spilt and Lily became a living sacrifice. You could say it was almost holy.

***

I was jolted from my thoughts. There were footsteps and Tiggy woofed and scratched at the door to the jetty. Next there was loud hammering.

I picked up the rifle and positioned myself behind the door. And so, the final act had begun.

Chapter Thirty-Four

Lily

I pushed the boat out, through the panelled corridor, onto the lake. To start with, my feet reached the bottom, but as I emerged into the open water, I stumbled and swallowed a great gulp of ivy-green water which left a residue of silt on the back of my teeth. I was hauling myself inside the floating tub just as Grace waded in. She grasped hold of my ankles, digging her fingernails into my skin and I kicked back at her with every ounce of strength I had. Before I lost momentum in my upper body and just before my brain had time to remember I couldn't swim, I dropped inside, landing on Nina's soft body. She groaned.

The panic at being surrounded by water had left me struggling to breathe. My nightmares might have vanished, but water was still a huge terror. One lesson on how to float with Flo had not turned me into a swimmer. Grace was at a distinct advantage; first, she could swim and, secondly, she knew how scared I was of water because she'd fed my phobia.

Grace was clinging to the boat like she was a crab, pincers hooked onto a nylon washing line dangled over the pier wall – desperate to retrieve the bait. She began to rock the boat, the tilting motion enabling her to claw her way closer. I grabbed the oar, sat up and whacked Grace's fingers until she screamed and was forced to let go.

The rage on Grace's face took on demonic proportions; her eyes disappeared to arrow slits and her mouth twisted into a knot.

Still gasping for air, I rowed into the centre of the lake, relying on adrenalin to power my body into movement.

When Grace saw I was out of her reach she submerged her whole body and retreated back under the boat house; a crocodile, biding its time. Classic reptilian behaviour; why waste energy in a fight when it was much more efficient to wait until the prey was tired and then go in for the kill?

It was bucketing down with rain.

After a few minutes my sister appeared on the jetty, her hair smooth against her skull, her roots brilliant white; eyes darting from side to side. Her lips were moving but no sound came out. Who was she talking to? Then I saw it and the oar almost slid from my grasp. She had a rifle tucked under one arm whilst an umbrella dangled from the other. She smiled at me and waved the gun in the air before sitting down and laying it next to her. It was as though she was setting out a stall at a fete. She patted a curious black object next to her thigh then put up the brolly, clamping the handle between her knees.

"You'll have to come in soon," she said, cupping her hands around her mouth, her voice competing against the storm. "The whole area around the lake is fenced – you'll never be able to get out. After all, dear Uncle Frank couldn't have us running away again." She laughed; a screeching sound. "I'll give you forty minutes to make your way back in before I start shooting."

And there we were; in a floating, wooden shell, bobbing up and down on the middle of the lake. Torrential rain pressed against the ridge of my spine and it felt like someone was shaking a box of dressmaker's pins onto by back. Nina was lying on her side and I covered her face with my upper body, spreading my arms wide and transforming my cardigan into a make-shift tent. I sang to her and every so often she opened a glassy eye, presumably to check I was still there, but the longer we drifted on the water the less the frequency of her stares.

I couldn't let Nina die. I wouldn't. Surely Flo would have raised the alarm when she realised her Mum and Frank were both missing? Were police cars on their way?

Suddenly I was blinded by a white light. At first, I thought it was lightning, but the dazzling illumination remained, coating my body in its brilliance. Grace was shining a powerful torch onto the boat and it created a silver a pathway across the water.

There was the sound of gravel shifting and a silhouette raced up the wooden steps. I couldn't see who it was, but they were slender and moved with stealth. My heart shuddered – was it Flo? Tiggy barked and Grace got to her feet and stood to one side of the door. There was loud banging, the door burst open and at the same time Grace raised the butt of the rifle. CRACK! The person fell to the ground and Grace rained more blows down upon them.

Grace shouted something to me, but her voice, drifting across the water from the boat house, was muffled by the gentle lapping of the lake and the grotesque cry of an amorous frog.

She pointed the rifle at the body on the deck and waved her arm in a beckoning gesture. She had gained herself another bargaining chip – she knew I couldn't stand by and watch someone else die – I already had too much blood on my hands.

My stomach lurched at the inevitable; I would have to row back to the boat house and face whatever punishment she chose to inflict. The help that I had desperately hoped would arrive and whisk us to safety had unwittingly handed Grace every last ounce of power. There were no blue lights flickering through the trees or sirens clanging in the distance.

"Don't move," hissed a familiar voice. I pressed my hand to my forehead. I must be hallucinating. I kept my head still but rolled my eyeballs around, trying to work out where the sound was coming from.

"*It's Friday I'm in love,*" sang the voice. It was coming from the water behind. I was going out of my mind. The boat moved forwards an inch.

"Flo? But I thought…"

"Your voice?" she exclaimed, almost laughing. "Shit –

how did that happen?"

"I can't explain. I had a vision. A man. I know it sounds crazy, but it's like he unlocked something inside of me. It's like he has given me back my voice."

"Nothing happening here sounds crazy because it's all off the scale fucked up. Throw the rope out to me, I can't tread water any longer."

"I'm so glad you are here," I said, guilt blistering out of my pores. I lowered the rope with slow movements. "I wanted so much to tell you what was going on, but I couldn't – I was such a coward." My voice trailed off.

"You are not a coward. Grace is a monster. I know she killed Amelie to frame Dad and get her revenge on his involvement with your father's death. She's been keeping you a prisoner for years and now it's time to cut her loose."

"But…he's not dead. My father, he's still alive. I can't explain it all now. How did you even get here?"

"I swam."

"Nina. She's in a bad way and whoever came to rescue us just now is lying unconscious on the decking."

"It was Annie–" said Flo, her voice breaking. "Mum… Will she be okay?"

"She needs help urgently. And Frank," I gulped, "I'm so sorry Flo, but he's dead."

Flo was silent for a few seconds. It was too much for her to take in. Water sloshed against the sides of the boat. We watched Grace disappear for a few minutes then return, carrying a rope.

"This is so fucked up," said Flo. "I saw what she just did to Annie. She was waiting to meet with Grace, but Grace must have seen us arrive together because she changed the venue. As soon as we realised, I got in a taxi and came rushing back here. I heard screaming down by the lake and saw you pushing the boat onto the water with Grace trying to grab you. I thought Annie would be following right behind me, but she took forever to get here so I decided the best thing to do was to swim up behind the boat. That way, I wouldn't be seen. I thought I'd be able to hide you in the bottom of the boat and then make a big show of swimming to the furthest bank, tricking Grace into thinking I was you. She would have had to leave her post to come and find you and then you could have rowed to shore and made a run for help. The gun and the frigging spotlight have put pay to that – she's watching our every move. No one's going to get through that door onto the jetty without her hearing them."

"She's tying Annie up. Flo, Annie's on her feet. She's okay." I let out a huge breath. "Okay. What are we going to do now?"

"You are going to row close enough to hold a conversation with the mad bitch. Once she's busy talking to you, I'll swim under the boat and through to the other side of the jetty. You need to keep her chatting and distracted. Once I'm in position, tie up the boat and get her to give you a hand onto the decking. That's when I'll attack her. From behind."

"Okay," I said. "Let's do this."

I turned the boat around and rowed in, towing my hidden extra cargo. My shoulders and arms ached from the effort, but I kept going. Soon, I could hear my sister hollering at me. Sweat trickled into my eyes making them sting.

Nina groaned. "Flo's here," I whispered. "It's all going to be okay."

A flicker of a smile clung to the corner of her mouth and made my heart flutter.

When I was about two metres from Grace, I stopped rowing, turning as I slowed.

I stared at Annie, who was gagged, trussed up and tied to a wooden post. One of her eyes was screwed shut, whilst the other focused upon me. Grace was bent over, re-adjusting the angle of the torch.

"As you can see, the lovely Annie's here," she said, standing upright and placing her hands on her hips. She turned to Annie. "Thought you'd got me, didn't you?" She wagged a finger at her then turned back to me. "I don't suppose you've seen your step-sister on your travels. She's bound to be prowling around here somewhere."

"You've got to stop this, Grace."

236

Grace's jaw fell open and then she threw back her head and cackled. "So, you've found your voice. Well, well, well. What brought about that miracle?"

"It came back when you found the chopped-up skeleton in the water."

Her body went rigid.

The boat dipped and I pictured Flo sucking in a deep breath before submerging her head. The water to my left rippled and I saw a green-white shadow slip away under the surface. I had to keep Grace talking.

"You won't believe it," I shouted, "but since then I've been haunted."

"What?" Her eyes twitched from side to side and her mouth hung ajar. She took a step closer to the edge of the jetty. I needed to keep her face trained on mine.

"I know it sounds crazy, but it is the ghost of a young man."

"What does he look like?"

In the distance I saw Flo's head bob up out of the water. "He's tall with golden skin and long white-blonde hair. When he smiles," I waved my hands in the air, "well, it's as though he could light up the whole world."

Her hands trembled. All thoughts of hostages and bargaining chips seemed to vanish.

I had her hooked.

She knew my guardian angel.

"Is he here?" She whipped her head from left to right – her eyes glinting in the artificial light. Flo's silhouette was clawing up one of the wooden posts. My stomach churned. Grace had to stay focused on me.

"No," I snapped. "He's not here at the moment."

"When did you last see him?"

"In the woods. And then again under the boat house. He was the one who guided me onto the water."

"He's been guiding you to me," she said, pressing her hands together in prayer. "It's me he's trying to communicate with. Not you."

Tiggy barked and went over to where Flo's fingers were

237

curling over the edge of the wooden boards.

"Tiggy," I shouted, my voice stern. The dog spun around and pattered towards me.

I rowed the boat a metre closer. I could see Grace's breath rising up into the cold air.

She threw back her head and laughed, a horrid mechanical sound. "Did your ghost tell you his name?"

I shook my head.

"Gil Walton."

I kept my face trained on hers. The dog was running from side to side, barking and wagging her tail.

"Gil Walton, otherwise known as Myrtle – the creature of the lake. The dead body you saw under the water." She laughed until tears ran down her cheeks. "It was Gil, your nanny, not a fucking mermaid." Hazy images of a young man lifting me up into the air and spinning me around, flooded into my mind. Grace's cries of laughter morphed into sobs. "Every time you had a nightmare you saw him. That's why I wanted to listen. He was mine," she jabbed an index finger against her chest. "He belonged to me and yet each time it was you who got to see his face and hear his voice." Her speech was stilted, her ribcage jerking in and out.

My mind was racing. My mermaid was Gil – a nanny I could barely remember.

"I killed him." She thumped her fist against her chest. "I did. He loved me and Dad took him away from me."

And then I saw him. Gil was standing behind Grace holding his arms around her; his skin golden and shimmering.

Flo was out of the water.

I threw the rope onto the side.

"He's here," I whispered. "Don't move a muscle."

Grace froze. "Where?"

"His arms are around you. Can you feel them?"

Annie flinched and in that split-second Grace turned. There was a roar as she flung herself on top of Flo. The dog was running in circles, barking and wagging her stumpy tail. I leapt onto the deck and jumped on top of Grace's back so that all three of us were rolling around on the planks. After a few minutes of wrestling, Flo and I had Grace pinned face down, hands behind her back. Annie nodded her head to her back pocket and Flo reached inside her jeans and pulled out a set of handcuffs which she slapped around Grace's wrists.

"There's more rope in the boat house," I said, my kneecaps grinding into Grace's spine. Flo fetched it and busied herself tying Grace's ankles together. Then she undid Annie's bindings. Annie gave each of us a quick hug then pulled out her phone, waving it at us. "I'll go and find a signal," she called out as she shot off towards Toad Cottage.

Grace's stream of filthy threats stopped. She twisted her head and stared into my eyes. Bubbles of saliva frothed at the corners of her mouth.

Gil stooped down, kissed her cheek and whispered into my ear.

Then he vanished.

"He's gone," I said.

"He was never there you bitch."

"He was and he said to tell you this: *My Lady of the Lake, forgive me.*"

And there, right in front of me, Grace's face changed. It was as though the years had melted away. I recognised her – she was my sister. My grumpy teenage sister who, once upon a time, had amber eyes which were filled with light and hope.

Chapter Thirty-Five

Flo

I was leaning into the snack machine, running my finger along the rows of sweets and tapping a pound coin against the smeary glass with my other hand.

"Twix, every time," said Annie, appearing out of nowhere.

"Christ!" I bumped my forehead against the glass. I turned around and gave her a gentle hug. She was covered in bruises and I didn't want to add to her discomfort. Annie's hospital gown flapped around her ankles like a tent – it made her seem even smaller than normal. A large piece of fabric gauze was stuck to the side of her head and she smelt of antiseptic.

"Hey, it's so good to see you, Annie. Do you want something? Maybe a coffee?"

"No thanks. I'm awash with all sorts of drugs – I'd best not add caffeine to the mix. It's hard enough to sleep on the ward as it is."

"Will they let you out soon?" I punched in the code for my selection. I put the coin into the slot. "What a rip off," I muttered to my reflection in the glass. The green digits blinked, and the bar of chocolate fell to the ground with a tinny thud.

"Should be back home tomorrow morning," said Annie. "How about Nina? I see she's off the oxygen."

"Yes." I stooped to get my hand inside the drawer. "It's brilliant, but she's going to be in here for a while – her knee is fucked." I stood back up waving my choccy and pointed to a couple of chairs squashed into a corner. We sat down at right angles to each other, our knees almost touching. Annie's breath smelt metallic and her eyes were bloodshot.

"I had a little chat with your Mum last night. She's been through a lot." She smiled. "I guess that's the understatement of the year."

I swallowed but didn't say anything. Annie squeezed my hand.

"What have they told you about Lily?" I bit the top of the Twix wrapper with my teeth. "Please tell me your lot aren't charging her. Are they? I mean, what she must have been through is horrific."

"No. *My lot* aren't charging her, but there's a quite a bit of ground to cover. They've taken her to a special interview suite so they can hear her story and take care of her at the same time. Her body was dependent on those sleeping pills so coming off them has given her some serious side-effects which she didn't even know were happening to her. Hallucinations and the like. It will take a while for her to recover."

I welled up. "She's had such a shit life. All this time we were together, and I didn't notice what Grace was doing to her." I took a big bite of biscuit.

"How could you have noticed? Grace manipulated all of us."

"You saw through her," I said, holding my hand over my mouth, crumbs spilling all over the front of my sweater.

"Only because I was pre-disposed not to like her." Annie reached out and dusted off my jumper. "Grace was a project she'd been planning for years. She'd stalked Tom for a long time – finding everything out about him so she could wheedle her way into your lives." She reached forward and tucked a strand of my hair behind my ear. We stared into each other's eyes, neither of us able to speak for a few seconds.

"It's over now," she said. "She's signed a confession for the murders of Gil, Amelie and Frank *and* to the attempted murder of Nina. That's just the start of it – there will be other charges too."

"Do you think she would have killed me, you and Lils as well?"

Annie nodded.

"That's so messed up."

"She's had a sad life." Annie leaned her back into the sofa. "Frank started manipulating her when she was fourteen and her Dad was too weak to notice. He'd been blackmailing James into getting the Government to endorse Zolis. First he said he was going to leak Gil's gay relationship with James to the press, and then, when that didn't work, he threatened to expose Grace as a murderer – James didn't think he had a choice. In the end, unable to cope with what had happened to Gil, he went insane and ended up handing over the estate to him, too. For the past ten years Frank had been embezzling off the girls' inheritance."

"Fatty Fucking Fanshawe." I folded the biscuit wrapper into a tiny, neat triangle. "I mean, I never liked him, but what an absolute thieving arsehole. Fancy letting your niece believe she was responsible for killing her Dad. I mean that's got to mess with your head. No wonder she turned into a complete psycho."

A couple of nurses dressed in overalls, walked along the corridor bitching about someone called Pippa who worked in radiology. I got up, my knees clicking, and threw the wrapper into the bin. They smiled at me before turning the corner and their rubber clogs carried on squeaking long after they had disappeared.

When I went back, Annie had her feet up, hugging her knees to her chest.

"Mum's horrified. Feels she should have known what sort of a man Frank was. But at the same time, she's mourning him."

Annie rested her chin onto her knees. "But he didn't do anything to you, did he?"

"No way! But he was creepy – the clothes he bought for me–." I swallowed. "I mean, Mum made me wear them to be nice, but they were so weird and childish. I just thought he was old-fashioned and stuck in the past." I clenched my fists. "I had no idea what a manipulative prick he was."

"When Grace murdered Amelie I don't think she realised

242

how much it would throw her into the limelight. Frank spotted her immediately although Lily told us he claimed he had known where they had been living for a while – that he was just biding his time, making sure when a crisis situation arose, they would have no alternative but to return to him."

"Why did he want them to stay hidden?"

"Because he'd been carving up the Aldeburgh Estate. He'd stolen their inheritance to pay for his own lavish lifestyle, using Zolis to hide the path of the money he was siphoning off. When his nieces appeared on the news in relation to a murder committed by Tom Marchant, he needed to get them back under his control – stop them drawing any attention to him. There were more blackmail opportunities, but on both sides this time. He knew Grace had killed Amelie – he'd watched his nieces dispose of the body down by Cupid's Wood. But he also knew it wouldn't be long before Grace realised he had been spending their money."

"Is there any left?"

Annie shrugged.

Dad appeared, holding a rather crumpled bunch of flowers and a bag of white grapes with "seedless" written in large capital letters on the cellophane. He was out of breath, his face all pink and shiny.

"You took your time," I grinned. Annie's pale skin flushed, and she busied herself, tucking her gown around her thighs like she was crimping pastry.

"It took me forever to find a parking space," he said, shaking his head.

"Even though Mum's in a god-awful state, she'll not take kindly to those flowers. She can spy a cheap, hospital gift a mile off."

The tips of Dad's ears glowed. "Well…they're not actually for her." He coughed and shoved them in front of Annie's face.

"Oh!" she said, pressing her lips together. "How, er, nice." She caught my wide-eyed gaze and we burst into laughter.

Dad sat down and rubbed his forehead.

"Sorry, Dad."

"Amelie's parents came to see me."

"Shit."

"They came to apologise for thinking I'd murdered her." He spread his hand on the sofa and stared at his fingers. "Those poor people," he said, his voice breaking with emotion. "They are overwhelmed with guilt. They were already going through a very difficult time. They were getting a divorce and Amelie wasn't dealing well with the news. She'd just started opening up to me a bit." *The hug.* I cringed.

"But then this? I mean, how do you cope with finding out your daughter was murdered just because she happened to be a student in my class who was quiet and thoughtful and who bore a slight resemblance to you, Flo?" He swallowed several times. "I...I told them the evidence against me was overwhelming – that they could hardly be blamed for believing what the police dug up." He reached out and caught my hand. "But you never believed it was me, did you?"

I opened my mouth then shut it again; he didn't need to hear that I'd had my doubts – it didn't matter now. I smiled and squeezed his hand tight. Then he turned to Annie. "And I know you didn't either. Not really."

Annie tilted her head onto one side. "I may have wavered for a second, but deep down I always knew it couldn't have been you." Her eyes were shining with tears and she snatched up his hands in hers and kissed the back of them.

My cue to go and check on Mum.

One Year Later

Emily

I sat on the bench staring out at the pond, white winter sunlight streaming onto my face. Sparkles danced on the water like fallen stars and a family of gangly mallards played follow-my-leader around the rush-lined edge. I was wrapped up in blankets, a scratchy woollen scarf wound around my neck which my incompetent nurse, Bradley, helped me to make. Finger knitting. I wasn't permitted anything with a sharp point and the garment was full of holes; careless dropped stitches. I had the honour of being allowed out by the 'nature pool' on a daily basis. More so than most of the other patients because the moment I set eyes on the water, I grew calm and sedate.

This therapy was better than any medication they had to offer.

Another patient sometimes sat next to me – a middle-aged man with receding grey hair and saggy skin which hung off his bony frame. He also gazed out towards the lake as though searching for something. I didn't think we looked alike, but there was something shared in the way we carried ourselves; how we both wrinkled our foreheads when the sun was too bright; how we interlocked our fingers a certain way and held them in our laps.

If he recognised me, he didn't show it. Neither of us spoke.

Bradley had brought a fistful of stale bread from the kitchen and asked me if I wanted to come with him, down to the water's edge.

I wished he would drop dead. I didn't want him anywhere near me, interrupting my vigil.

He held out a fat palm to me, but I turned my face away. He shrugged. "Suit yourself," he said, a large grin spreading across his square face. "You and your Dad can watch me from where you're sitting." He lumbered off, quacking like a cartoon character, forcing the ducks to make a noisy retreat.

I had plenty of time now to dissect my childhood and, on balance, I had decided that almost all of it was ruined by adults; even Mummy couldn't stay alive to keep me safe. When the police interviewed me, they asked why I had persisted with the notion that Tom was responsible for everything that went wrong in my life. I said nothing. How could they possibly begin to understand what he did to me? I thought back to that awful day when he showed me that my life had no worth. The last piece of the humiliating puzzle.

**

It was the middle of the night. I heard the handle rattle then my bedroom door creaked open.

The room filled with wheezing and I pulled the bedclothes over me, tight. The mattress sunk and I felt his body press against mine.

"I know you're awake, my darling," whispered Frank. I kept my body still – my short breaths flowing around my face turned my cheeks hot. Saliva pooled in my mouth as I forgot to swallow.

"You know how special you are to me," he said, running his hand across my thigh – the sheet protecting me against his flesh.

His hand shot up and circled my neck – he clamped it there and I twisted my head from side to side and kicked my legs.

"Now dearest." He pressed on my throat until I started to gag, I was struggling for breath.

"Stop this." He leaned his body onto my lower half. I stopped my kicking and he lifted a tiny bit of pressure from

246

around my throat. I was sucking in the sheet along with the air and it grew wet with my spit. The back of my throat filled with phlegm and I thought my rib cage would burst. The panic coursing through my body left spots of white bursting behind my eyes.

"I'm not going to hurt you," he said, slipping his hand underneath the sheet.

That was the first time he raped me.

The next morning he was at the kitchen table, shovelling scrambled eggs into his mouth, and reading the newspaper. I was still wearing my pyjamas.

"Morning, sweetie," said Daddy. Gil was eating toast and passing Cassie banana slices dipped in Nutella at the same time.

Frank looked up at me, a brief smile. "You look tired, dearest," he said, before returning to *The Times*. "Not enough beauty sleep, hey?"

Daddy laughed and got up, glancing at his watch before pecking Cassie on the head.

Frank pushed his plate to one side. "I'll give you a lift to the station. I've got a busy day too so maybe we can talk about that little business proposal on our way." Daddy blew kisses at all of us and was out through the door, Frank striding to catch up with him.

"Em, you'll need to hurry with breakfast if we're going to leave on time." He turned to Cassie. "Poppet – you go brush those teeth and I'll be along in a minute to check you've done a good job. And don't think I won't know if you've just smudged toothpaste onto your tongue." Cassie ran off to the downstairs bathroom giggling.

"I don't feel well," I said. It wasn't a lie. I didn't – my whole body was sore and bruised.

He came over and pressed his hand to my forehead. "What sort of ill? You don't feel hot." How was that possible when I was burning inside?

I couldn't meet his gaze. "Achy – you know."

"Hmm," he kissed the top of my head. "You look pale. You on your period?"

"No."

"Okay. Well why don't you go back to bed for a bit? Frank's right – you do look tired. I'll take Cassie to school and when I get back, we'll see how you are – maybe after a bit of a snooze you'll feel like heading in." Cassie was hollering for him.

"Coming," he shouted. He rolled his eyes and tousled my hair.

I sat there, gazing out of the window. Every movement was an effort – as though weights were attached to my limbs. Cookie came in to clear the plates and as soon as I told her I wasn't feeling well, threatened to make me a bowl of her disgusting salty porridge because she was adamant it could cure whatever was ailing me.

I went back to Cassie's bedroom and got into her bed. I couldn't bear to climb back into mine – not until I'd stripped it and boiled the sheets. Myrtle was under the pillow and I held her to my face, crying into her velvet tummy. When I was done with the tears, I decided to get up – there was no way I was going to fall back to sleep.

I showered then dressed, grabbing my jeans which were slung over the chair. There was something in my back pocket. I pulled out Tom's card and smoothed my thumb over the dark, slightly raised, numbers.

What was it he'd said? "Call me anytime, Kiddo – I mean it."

He'd said he could help, and he had sounded so kind; he would know what to do.

I picked up my phone and dialled.

"Hello." It was a woman's voice. I hung up, my heart racing. Maybe I'd mistyped the digits. I tried again. The same voice; "hello – who is this, please?"

"I want to speak to Tom Marchant."

"Okay – I'm his secretary. He's actually in a clinic at the moment. Can I take a message?"

"I really need to speak to him. Now."

"I'm sorry, but that's not possible unless it's an emergency."

"It is an emergency." I screamed the words.

She sucked in her breath. "Okay, okay. Please calm down. Let's start with your name…"

"I don't want to tell you my name."

"Well, how will Dr Marchant know who's calling."

I gulped.

"Okay, I can hear you're distressed." She spoke the words slowly, like I was stupid. "I'm going to knock on Dr Marchant's door and see if he'll talk to you. Just give me something for him to go on – a detail so he knows what it's about."

"Tell him he met me at the opening of the new clinic. I was hiding in one of the rooms and he gave me his card – said I could call him any time."

"Okay – I'm putting you on hold." She pressed a button.

I heard knocking on a door. She hadn't hit mute.

"Jean?" came Tom's distant voice.

"So sorry, Tom," she said in a loud whisper, "I really didn't want to interrupt, but there's a kid on the line – sounds disturbed."

"Excuse me – I won't be a minute."

There were footsteps and the gentle click of a door closing.

"Sorry," said Jean, her voice clearer.

"Who is it? One of my clients?"

"I don't think so. They said they met you at the opening of the clinic – said you found them hiding and gave them a card."

I could hear breathing.

"Oh yeah, sure – it's coming back to me. Some sad-looking, overweight teenager. I imagine he's probably being bullied at school. But, it's really not an emergency – he just needs a shoulder to cry on. Get his number and I'll call him back later today. Oh! And can you dig me out some of those diet sheets – the one's aimed at couch potatoes."

"Sure, sorry Tom. I'm so sorry I disturbed you, it's just he sounded distressed."

"Hey, Jean," said Tom. "You did the right thing. I'll sort

it."

"And you know what Tom, how about, in the future, you don't give your card out to everyone who sells you a sob story."

He laughed.

I hung up.

***

I have given up my voice. The night they took me, as I lay there on the jetty, I realised it was the only course of action left for me to do. After all, he returned Cassie's speech to her and I was sure if I waited long enough, he would do the same for me. Maybe, this time he would take me with him.

The wind rustled the barren branches and the tops of my ears prickled.

My Lady of the Lake, forgive me.

And here I will sit, day after day, for as long as it takes, scouring the horizon for a glimpse of my beloved's golden shadow.

Lily

After it ended Tom said he could help me unlock the rest of my hidden memories. I had found the trigger – the key with which I had chosen to lock Myrtle's casket all those years ago. But, with the emergence of Gil's body, all that really mattered seemed to float to the surface by itself. In time, the police and lawyers uncovered the horrid charade Uncle Frank had inflicted upon my poor Dad and sister and, regardless of my forgotten memories, all his deceit and cruelty came bubbling to the top. I figured it would be crazy to dig deeper and uncover more of the same.

I jostled amongst the swimmers, yellow cap and goggles fixed firmly to my crown. The wall of shiny black wetsuits which surrounded me smelt like damp plimsolls in an airing cupboard. I was hemmed in by bodies and they radiated warmth although the tip of my nose tingled in the cold breeze. I looked to where Annie, Flo and Tom were standing on the bank – smiling and laughing. Annie's bobble hat jiggled as she handed around cups of coffee poured from Tom's thermos. Flo and her Dad held a banner between them that said Go Lily in bubble writing which spiralled out of an angry dolphin's blowhole. Flo's voice soared over the rest of the crowd. "Goooooo Lilllllllly!"

The klaxon sounded and I was almost lifted and carried into the water by the advancing crowd. My feet prickled as the freezing water seeped into my jelly shoes, but the adrenalin pumping around my body kept me charging forwards. Soon I was knee deep in the wake churned up by the professionals, my body flecked by their foam. I strode forwards then plunged my face into the water, my heart was pumping, its movement tickling the bottom of my throat. It took a few seconds and then I was in my stride. *One-two-three breathe. One-two-three breathe.* The sounds around me were as though someone was flipping a switch on and off; a burst of cheering broken by the muffled rumble of legs kicking underwater.

Coach Flo thought I was a wonderful swimmer and that, with a bit of hard work, I would soon be standing on the podium receiving a gold medal. She was, of course, deluded. I was terrible.

Everyone assumed I learnt to swim to prove a point, but they were wrong.

I kicked and splashed, trailing my clumsy limbs through the water and veering from left to right, but it was my way of saying thank you; thank you to Gil and my new friend, the lake, for giving me back my voice.

THE END

Fantastic Books
Great Authors

darkstroke is
an imprint of
Crooked Cat Books

- Gripping Thrillers
- Cosy Mysteries
- Amazing Horrors
- Fascinating Historicals
- Exciting Fantasy
- Young Adult Adventures
- Non-Fiction

Discover us online
www.darkstroke.com

Find us on instagram:
www.instagram.com/darkstrokebooks

Printed in Great Britain
by Amazon